BLOOD ROYAL

*An evocative novel exploring the life of
Mary Queen of Scots*

Nathan, a pedlar and seller of embroidery
threads, first sets his eyes on the queen as an
infant being crowned at Stirling Castle. He
follows her life, being one of the many who
are drawn to her, and becomes more closely
involved in her life than a mere pedlar could
possibly imagine...

BLOOD ROYAL

Elisabeth McNeill

Severn House Large Print
London & New York

This first large print edition published 2010
in Great Britain and the USA by
SEVERN HOUSE PUBLISHERS LTD of
9-15 High Street, Sutton, Surrey, SM1 1DF.
First world regular print edition published 2008 by
Severn House Publishers Ltd., London and New York.

British Library Cataloguing in Publication Data

McNeill, Elisabeth.
  Blood royal.
  1. Mary, Queen of Scots, 1542-1587--Fiction. 2. Queens--
  Scotland--Fiction. 3. Merchants--Scotland--Fiction.
  4. Scotland--History--Mary Stuart, 1542-1567--Fiction.
  5. Historical fiction. 6. Large type books.
  I. Title
  823.9'14-dc22

  ISBN-13: 978-0-7278-7854-0

Printed and bound in Great Britain by
MPG Books Ltd, Bodmin, Cornwall.

Many thanks to Alex Merry whose painstaking and fruitful research provided much valuable information about Mary and her times

One

'Tomorrow?'

Paulet saw her hands shake slightly as she asked the question. Although she seemed icily calm, she was obviously thrown off her guard.

'Tomorrow,' he repeated and his voice was hard as he showed her the death warrant.

Mary shivered and gathered a woollen wrap round her shoulders. She had been asleep when her jailer, accompanied by the Earls of Shrewsbury and Kent, arrived to break the news to her. Shrewsbury carried an official looking document, and Mary saw her cousin's beautifully penned signature at the bottom of the page. Elizabeth's writing was as unmistakable and vainglorious as her portraits.

'But I need time to make my will and write my last letters. Delay it by a few days,' she said without a tremble in her voice and no trace of pleading. Her tone was always peremptory when she spoke to Paulet.

It did her no good.

'*Tomorrow.* You die tomorrow,' he said with

7

satisfaction, for he disliked the woman intensely.

'At what hour?'

'Eight in the morning...'

Her serving women gasped in shock. *Only ten hours*, was the thought in all their minds, but, unflinching, she continued to stare into her jailer's narrow, pinched face.

His pouched eyes met hers and did not waver. Dispassionately she took stock of him, noting the sickly greyness of his skin. Two spots of bright scarlet showed in the lower parts of his cheeks like the marks on the face of a fever victim.

He doesn't look well, she thought. *He's enjoying telling me that I am to die, but his own death is not far away.*

'So be it,' she replied calmly. A queen did not cry before a man like Paulet.

In spite of appearing composed however, she was in mental turmoil. For weeks she had been expecting the verdict of her trial, but a death sentence now was shattering. It was hard to believe that her cousin would condemn another queen to death. She wished they could have met, but though she tried, Elizabeth always held her off.

If we met I could have convinced her that I'm innocent. I could have told her I'm only standing up for my rights and for the true religion, she thought.

The women who shared her imprisonment were sobbing around her but she did not break down and join them in grief. Holding up a hand, she said sharply, 'Be quiet, be calm! I've been expecting this and I welcome death. Help me to dress. There's much to be done...'

Elizabeth Curle, the favourite among her companions now that Mary Seton had gone away, ran from the room to fetch the queen's doctor, Bourgoing, who came at a run with her two secretaries, Curle's brother Gilbert and the faithful Andrew Melville. The men were in tears too and Bourgoing kept repeating in his strong French accent, 'Imposs-ible, imposs-ible.'

'*Pas impossible*,' she snapped, 'Collect yourself. I knew this would happen, but not so soon. Help me by doing as I say and keep your tears for later. I'm weary of life and God will take care of me and forgive me.'

She did not say what there was to forgive, for she was sure her place in heaven was secure.

Driven by febrile energy, they all worked without ceasing through the late hours as she made a detailed will, the last of many, leaving keepsakes and small legacies to all who had served her during her imprisonment. There was not much left to bequeath and it pained her that the best of the jewellery she had once owned, and always treasured so much, had been stolen from her long ago by members of her own family.

A flattering portrait of herself was sent to a cousin who was a Jesuit priest at Douai and provision made for hiring horses to carry her servants away from Fotheringhay after she died. They must not be condemned to staying on in this cold, inhospitable place, she thought.

She composed a formally phrased letter to her

9

twenty-year-old son James, the King of Scotland.

What does he look like now? Whom does he resemble? she wondered, but would never know. How would he react to the killing of his mother? With indifference, most likely, for he'd done nothing to try to save her or intercede with Elizabeth on her behalf. Perhaps he was so unfilial because he had no memory of a mother. At their last meeting, when he was ten months old, he'd scratched her face in his baby struggles to get out of her arms.

Another letter of useless protestations of innocence was written to Elizabeth Tudor, and one to her brother-in-law, King Henry III of France.

To him she wrote, 'I am to be executed at eight in the morning like a criminal, but I am innocent of any crime.' At the foot of the page she signed her name and added a footnote: 'Wednesday at two in the morning.'

At last, exhausted, she leaned her head on one long, elegant hand and gave a little sob and said, 'I only wish I could speak to a priest. I would like to be shriven for the last time.'

Melville cursed, 'God damn Paulet for forbidding you that comfort, Madame.'

'But he can't take away my consolation in Christ,' she assured him.

Hollow-cheeked with exhaustion, she let her women help her into a high bed enclosed behind beautiful curtains she had embroidered with hunting scenes during the long years of her imprisonment.

Lying in the middle of the mattress with a serving woman on her right-hand side, and another on her left, it pleased her, as it had always done, to realize she was a good eight inches taller than the tallest of them. Only Seton had been her size, and that was one of the reasons they admired each other so much.

When her candle was snuffed, she closed her eyes and kissed the jewelled cross that hung around her neck, but it was impossible to rest because, malicious as ever, Paulet had ordered three guards to march up and down the corridor outside her room all night in case she tried to escape.

The thudding of their boots made sleep impossible.

Lying in the darkness, she tried not to anticipate what was going to happen in a few hours. The thought of her head being severed from her body made her shiver with dread and she stroked the skin of her throat with her fingertips and silently prayed, *Dear God, grant that it be quick. Don't let me feel too much pain.*

At last, with supreme self-mastery, she drove the horrible fears away, and turned her mind back to more pleasant things.

With love, she remembered her childhood and her mother, Mary of Guise. Only in France had she been truly happy, but she'd been exiled from there for so long. *Heaven must be like Fontainebleu,* she thought. It would certainly not be like grey, rainswept Edinburgh, a place she hated.

It pleased her to concentrate on happy memories, memories of dancing, hunting and listening to music, especially to poor Davie Rizzio's lute playing and his sweet singing voice.

Then she remembered her second husband, Henry Darnley, whom she had thought so handsome and charming before he showed his true character. Her three husbands paraded before her mind's eye. First came sweet-natured Francois, who died too young. He was followed by dandified Darnley, who only brought her disillusionment. The last was Jamie Bothwell.

Was it pity or remorse she felt when she thought about him? It was still hard for her to accept he was dead because he always seemed so invincible and his frowning face rose in her memory. He was certainly not handsome, with that scarred forehead and the cautious, knowing tawny eyes. He was a man of contradictions – a foul-mouthed fighter, but also a man of learning, a ruffian and a dandy all at the same time. For him she'd abandoned all qualms of pride or morality.

When the castle clock chimed five she shivered and began to wonder what she should wear on the scaffold. It was important to present oneself properly as a queen and a martyr for the Faith when dying so publicly. No rich fabrics, elaborate ruffs or laces for her, but a gown of black and a widow's stiffly starched white headdress.

Elizabeth was always adorned like a popinjay. 'Gloriana' her subjects called her. Her father too had pranced and preened in magnificent finery even when his body was gross and swollen.

12

Is it unholy that my last thoughts are of clothes? she wondered. Only a confessor could answer that question and grant her absolution, but that comfort was denied to her.

She fell into a fitful doze but, in what seemed only minutes, started awake again because a hand gently shook her shoulder and Elizabeth Curle's voice said, 'Wake up, Your Majesty. It's seven o'clock.'

Two

February 8th

The landlord of the inn in Fotheringhay was afraid of the big man who slept in his upper chamber.

'Bull's my name,' the fellow had said when he stamped into the house, and drinkers sitting around the fire with their tankards of ale looked up in surprise at the size of him, for he seemed to fill the doorway and his top of his head brushed the rough-hewn rafters of the ceiling.

He was accompanied by a smaller, shifty-looking fellow who carried a long wooden trunk on one shoulder.

The landlord hurried to get them upstairs, for everyone in the place knew what Bull had come to Fotheringhay to do, and shied away from the idea of it.

13

'Do you think the axe is in that trunk the other fellow's carrying? What sort of way is it to earn your money cutting the head off an old woman?' whispered his wife.

'I've no choice but put him up,' grumbled the landlord.

'The sooner he does his job and gets out of here, the better,' she agreed.

They were surly and unfriendly when Bull and his companion came thumping down the stairs demanding more ale at seven o'clock next morning.

Satisfied by three tankards full each, they left and followed a path from the inn to the castle, trailed all the way across the dried-up moat by curious youths, little boys and a string of snarling dogs. Older people they met avoided their eyes as if they did not want to acknowledge their existence.

Bull was indifferent to their distaste, for he was used to being treated like that. This was not the first time he'd used his axe to enforce a bloody law.

He and his companion, who was still burdened by the box, had almost reached the castle's outer gate when an old packman in a black cloak with a pack on his back stepped boldly into their path.

'Be quick. Be merciful,' he said.

Bull pushed him roughly aside before he noticed that the man was blind. The pupils of both the packman's eyes were clouded with white. He was old too, because his long, straggling hair was grey under his battered black felt hat.

14

'Make it quick. One blow. Do not torture her,' the packman said again.

'I'm not a butcher,' snapped Bull and tried to push him over, but surprisingly the packman stood firm. He was not as feeble as he looked.

'I'll give you something if you do it in one stroke,' he said and held out his clenched hand towards Bull, who accepted the offering. It turned out to be a golden angel, a coin of high value.

'She must matter for you to pay so much for her quick dispatch,' he said sarcastically.

'She's been cursed by ill fortune from birth. Be merciful towards her,' was the packman's reply.

The executioner only pursed his lips and stuck the coin in the purse at his waist as he strode away.

Nathan the packman stood staring after the sound of the executioner's heavy tread. There was a bleak look on his deeply lined face. The young woman who stood beside him took his arm and said softly, 'Come away, father, you've done your best for her. He's going through the gate now.'

The girl was unusually tall and lovely, in the first bloom of womanhood, but she was poorly dressed in a rough fustian skirt and blouse, with a woollen shawl over her shoulders. Her hair was hidden beneath a peasant woman's white head cloth, tied tightly in a knot under her chin.

'He took the money didn't he, Sarah?' Nathan asked her.

'Yes, he put it in a pouch on his belt.'

'How did he look when he took it?'

15

'Grateful,' she lied.

'So do you think it will do any good? I can't bear to think of her suffering.'

'I'm sure it'll help. He's very big and strong, not the sort to miss his aim by accident.'

'But does he look compassionate?'

Bull looked anything but compassionate for he seemed brutal in every way, but the girl lied again. 'I'm sure you touched his heart,' she told her father, who gratefully took her arm and leaned on her. She was much taller than he was.

'I hope you're telling me the truth, child. I can't bear to think of my Queen suffering more than is necessary. I want it to be very quick,' he said.

'You gave him a golden angel. You've done your best,' she reassured him as she tried to steer him out of the mob that was following Bull through the castle gate. When he felt her pulling him gently in the opposite direction to the crowd, he shook his head and said, 'No, no, Sarah, I must get inside the great hall. I can't see anything but I want to be there. Will you tell me what happens? Please do this for me. I've followed her through life and don't want to abandon her now.'

Sarah groaned. The last thing she wanted was to witness the grisly event that was about to take place.

'It'll be hard to get in. There are guards on the gate turning people away because they're afraid of an outcry,' she told him.

'I'll get in. Just lead me to the gate. How many men are guarding it?' His voice was determined and she knew it was pointless to protest. When Nathan made up his mind, he usually got what he wanted.

Two heavily armed men stood with long pikes crossed across the portcullis gate and Nathan fumbled in the purse at his waist as Sarah led him towards them. She caught another glimpse of gold, which did not escape the guards either, and one of them demanded suspiciously, 'Where do you think you're going?'

'To see the execution,' replied Nathan.

'But you're a blind man, aren't you? You won't be able to see anything.'

'I want to be there when the woman who plotted against Queen Elizabeth suffers for her sins,' he said sanctimoniously.

The guards were not impressed by this.

'Huh, everybody in town wants to get in, but we've been told to keep them out,' said the younger of the two. His eyes were fixed on the girl leading the old man along. *That's an impressive looking woman in spite of her shabby clothes*, he thought.

Nathan performed another sleight of hand and two more golden angels went from him to the armed men. Sarah was astonished that her normally prudent father should be dispensing large amounts of money so freely.

For a few seconds the men mentally debated keeping the money and still barring the gate, but she smiled at the younger one and whispered, 'It matters a lot to my father.' He visibly weakened, turned to his companion and said, 'Let them in. The poor old soul is stone blind. He's not going

17

to cause any trouble.'

The senior guard pocketed his coin as he stood aside, lowering his pike to let them hurry under the arch of the ancient gateway.

'Every man has his price,' Nathan whispered to his daughter as they walked into the courtyard.

Sarah knew it was her smile as much as his money that won them entrance, but said nothing, because she was fully employed steering her father through the crowd filling the inner keep. Nathan cleared a way for them by waving his walking stick in front of him till they reached the front of the throng at the door of the great hall.

As a huge clock on the wall above struck eight, people in the crowd began shouting, 'Let us in, let us in!' and hammering on the wooden panels of the enormous door. It slowly swung open and admitted an avalanche of bodies.

Sarah found it hard to keep her feet in the rush, but a couple of men in the crowd recognized Nathan's blindness and propelled him forward as she clung to his arm. Because she was taller than most of the onlookers, she had a clear view, and a terrible one she found it.

People were pressing around a high wooden scaffold draped in white linen. In the middle of its raised platform stood an enormous block with an indentation in its surface. 'That's where she'll lay her neck,' Sarah thought, with sickening realization that grew worse when she saw a gleaming, long-handled axe propped against the block.

She tried to turn away. This she did not want to

watch, but Nathan held her arm firmly and pleaded, 'Tell me what you see.'

'I see a high scaffold covered with white cloth. I see an executioner's block and a big axe...'

'Aieee,' he moaned, but this sigh was muffled by a roar from the assembled crowd as Bull, dressed in black with a hood over his head, climbed the steps to the platform. Two holes had been cut in the hood for his eyes, which shone through, bloodshot and dangerous as the eyes of a rabid dog.

Like an actor, he took a bow and began rolling up his jerkin sleeves while Nathan hissed urgently in Sarah's ear, 'Go on, tell me what's happening now. Tell me everything. Don't spare me. Tell me the truth.'

He grasped her hand so urgently that she knew she must do as he asked. It mattered to him because he loved the woman who was about to die.

Mary, one time Queen of France and Scotland, was late for her own death. Doctor Bourgoing, who had looked after her faithfully through her years of imprisonment, brushed away the guards who were trying to hurry her on to the scaffold and said, 'Let me give her a bite of food and a glass of wine first. She has eaten nothing since last night.'

'Does that matter now?' sneered one man and the doctor turned on him with a snarl. 'Yes, it does matter. She's a high born lady. Treat her with respect.'

He took Mary into a side room and gave her a

piece of dry bread and a glass of wine.

'I don't want anything,' she said.

'Drink it. Treat it as a holy sacrament,' he told her.

She did as she was told, but screwed up her face when she tasted the wine. 'It's sour,' she complained.

'I know. Paulet doesn't waste money on good wine,' he agreed, but in fact he had laced her drink with valerian, for he wanted her to be as calm as possible during the coming ordeal.

When she finished the draught, he courteously extended his arm to her and said, 'Let me lead you in, my Queen.' Even the most officious guard did not try to stop him.

An outbreak of catcalls from the back of the hall told the crowd that Mary was arriving. There was an altercation in the doorway while her attendants loudly protested at not being allowed to mount the scaffold with her, and an even bigger one when she asked for a priest.

Her voice was high and clear and she still spoke with a French accent, though she had been many years out of that country.

'Grant me the services of a priest. Surely you cannot deny me the solace of my faith,' she cried, but again it was denied. Instead Paulet offered to summon a Protestant clergyman and she spurned that.

With help from the guards, because her legs were grossly swollen with the beginnings of the dropsy that had killed her mother and she found it painful to walk, she slowly mounted three steps to the block. As she climbed, even the rowdiest members of the crowd fell silent, overcome by unexpected feelings of pity and solemnity at the sight of her tall, black-clad figure standing high above them. Those who had been shouting most enthusiastically tried to look away and not catch her eye as she scanned their faces.

'How does she look?' Nathan asked Sarah in a whisper.

'As stately as a queen. But she seems ill and old.'

'What is she wearing?'

'A plain gown of black, with a long white headdress. Its tail touches the ground at the back. Her hair is red and plainly dressed.'

'Widow's clothes. She's a widow three times over after all. And she has always had fine hair. Is she wearing fine jewellery?' he asked.

'Yes, there's a big jewelled cross around her neck, a long pomander and another necklace with a silver lamb hanging from the end of it.'

'Her Agnus Dei. She's very pious,' Nathan said.

'The executioner is trying to take it away from her. He's very rough. She's kissing it but she has to give it to him.'

'It's part of his wages.' Nathan's voice was bleak.

'Now he's telling her to take off her gown.' The outrage in Sarah's voice showed her shock at Bull's discourtesy.

At that point, two of the queen's serving women succeeded in desperately fighting their

21

way on to the scaffold. 'Leave her alone. Don't touch her. We will disrobe the queen,' cried the youngest of them, a woman with a red and angry face.

Standing one on each side of Mary, they helped her off with her black gown, revealing a dark red petticoat beneath a white bodice.

'Her petticoat is scarlet,' Sarah whispered to Nathan.

'Defiance,' he whispered back.

Bull stepped up to rip off the detached sleeves of her gown, but the women intervened again and slid them gently from her arms, replacing them with sleeves the same colour as her petticoat.

'She's dying like a scarlet woman,' Sarah said in disapproval.

'No, she'll have chosen the colour because it doesn't show blood,' Nathan replied solemnly.

'But the white linen on the scaffold floor will,' said Sarah, wishing she could close her eyes.

Mary stepped forward, stately in her underclothes, and stared defiantly down into the rows of faces turned up towards her.

'I am innocent of any crime,' she cried in a strong and unwavering voice. 'I am not afraid to die. My God will take care of me.'

The crowd hushed as her ladies began weeping. She turned to them and said in French, 'Don't cry, rejoice for me. I am weary of this life.'

Paulet was agitated because he was afraid that she was arousing too much sympathy, so he waved a peremptory hand at Bull, telling him to get it over with. The executioner and his companion knelt before the queen to ask forgiveness for what they were about to do, and she told them, 'I forgive you.'

The crowd sighed like a wind rushing through trees.

'She's kneeling down on a cushion. One of her women has put a folded cloth on her head. Oh dear God, she's put her arms onto the block to steady herself. If she doesn't draw them back they'll be chopped off too,' Sarah gasped in her father's ear.

'She's dropped her arms now. She's praying in Latin...'

Mary's voice rang out three times as the axe was raised above her head, 'In manus tuas, domine! In manus tuas, domine! In manus tuas, dom...'

A shocked silence fell on the crowd as the terrible thud rang out. Sarah groaned, quailed and slumped against Nathan. Bull had botched the execution. His axe inflicted a terrible wound but missed the neck completely. Mary cried out in anguish, 'Sweet Jesus!'

Someone in the crowd yelled, 'You've only cut the side of her head, man. Do it again, for God's sake!'

Panicked, he stepped back and hurriedly raised the axe once more. It came down with another terrible thud, but again the head did not roll off. A strip of sinew at the back of Mary's neck was unsevered.

A terrible groan swept the hall and Sarah did not have to tell Nathan what had happened. They

23

grasped hands and leaned against each other in tears.

'I can see her face. Her lips are moving. She's trying to speak!' sobbed Sarah.

Bull took a third swipe and the watchers groaned at last, 'It's done, it's over.' The Queen's head was lying on the ground.

'This is terrible,' sobbed Sarah and people around her gave a strange, animal-like wail that echoed off the stone walls and drowned out the frenzied keening of Mary's retinue.

Calling, 'God Save the Queen!' Bull bent down to lift up the severed head. When he pulled at the hair, it came away in his hand. Queen Mary of Scotland had been wearing a wig and her real hair was no longer glorious red but grey and thinning.

At the same time, a small dog appeared from beneath her skirts and, whining, tried to cuddle into her shoulder. Pulsing blood stained its grey coat. Terrified, it began licking her skin.

Thinking that Bull was about to kill it too, Elizabeth Curle rushed beneath the poised axe and snatched up the dog, cuddling it to her chest. The blood on it stained her clothes.

This was too much for Sarah to endure, and she covered her eyes with her hands and said, 'Don't make me watch. I can't bear any more. I can't!'

Nathan was not listening to her. Like a man possessed, he threw up his arms and his voice rang out above all others. *'Baruch shem k'vod mal-chuto l'olam va-ed*!' he yelled, while tears rolled down his furrowed cheeks and into his white beard.

'Hush, the guards are looking at you,' Sarah told him, afraid that he would attract unwanted attention from Mary's jailers, but others were yelling at the same time and his outburst was ignored.

Only a few people cheered the Earl of Kent when he climbed the platform and called out, 'Such is the end of all the Queen's and the Gospel's enemies!'

As the hall cleared, Sarah held her father's arm and led him back through the gateway to the path back to the outside world. No one tried to stop them.

'What did you shout when the Queen was dying?' she asked when they were well clear of the castle.

'It's Hebrew, the language of my people. I thought I'd forgotten it but it suddenly came back to me,' he said.

'What does it mean?'

'Praised forever be your glorious Majesty. We say it in worship of God, but I thought it was right for her too.'

Three

From a grey and threatening sky, rain lashed down on to the high stone walls of Linlithgow Palace and a screeching wind howled like a banshee around its towers and parapets.

A flurry of hurrying women ran to and fro from the Queen's chamber on the first floor of the central building, but when one passed through the press of people waiting in the outer chamber, she only shook her head and said, 'Not yet.'

Anxious courtiers looked at each other and frowned.

'She's very slow this time,' said a man.

'It'll be all right. She's delivered before,' the woman by his side assured him.

'Yes, she delivers but they don't survive long,' added another.

'The French ones did, but they're no use to us,' chipped in another voice.

Talking stopped when, from the other side of the Queen's door, came a prolonged and agonized yell. 'Awww, aww!'

'It's coming,' cried the onlookers in chorus

26

and pressed forward, anxious to miss nothing. The yell was followed by a silence that hung over them like a pall. The wind outside was all that could be heard till a woman of the chamber looked out to say, 'The child is born. It's healthy.'

'What is it, what is it?' the crowd chorused.

'A girl.'

Everyone groaned. A girl was not what they wanted.

Mary of Guise, wife of the King, lay back against the pillows and held her newborn daughter close. This child would take the place of two little boys she had tragically lost within a few hours of each other during the past year, and also fill the longing she felt for Francis, the only surviving child of her first marriage whom she'd left at home in France. It didn't matter that this was a girl. It was a child to love and she badly needed that.

She stroked the baby's cheek and saw that the fluff of hair on the little head was bright red. She uncurled the clenched hands and was delighted that her daughter had long elegant fingers. Her legs and body were long too. She would be a tall, tawny-headed woman one day.

'Send news of his daughter's birth to my husband,' she said to the doctor leaning over her bed.

'It's been done. A messenger has already gone to Falkland to tell him that he has a fine daughter,' was the reply.

Mary knew very well that the sex of his child

27

would be a disappointment to her husband, but did not really care what he thought. In fact, she did not like the man much, but matters of liking or disliking did not enter into royal marriages. After her first widowhood, offers had been made for her hand by two kings, Henry VIII of England and James V of Scotland. Henry had a bad matrimonial reputation because of the execution of Anne Boleyn, and, when refusing him, Mary had quipped that though she was tall, she only had a small neck and did not want to lose it.

The Scottish marriage was a diplomatic alliance organized by her powerful family, the French house of Guise, and they chose James Stewart, a twenty-five-year-old widower. She was a widow of twenty-three when the arrangement was made, and it did not matter that she found the bridegroom physically and temperamentally unattractive, with his skewed left eye, and vainglorious, licentious and hysterical nature. They led separate lives, only sharing a bed for the purposes of procreation, and he had not taken the trouble to be with her while she was delivering their third child.

Instead he'd gone off skirmishing against the English at Solway Moss, and, from all accounts, lost the battle. In defeat, he did not come back to Linlithgow but retreated to his hunting lodge, Falkland Palace, thirty miles away.

She suspected he was indulging in one of his periodic emotional collapses, an indulgence for which his stoical, practical wife had little sympathy.

'I hope this daughter does not inherit his temperament,' she thought, as she watched her child being taken away by the wet nurse.

Mary's scepticism about her husband's justification for taking to his bed at Falkland was shaken four days later when she received the news that he was gravely ill.

'Does he want me to go to him?' she asked. Though still recuperating from the birth, she could be carried across country in a litter if necessary.

The messenger shook his head. 'No, it's best you stay here with the baby, Your Majesty. The doctors think what ails the king might infect you.'

'What exactly ails him?'

'A purging fever.'

'The plague?'

'Perhaps.'

'Or the pox?'

'Perhaps that too. The doctors don't know. They think he might be dying of despair.'

'Did he not rally when he heard he had a daughter?'

The messenger shifted his feet uneasily because he knew that James had groaned at the news and said, 'My kingdom cam' wi' a lassie and it'll gang wi' a lassie.'

He would not tell that to the Queen because it sounded as if the King was condemning his child to the same tragic life as himself. The Stewarts had indeed come to the throne of Scotland through the daughter of Robert the Bruce, but none of them enjoyed a peaceful

29

reign and the man dying at Falkland would be the first in over 200 years to actually die in a bed, if he did die, which seemed more than likely.

Mary of Guise knew a time of decision had come for her. She must get up and start making sure that nothing would stand in the way of her daughter inheriting her father's throne if he died.

First the child must be christened, even if her father was not present. Untrue rumours were already flying around that the newborn baby was sickly and near to death. Of course, rumour mongers had their own reasons for spreading these stories. The powerful Scottish lords did not want a female child on the throne, and England's King Henry VIII would be more than happy for his northern enemy to be thrown into a state of ruler-less confusion.

As soon as the winter storm outside abated, Mary ordered her maids to dress the child in a robe of white taffeta, and wrap it up warmly for the short trip to St Michael's Church alongside the Palace. There her daughter was swiftly baptized according to the rites of the Roman Catholic Church and christened Mary, though her mother always called her Marie.

The ceremony was over not a moment too soon, because when the christening party returned to the warmth and safety of the palace, a sweating horse and rider came clattering through the gate to announce that the baby's father, King James V, was dead. His daughter Mary, the new queen, was seven days old.

Marie of Guise did not waste time weeping,

but summoned the English ambassador to Linlithgow and insisted on stripping her child naked so that he could see it was physically perfect and in good health. That information was sent to his master Henry Tudor, and the ambassador added a note saying that the child showed signs of being as impressive as its mother, who was almost six feet tall.

Henry's response was swift. Within days he proposed an alliance between the new queen and his five-year-old son Edward. This suggestion was enthusiastically received by many of the Scottish nobility, though not by the Francophile Queen Mother or her chief ally and adviser, the Roman Catholic Cardinal Beaton of St Andrews, in whose opinion Henry was a heretic and an enemy of the true church.

The chief supporter of the English marriage was the Earl of Arran, next in line to the throne after the newborn baby. He was a Protestant, the religion that was rapidly taking over Scotland.

Mary of Guise played her hand with cool skill. Because it was dangerous to antagonize Arran too much, she pretended to agree with his wishes and allowed her baby daughter to be affianced to the English prince.

To make sure that she could not back out of the agreement, Arran imprisoned her and the baby in Linlithgow Palace. She stayed quietly, not protesting when the news was brought to her that a contract had been signed at Greenwich officially pledging the two children in marriage.

But secretly she told Beaton, 'This I will not have.' She had other plans for her child.

By bribery, the mother and baby escaped from Linlithgow in the middle of the night and fled to Stirling Castle, which was Scotland's most impregnable stronghold. None of Mary's enemies could get at her there.

The first thing she had to do was make sure that her daughter was openly acknowledged as the ruler of Scotland, and for that, the child must be publicly crowned.

Four

September 9th, 1543

It was a bright, golden autumn morning. Oak trees heavy with fat acorns and rustling with leaves the colour of burnt sienna and ochre lined the road as twenty-year-old Nathan strode along beside his father Ezra, a Jewish 'smous' or packman.

They were on their way to Stirling, because someone in Perth had told them that the baby queen was to be crowned in the castle at noon. Ezra was determined to be there too. He was fifty years old, fit enough in body but his sight was failing, so he needed the help and guidance of his son when he was on the selling rounds, which he undertook for six months of the year.

On their backs they carried bulging packs full

32

of exquisite lace from France and Belgium, beautifully coloured silk threads, embroidery canvas and fine linen, needles, pins, tiny silver scissors, thimbles, and hanks of brightly dyed wool.

'A royal crowning'll be a grand show. You'll never see anything like it again,' Ezra told Nathan, who laughed and replied, 'I didn't think you were a royalist, father.'

'I'm not, but those high born women who'll be in town today have plenty of money and good taste. We'll sell a lot in Stirling.'

'We might be better off touring villages. There'll be such a crowd in Stirling, we'll never get near the grand ladies to sell anything,' said Nathan, but Ezra grinned and disagreed, 'Oh, we'll sell. A good smous can get into any great house.'

As they walked, they bantered cheerfully. Ezra enjoyed baiting his son about getting married soon.

'You'll have to find yourself a wife. My eyes are going like my father's did and I won't be able to go on travelling much longer. Your mother and I'll go home to Amsterdam when you find yourself a woman to look after you,' he said.

'I can look after myself,' replied Nathan.

'Rubbish. You're too soft-hearted. You need someone with you to make you drive harder bargains, and besides you can't cook.'

'And you've someone in mind to do those things for me, no doubt?'

'I have.'

33

'And who is it?'

'Remember Leverson, who we buy our silks from in Leith?'

'Of course. Mr Leverson drives a very hard bargain.'

'And he has a daughter.'

Nathan paused, shifting the heavy pack on his shoulder as he asked suspiciously, 'How far has this notion gone? If she's as fat as her mother, I won't have her.' Mrs Leverson was like a butter ball.

'I haven't seen the girl but she comes from a good family. They're from Amsterdam originally, like us.'

'They're also a family that knows how to eat, that's for certain. I hope you've not committed me to anything.'

'Do you know a better family with a daughter of the right age?'

'I haven't looked around. Anyway, I'd like to fall in love first.'

Ezra snorted, 'Love! You'll soon learn that family and connections are more important than that.'

But Nathan remembered the songs that people sang at night around bonfires in country villages. They were often about love between a man and a woman, and already he knew what it was to be physically attracted to a girl, and to sleep with her as well if she was agreeable, as many of them were, for he was a dark-haired, handsome young fellow. He wanted to experience true love like people in the songs.

He was not to know that he was on the verge

of falling into an unlikely, unfulfilled and self-less fixation that would possess him forever.

Stirling was crowded. The castle was perched on top of a sheer wall of stone, precipitously high like the nest of a giant eagle. From its tallest flagpole, the royal standard of Scotland flew proudly, while strains of music floated down from the courtyard to the excited crowds in the streets below.

Ezra was well known in the town, for he had been going there for thirty years and many friends greeted him.

'Have you come to see the little queen being crowned, smous?' a man called out jovially.

'Has it happened yet?' Ezra asked.

'No, in an hour's time. In the Chapel Royal up there ... Her mother brought her here to us to be safe from the English. We're loyal to the Stewarts and the old religion in Stirling,' cried a man in a faded priestly cassock.

'Can people get in to witness the ceremony?' Ezra asked.

'Yes, they're letting people into the main courtyard. Her mother isn't keeping people out because she wants as many as possible to witness the coronation. Then there can be no denying it ever happened,' a bystander said.

'In that case, we'll add our testimony,' said Ezra, pulling his son forward.

The castle gate stood wide open, giving entrance into the huge main courtyard in front of the Chapel Royal, which had been built by the new queen's grandfather, James IV, who had a

35

mania for putting up fine buildings.

Using his walking staff as a weapon to clear a path, a skill that Nathan learned from him and was to put to good use later, Ezra cut through the crowd.

'Make way for a blind man,' he called and pushed forward, ignoring catcalls from people who questioned how a blind man expected to see anything, even from close up.

They were standing at the chapel door when the royal entourage emerged from the palace state rooms and formed up in a stately progress to cross the square, while the crowd parted before them like the waters of the Red Sea making way for Moses.

First out came the magnificent figure of Cardinal Beaton, the chief Catholic cleric in Scotland, a fleshy-faced, worldly looking man, magnificent in scarlet, who was accompanied by crozier bearers and young priests swinging censers.

Behind him walked the Queen Dowager, wearing scarlet too, though she should have been in mourning. Tall and magnificent in appearance, a hush of admiration fell over the gabbling crowd at the sight of her.

Following her were ladies in brilliant gowns, and men with magnificent ruffs above slashed doublets with feathered hats and swords at their waists, but the figure that caught Nathan's eye was a stout little nursemaid behind the Queen Mother. In her arms she bore an infant child clad like an adult in glorious robes.

The baby's gown of cloth of gold was studded

with jewels so glittering and valuable that the nursemaid was flanked on both sides by armed guards. Over the jewelled dress was a red velvet cloak trimmed with white ermine.

At the chapel door, the nursemaid tenderly handed the baby over to a richly dressed nobleman, who held her up high so the crowd could see her. The child's eyes stared out, wide open and obviously frightened, making Nathan feel a tremendous pity for the little thing who was about to be anointed queen, but had no idea what was being done to her.

With tremendous dignity and stately tread, the procession went into the chapel and, after they all passed, the ordinary people craned forward to watch what was going on inside.

Nathan had a good view. The baby was propped up on a gilded throne by the High Altar, and a nobleman stood beside her trying to hold her steady while another bent the fingers of her tiny hand round the shaft of the huge Royal Sceptre.

Her uncle, the jealous Earl of Arran came forward with the three-foot long Sword of State and tied it on to her little body. It was longer than she was.

Throughout all this manhandling, the baby stayed silent and frightened. Only when Beaton approached with the Holy Oil to anoint her forehead did she begin to cry, and her screams rang out, echoing off the hammer-beamed roof, while sympathetic people in the courtyard made noises of disapproval because their little queen was being put through such an ordeal.

The crowning could not stop for her to be

comforted. When the golden crown, its rim edged with velvet, was ceremonially lowered onto her head, she screamed even more loudly and tried to wrestle free, but was forcibly held in place while Beaton pronounced a solemn blessing and announced that she was now a properly anointed queen.

The singing of the choir drowned most of her howling, but she was inconsolable till her nursemaid rushed forward to cuddle her.

As the procession made its way out again, Nathan said in a heavy voice, 'That was dreadful.'

'The music was sublime,' protested Ezra.

'But the poor little thing was terrified. You're blind but you're not deaf. Didn't you hear her screaming?'

'She'll forget it in an hour. And now she is queen, her life will be glorious.'

'Will it? Is her mother's life glorious? Was her father's or her grandfather's? I feel sorry for her,' said Nathan.

Ezra sighed and said, 'Your heart is too tender. Even as a little boy you always wanted to save injured kittens and hungry puppies. A queen doesn't need your pity.'

But Nathan was moved by the ordeal of little Mary and haunted by the memory of her frightened, tear-filled eyes staring at the strange people crowding around her. If he could have kidnapped her and removed her from what he felt was an onerous destiny, he would have done it there and then.

Five

As they went about their business for the next few years, tramping the roads and paths of Scotland, Ezra and Nathan stayed in the north because they heard terrible stories from other travellers about devastation raging in the south.

'The English are looting and burning all over the Marches. They've sacked the Border abbeys and burned Edinburgh. No one knows when it's going to stop,' an old priest of St Machar's Cathedral in Aberdeen told Ezra, who had long been his friend and always called to see him when he was in the northern city. Despite the differences in their religious beliefs, they enjoyed philosophical debates with each other.

'What's causing this fighting?' Ezra asked.

'Henry Tudor went mad with rage when the Queen Mother repudiated the marriage contract between our little queen and his son. She wants an alliance with France because she favours the Roman Catholic faith instead of the new Protestantism.'

'But Scotland won't go back to Catholicism, will it?' Ezra asked.

'I'm afraid not, especially since Cardinal

Beaton burned the Protestant preacher George Wishart at the stake in St Andrews a month ago.'

Ezra shivered. A fear of religious persecution haunted the people of his faith wherever they went. 'That must have caused bad blood,' he said.

'It was a bad mistake. Both the Protestants and Beaton's supporters want to get their hands on the little queen, so she has to be hurried from place to place, and hidden for her own safety all the time.'

Nathan, who had brought his father to meet this friend, looked up with sharp interest, remembering the crying child with the huge crown on her head in Stirling's Chapel Royal.

'Where do they take her?' he asked.

'Sometimes to the west, sometimes to Stirling because that castle is easy to defend, now and again to an island in the middle of the Lochleven near Kinross. People think her mother will have to send her to France soon.'

'She'd be safer there,' agreed Nathan, and the priest nodded. 'Indeed she would, but getting her out of the country is a problem. English ships wait along the coast all the time hoping to catch her.'

'Poor child,' said Nathan fervently and his father told the priest, 'My son's heart was moved for the child when we saw her being crowned at Stirling. I think it's time he had a baby of his own. I want to get him married but he's not eager. We're on our way to Leith so I can arrange a marriage for him there.'

The priest shook his head. 'Don't go south.

After Wishart was burned, the English attacked Leith and broke down the pier. Find your boy a bride in the north if you can.'

But Ezra shook his head and said, 'I've a particular family with a daughter of marriageable age in mind. She'll bring a good dowry with her too and I can't go on travelling much longer. Nathan's my only son, so it's his duty to continue our family.'

Nathan groaned, 'But not with that Leverson girl who we met last time we were in Leith. I don't care if she has a king's ransom for a dowry. She's too fat, and I don't want her.'

The priest laughed and said, 'I wonder which of you will win!'

Nathan did not laugh. He knew that, like it or not, he was going to Leith, but was determined to make up his own mind about what happened after that.

They journeyed south, selling their goods on the way, till, at the end of May, they found themselves on the outskirts of St Andrews, where they had good customers because the women of university men had leisure to sew and money to spend.

The pleasant town clustered round a twelfth century tower dedicated to St Rule, which Nathan often climbed as a boy and counted 151 steps on the way up. In the bright morning sunshine it looked impressive as they walked towards it down South Street, but suddenly Ezra put a hand to one ear and exclaimed, 'What's that?'

'What do you mean?' asked his son.

'That noise, don't you hear the noise?'

When he lost his sight, Ezra's hearing sharpened, and he often heard things before his son did. Nathan paused and listened hard too, before realizing his father was right. From somewhere came a roaring sound – the yelling of a distant mob.

'Are the students rioting perhaps?' he said, almost enviously. Every time he visited St Andrews, he wished he could be one of the confident-looking young men in their distinctive scarlet student gowns.

'No, it's coming from the castle, not from the colleges. Let's see what's going on.' Ezra was always curious.

They turned left into Castle Street, but it was blocked by townsmen and students, all looking confused and alarmed.

'What's going on?' Ezra asked a shopkeeper in a white apron, who said, 'Some men captured the castle and they've killed the Cardinal.'

'Killed Beaton?' Ezra gasped. Everyone knew that Beaton was the Queen Mother's chief adviser and the most powerful man in the land.

'Use your eyes,' said the aproned man, pointing towards the castle wall looming above them. They saw a shocking sight – the stark white naked body of a man swung from the battlements by a rope tied round his ankles. Terrible lacerations and bloodstains marked the corpse.

'That's Beaton!' said the shopkeeper.

It was hard to accept that the vulnerable-looking corpse had been the magnificent churchman in heavily embroidered robes who presided over the little queen's coronation.

'What happened to him?' Nathan asked.

'He was in bed with his mistress last night and she left at dawn, but some Protestant lairds from Fife broke into the castle then and killed him in revenge for Wishart. They're still in there and our Provost is parleying with them, but they've taken control of the castle and won't come out unless they're allowed to go free.'

'How did they get in? Surely a man like Beaton was well-guarded?' exclaimed Ezra.

'Not last night. There was building work going on and a porter left the gate unlocked, so they just walked in. They put burning coals against Beaton's chamber door to smoke him out and he shouted they couldn't kill him because he was a priest – but they did. They killed him all right.' The speaker pointed again at the swinging body as proof of what he said.

Ezra, survivor of many threatening situations, took his son's arm, 'Let's leave here. It's not the place for us,' he said softly.

They hurried off to the little port of Crail, where Nathan's mother Miriam was waiting for them and they could hire a fishing boat to take them to Leith.

Fortunately the weather was fine, with the wind blowing in the right direction. During their day-long voyage, Nathan, still shocked by what he'd seen, sat in the keel looking at his parents. They were growing old and must be enabled to spend their last days in peace, for Ezra had walked the roads as a boy with his blind father. Now both his eyes were clouded with white membranes, like his father's had been at the end of his life.

'Will blindness come to me as well in time?' Nathan wondered, with a chill of fear.

As they sailed along, Miriam, who had not been told about the murder of Beaton, prattled excitedly about the family they were going to visit and the prospect of acquiring a daughter-in-law. 'Before you marry the Leverson girl, Nathan, I'll teach her your favourite dishes and take her to our winter cottage at Dunkeld. I wonder if she'll travel with you on your rounds? Not when she's carrying children, of course, but perhaps later, like I've done. It's a wife's duty to make sure her man is properly fed. I've always looked after your father. He'd never have lasted so long on the road if it wasn't for me.'

Ezra grunted and it struck Nathan that he'd never heard his parents having a prolonged conversation. He hoped that if they did marry him off, they'd choose someone he could talk to. He'd also prefer to marry a girl who could sing, because he was fond of music and often sang out loud as he walked along.

When they neared Leith, he stood up on the prow beside a fisherman, holding onto the mast with one hand. They both stared ahead till Nathan asked in surprise, 'What's happened to the long pier?' It had completely disappeared and all that was left were heaps of broken stones and boulders.

'The English ships blasted it out of existence,' was the reply.

'But how do we get ashore if there's no pier?'

44

Nathan asked.

'By wading in,' was the laconic reply.

'Without a pier, Leith's trade must be finished.'

The seaman laughed bitterly, 'Trade? That's gone too. People reckon they're lucky if they're still alive. I don't know why our rulers can't drive the English away from our coast. The old kings wouldn't have suffered it. That's what we get for having a woman on the throne.'

Nathan carried both his parents through the surf on his back and deposited them on the harbour side, before looking around in shocked surprise. Not only was the pier ruined, but so were most of the buildings along the waterfront. Only a circular stone watchtower at the pier head seemed to have withstood the terrible onslaught. Inns that always used to be thronged with drinking seamen stood deserted and roofless and people passing by looked totally demoralized.

Ezra, who could see none of this, was shocked when Nathan told him about the ruin of the once bustling port. 'Is Leverson's warehouse still standing?' he asked a passer-by.

The man pointed, not realizing Ezra was blind. 'Can't you see? That's it.' The formerly huge warehouse was roofless, but a few men stood in the open doorway, so Nathan ran over to them and asked, 'Where's Leverson?'

'Inside,' said one of the men, and yelled back over his shoulder, 'Hey Jo. There's someone here asking for you.'

Mr Leverson, still plump and prosperous-looking in spite of the wreckage of his business place, came out of the interior of the shed saying, 'Looking to do business are you? Come on in.'

'It's Nathan and Ezra, the pedlars who buy silks from you,' said Nathan, stepping forward.

Jo Leverson beamed, 'Nathan, you've grown so big and strong I didn't recognize you. I've a wonderful selection of silks for you. I kept them safe through all the trouble. Come in, come in.'

Stepping over a chaos of broken beams and debris, Nathan followed and found himself in a space fenced around by crates and wooden boxes.

'So you're still open for business?' he said in amazement.

'Of course. How else could I live? Where's your father?'

'He's outside with my mother. She's looking for an inn.'

'They can't eat at any of the places still standing. The food won't be kosher. Go and fetch them. I'll take them to my home. Your father has always been one of my best customers and I can repay him with hospitality now.'

He clapped a black hat on his head and they went out together to find Ezra and Miriam, who gladly accepted the offer of hospitality. Nathan suspected that the three of them might be in collusion, or at least had the same thing in mind – a marriage.

The Leverson family were securely housed in a basement in the Kirk Gate of Leith, not far from the harbour. Snug in their burrow, they had endured the English attack and were counting their blessings now that the bombardment was over, for not only were they alive but most of the goods in their warehouse were safe too, because the stout crates withstood the collapse of the shed roof.

Mrs Leverson was a fat little woman who held out her hands in welcome to the visitors and apologized for the fact she was living in a cellar, but was joyous that her family was safe.

'Have you heard what they've done to that cardinal? Isn't it awful! Were the English responsible? Will they burn down St Andrews too, I wonder? They set Edinburgh ablaze for days. We could see the flames from the street outside. It was terrifying. We're lucky to be spared and my husband had the sense to bring all our gold and silver in here when the trouble started. Sit down, eat, share our good fortune,' she told them.

The table was spread with fine linen and candles provided light for the diners, because there was only one tiny barred window high above their heads. A black-haired young woman called Ruth brought in a flask of wine and Nathan's heart sank at the sight of her, for she was even fatter than her mother and flaps of flesh hung down from the upper part of her bare arms. Though she had a pretty face, it was spoiled because her cheeks were round and red as apples and she had at last three chins. Making love to her would be like being smothered in a feather bed, he thought, and wondered how he could escape the marriage that he could see both

47

sets of parents were eager to arrange.

The girl dimpled as she handed him a goblet of wine. 'Drink, drink, you've come a long way and seen awful things,' she urged him.

He was so apprehensive that it was difficult to swallow and he saw Mrs Leverson looking suspiciously at him, obviously wondering if this boy was sick or, even worse, was one of those peculiar people like Protestants who did not approve of wine.

While both sets of parents made conversation, the sound of clattering dishes came from the kitchen, where food was obviously being prepared, and delicious smells began wafting into the room.

'My Ruth is a very good cook, you'll enjoy what she is making,' Mrs Leverson assured Nathan's mother, who smiled and enquired how old Ruth was.

'She's almost twenty.'

'Not affianced to anyone yet?'

'There's a family called Stern in Edinburgh's High Street whose son is the right age and they've made an offer, but Ruth says he's too thin.'

Nathan looked down at his legs, strong and stout in buckskin leggings, and wished they were thinner.

Ruth was much in evidence during the meal, while her mother proudly pointed out the special delicacies that she'd made and Nathan's parents responded equally enthusiastically. When the feast was over, he gallantly stood up to help carry empty plates into the kitchen, for the family seemed to have no servant, though they were obviously comfortably off.

The kitchen was even darker than the main room, but a huge fire burned in the grate and when he carried in his burden to put it on the table, he saw another girl standing by the hearth. As she stirred a pot hanging over the flames, she was singing quietly to herself in a sweet, clear voice. This girl was as slim as a fairy, dark-haired and wide-eyed, with a mouth that curved beautifully when she turned and smiled at him. He felt his heart leap at the sight of her.

'Hello, I'm Nathan,' he said.

'I know,' she said, 'My name is Esther.'

'Are you the maid?'

She laughed. 'Not all the time. Our maid ran away and the cook was killed during the English attack, so I'm helping my mother and sister.'

'You're also a daughter of the house?'

'Yes – I'm the baby.'

'Are you married?'

'Of course not! I'm only sixteen.'

'Would you consider marrying me?'

She walked nearer to him and stared up at his face for what seemed to be a long time. 'I like the look of you, but my mother and father want you to marry my sister. Your father spoke to them about it the last time he was in Leith.'

'I'd rather marry you,' said Nathan.

Six

1547

It took Nathan a year to convince his parents and the Leversons that he would not marry Ruth, but wanted to make her sister his wife instead.

His mother wrung her hands and moaned, 'But Leverson won't give Esther such a good dowry as her sister and she's so thin and young. She doesn't look as if she'll have strong children. The other one is more healthy. She'd survive a famine. I remember my mother telling me that when she was a girl in Russia, they used to be urged to eat as much as possible during the good times so they could live on their fat when the hungry days came.'

'I don't care about the dowry and I don't care if Esther's sister can live for a year on her fat, I'll not marry a woman who looks like a lump of dough,' said Nathan firmly and eventually both sets of parents realized that nothing would shift him. If the families wanted to unite, Esther had to be the bride.

The wedding was celebrated by a local rabbi in Leith on the same day as the little queen sailed from Dumbarton to safety in France.

* * *

Mary of Guise almost collapsed with grief when she parted with her beloved child, and, seeing her mother so overcome, young Mary began weeping too as she tried to run off the King of France's royal galley while the sailors were untying the ropes that tied it to land.

'Mama, Mama!' her voice was heard crying in anguish as the small fleet of French ships sailed off into the waters of the Clyde estuary.

None of the women of her court had ever seen the Queen Mother openly break down through any of her troubles, but now she howled like a hurt animal and tears poured down her face. She adored her daughter and they were very close, spending as much time as possible together. When the child suffered a bad attack of measles, her mother sat by her bed every day, praying and hardly sleeping till the fever abated.

'Madame, why don't you go to France with the Queen?' asked one of the sympathetic courtiers accompanying her, and she turned on him savagely, 'And what do you imagine will happen if I leave Scotland? My daughter's kingdom would be stolen from her, either by the English or by her own kin, that's what! I have to keep it safe till she's old enough to rule herself. I'm the only person in the world who is truly loyal to her.'

What she said was true. Ever since James V's death, she had devoted her enormous energies to making sure that Mary was acknowledged as Queen. To that end, she travelled the country, from north to south and east to west and, in spite of the turmoil caused by English attacks along the Border and from the sea, she encouraged new industries that enhanced the state finances which were badly depleted by the prodigal spending of her mother-in-law, James IV's widow, Margaret Tudor. Through her encouragement and enthusiasm, coal, lead and gold mining began in Scotland, starting industries that would flourish in the future.

Even her enemies, and she had many, acknowledged that she made a better ruler than any of the kings who'd preceded her.

Her ambitions for her daughter knew no bounds, and she looked beyond Scotland on Mary's behalf. The heir to King Henry II of France was Francois, a year younger than Mary, and her mother could think of nothing better than a marriage between them. That marriage would make her child Queen of France as well as Queen of Scotland one day.

This ambition was not approved of in Scotland. The great Protestant lords who sat in the Estates of Scotland were violently opposed to Roman Catholicism and, for them, the biggest barrier against a French marriage was religion. Mary of Guise's staunch support of the Catholic church made her rule already unpopular, and the idea of her daughter, the next ruler, marrying a Catholic prince was appalling. Eventually, by bribery and coercion, she managed to persuade them to agree to a marriage treaty between her daughter Mary and Francois, Dauphin of France. The treaty was signed in secret in a Haddington nunnery.

But a treaty was not an actual marriage and

Mary of Guise still had much to overcome before her dynastic ambitions were achieved. A major obstacle was young Francois's mother, Catherine de Medici, a scheming Italian woman who was jealous and suspicious of the power the Guise family held in the French court. It was unlikely that she would welcome Mary of Guise's daughter as a bride for her eldest son.

As soon as little Mary's ship disappeared from view on its way to France, her mother returned to Falkland Palace and shut herself up for days, weeping over the loss of her child and fretting for her safety. The weather was wild and messages kept arriving about storms preventing the royal convoy venturing into the turbulent open sea.

'What if my child is drowned? What if she never sees France? Have I made the wrong decision sending her away?' moaned the Queen Mother and her courtiers were powerless to reassure her.

She was not alone in worrying, for other people in her court had beloved children of their own aboard the storm-threatened ships. Four little girls from suitable families had been chosen to accompany the young queen into exile and their parents tried to hide their own anxieties as they reassured little Mary's mother.

Mary of Guise stopped pacing the floor of her chamber and wringing her hands when Mary Beaton's father, who was Keeper of Falkland Palace, arrived with the good news of their children's safe arrival in France.

After a prolonged voyage, the convoy had made safe harbour at Roscoff in Brittany on August fifteenth. The message sent back to tell the people at home that the precious cargo was safe said that, though most of the passengers on board the royal ships were violently ill while they tossed about in the middle of the North Sea, the little queen and her friend Mary Fleming were the only ones unaffected, even when the seas were at their most rough. They'd raced round the decks, daring each other to lean perilously over the sides of the ship and rousing terror in the hearts of the people detailed to keep an eye on them, for they knew that if the Queen fell overboard, the punishment meted out to negligent carers would be horrific.

'All our little girls are safe and well, Your Majesty,' Beaton cried, presenting the Queen Mother with a sheaf of letters that she read aloud as if they were the most precious messages ever received by anyone.

'Thank God, thank God. The commander of the expedition says my Marie is very well, and compliments me on her beauty and strong constitution. He says she is beautiful and perfect in every way. Thank God she has her feet on the soil of France at last. Now she will be safe,' she cried.

In Roscoff, Mary was met by her grandmother, Antoinette of Guise, who enveloped her in a huge embrace. Three of her uncles were there too, tall handsome men whose imposing presences brought her mother vividly back to her memory.

Mary arrived with four playmates of the same age, five years old. They were Mary Fleming, Mary Seton, Mary Beaton – a relative of the murdered Cardinal – and Mary Livingston. All of them, except Mary Fleming, were half French like the Queen, for their Scottish fathers had married French women.

Mary Fleming was the only pure-bred Scot, because she was a grandchild of James IV through her illegitimate mother, and had inherited his charismatic character and supreme handsomeness. She was the only one of the Queen's playmates to rival her in beauty.

All the little girls were charming, but the young Queen was particularly appealing and she unwittingly played her part in her mother's marriage schemes by delighting everyone, and especially the King, from the moment she arrived in the French court. In France, Mary found her spiritual home. The grey skies and drizzling rain of Scotland, with its grim castles and cold, sparsely furnished chambers, were forgotten when she found herself in elegant and comfortable French royal palaces like St Germaine en Laye or Fontainebleu.

Under the indulgent eye of her grandmother, she was given the suitable education for a girl, learning to play music and sing. By the time she was eight years old she was able to speak, read and write Latin, French, Greek and Italian, but hardly any tuition was given in the English language, though a tutor was employed to make sure she could speak good Scots.

Her general education was not scholarly or

intensive like the education given to Elizabeth Tudor, for Mary was trained in the skills and arts of an upper-class French woman, whose only care was to please a husband and reign over a fine establishment. The ability to make charming conversation, deliver clever quips and conduct herself prettily came effortlessly to her. She danced with great skill and looked magnificent on the floor because of her ever-increasing height and elegant bearing.

In her leisure hours, too, she followed the pastimes of a lady. In particular, she became a skilled embroiderer, producing lovely work. Throughout her life she was rarely seen without a piece of needlework in her hands. Poetry enjoyed a great vogue in the French court at that time and she learned to write passable verse.

Most important of all, she proved to be an excellent horsewoman, which endeared her to King Henry II, who had a limitless enthusiasm for hunting and admired the daring she showed on the field when she followed him in his fast and furious chases through the dense forests of the Ardennes.

Unfortunately, no attention was given in her education to diplomacy or statesmanship, for those were considered to be more suitable for male rulers. Everyone she met was loving and indulgent to her, so she trusted all on sight and grew up without any criteria for judging people. Throughout her life she was unable to tell the sincere from the insincere, and this lack of awareness was to be her downfall.

On the day that Mary of Guise received a letter

telling her that the King of France had given orders that the young Queen of the Scots be given precedence over his own daughters in court processions, she knew her campaign for the marriage of her Mary was succeeding.

Seven

1557

'The Maries', as Mary and her circle of Scottish playmates were called in the French court, sat beneath a huge walnut tree in the park at St Germaine on a blazing summer day. It was ten years since any of them had seen their native land and they were more French than Scots now. Apart from the Queen, they had not seen their parents since leaving home.

Mary of Guise, though a devoted mother, only managed one short visit to her daughter because, as Regent, she was afraid to leave the faction split kingdom of Scotland for long. The powerful Scottish lords, many of them illegitimate children of James V or descended from the bastards of his father James IV, plotted and conspired not only against her but against each other as well. Because she was not sure whom to trust, she ended up trusting no one except her religious adviser Cardinal Beaton. Her reliance on him gave rise to the popular rumour that she was his mistress. 'The Cardinal's whore' was what people called her.

Worries like that, however, did not concern her daughter, who took people at face value and was well disposed towards anyone who seemed well disposed to her.

'It's too hot even to sew,' she said, laying down her needlework and wiping her forehead with the back of her hand.

Mary Seaton laughed. 'You don't often complain of the heat. I thought you liked warm weather.'

'I do normally, but it's stifling hot today. I wish I could take off all my clothes and jump into the lake.'

'Don't be silly,' said practical Mary Livingston.

'I'm not silly. I saw Diane de Poitiers swimming in the river yesterday and she was completely naked. The King was there too, in a little boat. She looked lovely, like a sea nymph,' Mary told them.

'Is that true?' asked Mary Livingston in an incredulous tone.

'I swear it. I was out riding alone and saw them. They didn't see me.'

'But she's an old woman! She must be at least fifty!'

The girls were horrified. Their own mothers were younger than fifty and the thought of seeing them naked was shocking.

Not to Mary Stewart though. She remembered the sleek look of naked Diane climbing into the King's boat and bending to kiss him with her breasts brushing his face.

'I don't think you should spend so much time with La Poitiers. People say she's an immoral and dangerous woman,' said Mary Livingston primly.

'Oh, don't be so proper. She's fascinating and she likes me. She talks to me as if I'm a grown woman,' Mary protested.

'That's what I mean.'

'But I nearly am. I'm sixteen and getting married next year. Then I'll know everything. I'll be able to tell you what it's like to go to bed with a man.'

Mary Fleming, who had already had that pleasure but kept quiet about it, said sharply, 'I wouldn't be too sure about that.'

'What do you mean?' asked the Queen.

'I heard some of Queen Catherine's women talking and they said the Dauphin hasn't developed yet. When you marry him, La Poitiers might have to give him one of her special potions, like she did when Queen Catherine couldn't conceive. Her special herbs did the trick. Catherine gave birth to Francois and went on to have nine more, though they're a motley crew.'

The girls laughed. Although they were young, they were well aware of all the court scandals and knew that one of Francois's brothers already insisted on dressing in women's clothes, while another was clearly deranged, and a sister talked about sex in the grossest terms. She'd told Mary Beaton that she regularly coupled with one of her brothers and had done so since they were very young.

'Unfortunately, it isn't Francois she sleeps with,' said Beaton.

'What do you mean – *unfortunately*?' asked Mary Livingston.

'Because if it was him we'd know he's not incapable.'

'That's only gossip,' said Mary apparently lightly, but she was apprehensive about her sexual ignorance. What would happen to her if she failed to bear a royal heir? she wondered, and made up her mind to seek out Diane to ask for advice. It was not a subject suitable for one of her long letters to her mother.

On fine evenings, before the sun went down, King Henry and his mistress Diane were in the habit of taking a ride around the huge park. That night, when they were returning to the stables, Mary waited beneath a clump of trees and rode out as they passed. Diane greeted her in a friendly way. 'Alone, my dear?'

'None of my Maries wanted to ride with me. They say it's too hot,' was the girl's reply.

Diane laughed, 'But not for you?'

'No, I need exercise and I thought I might meet you. I always enjoy our conversations.'

Diane looked sharply at the girl and knew there was a purpose to this meeting, so she turned to her lover and said, 'I'll finish my ride with this young lady, my dear. Go in and I'll join you soon.'

She turned her horse around and she and Mary rode off together in the direction of the lake.

'I saw you swimming here the other day,'

Mary said.

'Did you? Were you shocked?'

'No. I hope I can do things like that when I'm married.'

'Are you looking forward to marrying?'

'Oh yes. I believe in love. I love Francois because he is my friend. And I want to be a real woman...'

'Sometimes it takes a little time...'

'What do you mean?'

'Well Francois is a year younger than you. He's still only a boy. You might have to be patient.'

Mary turned her beautiful red head and stared into the other woman's face. This was what she wanted to talk about. 'Will it be all right for us? I know what is expected of me. If I don't have a son, I'll be blamed. Henry Tudor put away his first wife because she could only bear daughters,' she said.

'Henry Tudor was a man who blamed everyone but himself for anything that went wrong. But royal marriages – in fact any marriages – can be difficult, you know. When I first married, I was the same age as you and my husband was nearly forty years older. It was a shock to me. I didn't know how to give or receive pleasure with a man for a long time.'

'What did you do?'

'I asked other women. You can usually tell when a woman has the capacity to enjoy herself in bed.'

'One of my Maries said you helped the Queen conceive when she was first married. If I can't conceive, will you help me?'

'I don't think there's any reason for you not to conceive. You're a healthy young woman, and you have normal feelings, don't you?'

'Yes, sometimes when I see young men in the stable yard or working in the garden, they look so *animal* that they make my heart turn over.'

'You're a Stewart. They were amorous people and so are the Guises. Don't worry. If you have any problems it'll be because of Francois. Tell me and I'll help you manage him. I can explain things. Don't be afraid. Remember, this marriage of yours is an alliance of two powers. It's diplomatic more than romantic. Once you have a child, you can discreetly take lovers if your husband doesn't satisfy you.'

'Satisfy me?' Mary sounded puzzled.

Diane did not elaborate on that, but asked, 'Do you really like Francois?'

'Oh yes, very much. He's been my friend ever since I came from Scotland. We played together in the nursery. I feel sorry for him because he is so often sick and that itch of his drives him mad sometimes.'

'I'm sure your sympathy will help him and I hope you go on playing together,' laughed Diane. 'Don't worry my dear. Everything will work out.'

Eight

1558

Behind a parade of musicians and a line of gorgeously dressed heralds, King Henry II led the glorious procession of his family into the vast cavern that was the aisle of Notre Dame cathedral and courteously helped his wife Catherine to take her place of honour. Her gown was so stiffly embroidered and boned that it could stand up on its own, which made it difficult for her to bend the skirts enough to sit down. Nor could she turn her head, because of the huge layers of ruff around her face.

'The woman always overdresses,' he thought. 'That's because she's not of the noble class. She looks like an Italian merchant's daughter, which is where she comes from, of course.'

He preferred women to dress simply and elegantly, like his mistress Diane, who always wore black though not in mourning. He knew that today's bride had been advised by Diane on what to wear and looked forward to seeing her.

With satisfaction he surveyed the packed cathedral, though he did not actually like Notre Dame. It was too enormous, stark and echoing for his taste, but the alliance between his eldest son and the Queen of Scotland was a most important international occasion and the Chapelle Royale, his favourite place of worship, was too small to accommodate the vast crowd who attended this wedding. The marriage of the Dauphin was to be the most magnificent and lavish ever witnessed.

Mentally the king rubbed his hands and exuded satisfaction at the thought of the terms he had extracted from the Scots before he finally agreed to marry his son to their queen. Less than a fortnight ago, at the beginning of April, young Mary had signed an agreement promising that, in the event of her death, the kingdom of Scotland would pass to her husband, and also when, *not if*, he told himself, they had children, they would be first in line to inherit her domain as well as the kingdom of France.

What a jab in the eye that is for the English, he silently rejoiced.

Music from the vast choir soared gloriously to the cathedral roof as the bride walked up the aisle. Young Marie, for he preferred calling her that instead of plain Scots Mary, was a beauty and every inch a queen.

Diane's advice had been good, for the bride was dressed in a white diaphanous gown that flowed behind her like a mist and her glorious red hair was covered with a transparent white veil.

Catherine, his superstitious wife, nudged him in the ribs and hissed, 'Look! How terrible. She's wearing white! Doesn't she know that's the colour of mourning? I hope she won't bring ill luck to this marriage.'

He glared at her and snapped, 'The girl looks lovely, and far more royal than our son.'

Unfortunately that was true. Francois, the bridegroom, and Henry's heir, was waiting at the altar, his white face blotched with eczema scars and his nose running in a perpetual stream as it always did. Though he was only a year younger than the composed and beautiful bride, he looked half her age and was half her size.

Not far from Henry stood the bride's mother, Mary of Guise. Poor woman, she had deteriorated in health and beauty since the last time they had met. How old was she? No more than forty-two or three, younger than he was himself! Her face was thin and haggard, but her body was horribly bloated as if she had dropsy. The strain of ruling Scotland for her daughter was obviously wearing her down. It would not be long before his son inherited that kingdom as well as his own.

After the ceremony, wine flowed at the magnificent wedding banquet in the Palais de la Cite and as she sat at table, Mary of Guise fought to quell the nausea that swept over her as she watched an enormous array of dishes being borne in from the vast kitchens.

Diners were presented with a variety of roast fowls – ranging from turtle doves and quails to peacocks, geese, swans and pigeons. A line of serving men paraded between the tables, carrying platters of silvered and gilded calves' heads, or roast suckling pigs glazed with honey.

Spiced and citrus-flavoured sweetmeats were

eaten between courses. They were made from sugar, which was very expensive and had recently supplanted honey as a sweetener. Another new favourite that graced the feast was marchpane, made from pounded almonds, sugar and rose water and decorated with gold leaf. Excess and expense were demonstrated in equal measure.

Only the young had any energy left when darkness clouded the spring sky and musicians could be heard striking up in the vast pillared space of the Men of Arms hall, which was cleared for dancing.

The bride felt vigour surge up in her when she heard the music. She, who loved to dance, sweetly asked her bridegroom to take the floor with her and they stepped out together. Buoyant as she felt on her wedding day, it was undeniable that Francois was not a hero bridegroom from myth or legend. Stark red blotches marked his face and even as he danced, he was surreptitiously scratching himself with frantic fingers. *Was his skin disease infectious?* Mary wondered. She hoped not, because tonight she would be ceremoniously put into bed with him.

King Henry took control of the situation when he saw the shadow on the bride's face as she and her new husband returned from the floor.

'They're playing a pavane,' he said, rising to his feet and extending his hand to her. 'Let us take the floor, daughter.'

The music, played by lutes, violas, oboes and flutes, was slow and stately as they bowed to each other before treading the measure. In a few moments, others joined them and soon the floor was crowded with dancing couples.

Mary threw back her head and the white veil slid on to her shoulders, revealing her incandescent hair. More than one man stared at her with lustful admiration and wondered for how long puny Francois would retain her affections.

A man who stared more fixedly than the others was young James Hepburn, who was attending the wedding as a hanger-on of Mary's mother's retinue.

The musicians were playing a galliard, a fast tune that demanded agility and abandon, when Mary found herself dancing opposite him. He seemed to draw her as if by magic.

He held her eye, and somehow she did not seem capable of breaking the connection. He was sandy-haired and unsmiling, brooding-eyed and dangerous. He reminded her of a hunting hawk.

'Look away, look away,' she told herself, but could not. With eyes locked, they danced on, oblivious to other people around them. At last the music stopped, and when the King stepped in to lead Mary back to a seat beside her wan-looking mother, she whispered, 'Who's the man in the slashed green doublet, mother? Is he in your entourage?'

Mary of Guise followed her daughter's gaze and said, 'That's James Hepburn, the fourth Earl of Bothwell. His father's not long dead and he's one of the Border lords who're always fighting each other.'

'Is he a supporter of yours?'

'I'm not sure. He's a Protestant but he's backed me up on several occasions. People say he's a dangerous man to cross though.'

Young Mary sighed, 'He does look dangerous, that's true.'

Her mother's head turned sharply. 'Avoid him, he is VERY dangerous, especially with women.'

Very dangerous with women ... What did that mean? Mary wondered as she watched the man in green solemnly stepping the measure of a slow saraband. He pointed his toes and bent from the waist like a swordsman, lithe and supple, but still unsmiling. She thought he exuded some sort of promise, or was it a threat?

Nine

1559

'You might be a grandfather soon. Young Marie Stewart thinks she's having a child,' Diane de Poitiers told her lover, Henry.

He looked up, eyes alight. 'Does she? Do you think it's possible?'

'I don't know. You and I have the same doubts about Francois, but she says she didn't bleed last month. She's young, and sometimes young girls are irregular and she's willing herself to have a child, so she might be imagining it. She's started wearing loose gowns though and has ordered a new wardrobe because her waist is bigger, but I've noticed her taste for marchpane. Perhaps that's what's fattening her.'

'She can have as many gowns and as much marchpane as she wants if she is carrying a child, but you're not convinced, are you?' said Henry.

'No. I've asked her about their love-making and it seems as if they do nothing more than fumble.'

'Have his balls dropped yet?' asked Henry outright.

'I tried to ask but she doesn't seem to know what I'm talking about. For a girl from the Guise family, she's very naive.'

'Neither the Guises nor the Stewarts are famed for innocence. Get Doctor Pare to examine my son, but from the look of him I don't think he's developed into a man.'

'Neither do I, but it's best to indulge Marie in her fantasy. Perhaps one day it'll come true and Francois will be turn out to be as lusty as his father,' said Diane, patting her lover's cheek.

Mary and her friend Elisabeth, Francois's sister and the eldest daughter of Henry, were holding hands and giggling in the long hall of Fontaine-bleu.

'How many gowns are you taking to Spain?' Mary asked.

'Dozens. My mother's seamstresses have been sewing for weeks. I'm leaving all that to her.'

'Are you looking forward to being married?'

'Oh yes. I'll be a queen and have my own

court, the biggest in the world.'

Mary's face clouded. 'It's sad that you'll have to live in Spain and we'll not see each other any more. I'm going to miss you.'

'And I'll miss you,' said Elisabeth. 'You've been my best friend ever since you came from Scotland.'

'Do you think you'll like Philip? Have you ever seen him?' Mary asked.

'Only his portrait. He's thirty-two, quite old. His last wife was Mary Tudor. When she died, he wanted to marry her sister Elizabeth, but she refused him and now he's chosen me.'

'Diane says all you have to do is give him a son, then you can do more or less as you like,' said Mary. To her, a bridegroom of thirty-two was immensely aged. At least Francois was almost the same age as herself.

'He already has a son called Don Carlos. They wanted me to marry him but he's mad, and people say his father keeps him shut up in a tower. I cried and my father refused Carlos. Then Philip offered to marry me himself,' said Elisabeth.

'At least they didn't force Carlos on you,' said Mary, squeezing her friend's hand. She was glad that the excitement caused by Elisabeth's marriage meant that the gossips had stopped scrutinizing every move she made and every mouthful of food she ate. They were obviously wondering – when is the Dauphin's wife going to fall pregnant?

Catherine de Medici was determined that her sixteen-year-old daughter's marriage would be

70

splendid. Though the bridegroom was not attending the ceremony in person, the French royal family intended to make it a wedding never to be forgotten or overshadowed. Three days of feasts and balls, processions of musicians, parades through the streets of Paris and knightly displays, jousts and tournaments were planned.

'I'll show the Spaniards how glorious the Valois court is,' vowed Catherine.

Her husband was happy to spend lavishly, and was especially looking forward to the jousting, because he prided himself on his prowess in the lists. He ordered a new suit of armour with a magnificent plumed and gilded helmet to wear when he rode out to overwhelm his opponents.

The day before the ceremony, Catherine asked for an audience with the famous astrologer, Nostradamus, or Michel de Nostradame, a half Jewish apothecary from Aix, whose fame as a seer had spread through France after he had correctly predicted important events to other ladies of aristocratic families.

He did not resort to the usual astrologer's mumbo jumbo or go into trances and give advice in a ghostly voice, but replied to questions with rhyming couplets or in single, succinct sentences. A summons from the Queen was not to be refused, but he did not seem particularly impressed when she swept into his presence.

'I want you to tell me the future of my daughter who is about to become Queen of Spain,' she said grandly.

'I need to know the day and time of her birth,'

he replied.

The information was produced and handed to him. He read for a while and then said, 'And the bridegroom's?'

She fidgeted while he pored over more papers until she could contain herself no longer and blurted out, 'Will my daughter have a son?'

'An heir to Spain Philip will not gain, but daughters fair will your princess bear,' he said.

'Will she outlive Philip?' Catherine asked, wondering if there might be another glorious marriage for her child.

'Four times will the Spanish monarch wed,' he told her.

She gasped. 'But my daughter is only his third wife.'

'Four times will the Spanish monarch wed. Another wife is at his death bed,' said Nostradamus.

Catherine looked round at the women who had accompanied her to the meeting and said sternly, 'None of you will speak of this.' They nodded in agreement, though they were horrified by what they'd heard and all wondered how long the poor princess would live.

The Queen stood up, sternly controlled, and was about to leave when Nostradamus put out a hand to stop her and said, 'Madame, I have something else to say. Do you want to hear it?'

She could not hide the fear in her eyes as she looked at him. 'What is it?'

'Give your husband some advice. Stop him jousting in the tournament. If he does, *He will pierce his eyes in a cage of gold, and die a cruel death.'*

'His eyes?' queried the Queen, 'but he always wears a helmet with the visor closed.'

'If he jousts, he will suffer an injury to his eye,' said Nostradamus implacably.

She pretended indifference. 'A man can live a long time with one eye.'

'If he jousts he will die a cruel death,' persisted the seer.

Catherine's composure cracked and she ran out to seek her husband and say, 'You must not joust after the wedding. The seer told me you'll die if you do.'

He scoffed. 'Only you would believe such rubbish. You're a credulous Italian.'

'Please, I beg you. Do not go into the jousting ring,' she sobbed.

'I'm the best in all France at tilting with the lance,' he told her and walked away, but her conviction bothered him and he told Diane about it that night. She soothed him by saying, 'Nostradamus is a charlatan. He's better at making up potions than foretelling the future. Who is your opponent in the ring?'

'Montmorency, the Captain of the Scots Guard. It won't be an easy victory because he's younger than I am,' Henry told her, but again she reassured him, 'But he's not as skilled. You're the best jouster in the land. I'll be proud to watch you prevail over him.'

The day after the wedding in Notre Dame, the court crowded round the jousting ring to watch their King show off. Diane occupied the seat of honour in the viewing stand, taking precedence over the Queen.

Henry was in his bedecked tent buckling on his armour, when his distraught wife rushed in and again tried to make him change his mind.

'Do not fight. Abandon this joust for the sake of me and your children,' she pleaded.

He laughed, 'Because a bearded herbalist says so? Don't be silly. Anyway, Monmorency and I are only fighting with wooden weapons. There'll be no killing and I'll have him off his horse in five minutes.'

He was only correct about the length of the fight, because it took exactly five minutes before disaster struck. By a fluke, Montmorency's wooden lance split when he struck Henry on the golden helmet and splinters went through the visor to pierce the King's right eye.

He rocked in the saddle. The crowd gasped and the Queen stood up with a scream. Henry leaned first to the right and then to the left but managed to keep his seat. The noise the Queen made rallied her husband, who controlled his horse and rode to the side of the tilting ground, where he was helped to the ground.

For a moment he stood upright, then slumped down unconscious for a few moments, but soon he stood up again and was helped away to his tent.

Diane de Poitiers was with him while his helmet was removed and she almost fainted at the sight of the terrible wound he'd suffered. His right eye was thrust through.

When the frantic Queen arrived a few seconds later, she roughly elbowed Diane out of the way, and ordered a bystander to fetch the famous doctor, Ambrose Pare, who was a teacher in the university on the Ile de la Cite.

Henry was conscious and able to talk when a grave-faced Pare examined him. Montmorency's wooden lance had splintered so badly when it made contact with the King's helmet that fragments of wood were implanted in a circle in his temple and around his eye.

'Can you see my hand?' Pare asked, holding up his palm.

The King nodded.

'Deo gratias,' sobbed the Queen, but Pare cast her a baleful glance, for he had graver fears.

'The eye is only part of his trouble. I'm afraid there's an injury to his brain,' he said and the patient closed his eyes, trying not to hear what was being said.

All festivities ended and another doctor, a famous anatomist called Andreas Vesalius, was also summoned to examine him. Vesalius was met by the icy Queen, who demanded, 'What can you do for my husband that Pare cannot?'

'Because I'm not sure what part of his brain has been damaged, I can't tell how far the splinters of the lance penetrated and what part of his brain is pierced,' was the answer.

'Have you ever seen an injury like his before?' she asked and he shook his head.

'Would it help if you did see one?'

'It might.'

'Then you shall. I've ordered three felons to be killed by wooden lances being driven into their heads at exactly the same angle as the lance

75

went into my husband,' she said, and the grue-some order was immediately carried out.

Vesalius and Pare dissected the dead men's heads and what they found made them even more pessimistic. 'His brain must be compro-mised. If an infection sets in, he is doomed,' they told the Queen.

She screamed like a mad woman and they shrank from her. 'Fetch Montmorency. If my husband dies, he dies too,' she yelled.

The unfortunate Montmorency guessed he would be blamed for the King's injury, and tried to escape from Paris in the confusion following the joust, but was spotted and thrown into prison to await his fate.

After ten days of suffering, Henry II was doomed. His life ebbed away, and hour by hour he deteriorated, growing delirious, developing a fever, and suffering innumerable seizures.

When it was obvious that his fate was sealed, Diane de Poitiers was ordered to leave his bedside where she'd spent all her waking hours. Queen Catherine took her place, though Henry wailed piteously for Diane to return and hold his hand. Denied access to him, she sat weeping in the outer chamber, listening to his cries.

He died on the eleventh day after terrible suffering, and when his last breath was drawn, Catherine stormed out of his room shouting, 'Bring Montmorency here to me. I want to see him die.'

Diane tried to intercede for the unfortunate man. 'Spare Montmorency, Your Majesty. It was a fair combat. The King would not want him to be killed,' she pleaded.

Catherine pushed her in the chest and shrieked. 'You'll die too if I see your face in this palace again! Get out, get out!'

When Montmorency was hauled into the courtyard, she ran downstairs and stood watching with a terrifying expression on her face while an axe man cut off the poor man's head. She wanted her daughter-in-law Mary to watch along with her, but the young woman refused. 'Scenes like that repel me,' she said. She did not even like seeing a cat toying with a terrified mouse.

Mary sat up in bed early on the morning after her father-in-law's death and looked at her sleeping husband.

The new King of France lay snuffling beside her. Not only was she the Queen of Scotland, but now she was also the Queen of France, and as far as a legitimate claim was concerned, she told herself she should be Queen of England too, instead of her cousin Elizabeth, who was a bastard, having been fathered by Henry Tudor when, in the eyes of the Church, he was still married to his first wife, Catherine of Aragon.

She hugged herself in delight as she thought about the glorious future that stretched before her, and knew it would be difficult to appear properly grief-stricken at her father-in-law's funeral.

Francois stirred by her side, snorting into the pillow, and a wave of distaste swept over her. Usually she was tolerant towards him and his myriad illnesses, as well as his childish mind, but now she felt as if she had gone to bed a child on the previous evening and was waking up an adult.

She knew it was her duty to act the part of a loving wife, and that was not difficult when she and Francis were out hunting or hawking, pursuits they both enjoyed and indulged in throughout the year, but more would be expected from a king and a queen. She knew enough about the machinations of courtiers to realize that her life would now be full of obstacles and hidden dangers, especially from her mother-in-law. Though Catherine seemed friendly enough on the surface, she would suffer no other woman to outshine her or usurp the power of her family, the house of Valois.

Another pitfall for Mary was her own family. Her mother's brothers and her grandmother Antoinette treated her like a puppet and pulled her strings on behalf of the Guise family. And they were formidable people who had dominated her since childhood. Would she be able to break away? Did she want to?

Francois opened his eyes and asked, 'Is the weather fair?'

She propped herself up on one arm and looked through the window opposite their bed. 'It's fine,' she told him.

'We can ride out with the deer hounds then.'

'You can't hunt today. Your father only died yesterday. The court is in mourning,' she protested.

He pouted, 'I don't want to sit with my weeping mother all day. I want to ride out and I want you to come with me. Tell her it's necessary for my health.'

'YOU tell her,' said Mary for she would not dare to break into Catherine's terrifying mourning. Only yesterday she earned a withering reprimand when she refused to accompany the royal party to watch Montmorency's execution.

Her excuse was that she might be in a delicate condition. 'I've missed a bleed. To watch that man die would make me faint and I could lose the baby.'

Catherine seemed to be able to read the girl's secret thoughts, however, and looked sceptical.

She knows I'm not carrying a child, and she knows why, thought Mary and wondered in despair. *Will Francois ever manage to make love to me? Will he father a child on me?*

Diane had given her succinct instructions about how to make a man's penis stand erect but, though she tried as hard as she could, Francois's member remained flaccid.

When she accepted that what she and Francois were doing in bed would never produce a child, she abandoned loose gowns and tolerated her husband's way of rolling her around as he ineffectually tried to penetrate her. She sometimes thought if she married a man like the one in the green doublet, there would be no need to scuffle under blankets. Longings burned in her.

Lying in bed beside her unsatisfactory husband on her first day as Queen of France, she determined that instead of going out hunting, she would seek out Diane again and ask for another

79

potion for him. It was essential to have a son.

It was still early and the palace was silent as she drew on her wrapper and ran through the corridors to the royal mistress's apartments where, to her surprise, she found a ferment of frenzied activity, supervised by Diane in black travelling clothes and looking more agitated than Mary had ever seen her.

Women were stuffing clothes and tapestries into big travelling trunks, which men securely tied up with ropes, and two boys staggered out under the weight of a huge painting of Diane naked in her bath, which Henry had commissioned from Francois Clouet, one of the court painters.

Mary had so admired this picture that she'd commissioned the same artist to do one of her, also in the bath, but Francois and his mother vetoed her posing naked, and the painter had used another model for the body. The only proper portrayal was of her face.

At the sight of Diane's picture being hauled away, Mary exclaimed, 'Are you leaving us?'

Diane whirled round and said sharply, 'If I don't go now, I'll soon be as dead as poor Montmorency.'

'Where are you going?'

'To Chenonceaux. It's mine. Henry gave it to me in his will.'

'I'll visit you,' promised Mary, and Diane patted her gently on the cheek as she said, 'I hope you do.'

They were taking farewell of each other when a messenger from Catherine walked into the chamber without being announced and told Diane, 'Queen Catherine demands that you return to her all the jewels the late King gave you.'

Diane stared back, face impassive, but after a few seconds turned to her women and said, 'Give this man my jewel box.'

'Don't. I'm the Queen now and I say you can keep them,' interrupted Mary.

Diane shook her head. 'I'll do as she demands. Jewels are nothing to me. Goodbye my dear, don't endanger yourself by advocating my cause. I'll be safe because I still have friends, even in this court.'

When her friend left, a furious Mary ran back through the palace, heading for Catherine's suite. The Queen Mother was up and dressed in deepest mourning and she stared coldly at the young woman. 'What do you think you are doing, wandering the palace in night clothes?' she asked.

'I went to take my farewell of my friend the Duchesse de Valentinois and was there when your messenger seized her jewels.'

'Duchess de Valentinois? You mean the whore de Poitiers, don't you? I took back crown jewels that my husband gave her. They belong to the royal family,' said Catherine fiercely.

Though she was much taller than her mother-in-law, and not normally timid, Mary shrank back when Catherine advanced with a mad look in her eye. In such a heightened mental state, there was no knowing what she was capable of doing.

'I know where the whore is going. She thinks

81

she can enjoy Chenonceaux, but I'll only allow her a few days and have her out of there too. My husband should never have given her the chateau. I wanted it and now I'll have it,' she spat.

Mary ran back to her own chambers and sent a messenger to warn Diane that Catherine planned to evict her from her seclusion.

A short time later a letter came back saying that Diane thanked her for the information and had moved for safety to a distant part of France, to the small chateau of Anet, which was her own property and could not be appropriated by any-body else. There she would stay for the rest of her life.

The burial of Henry in the abbey of St Denis was swiftly followed by the coronation of his son in Notre Dame.

As all eyes followed Francois to the royal throne, people were already plotting to take control of him because it was obvious that his mind was simple and whoever controlled him, controlled France. He was doomed to be shuttled about between his mother's supporters, and the Guise uncles of his wife.

Mary, because she had already been crowned a queen in Scotland, was not to be re-crowned in France, but sat in front of the altar flanked on both sides by her uncles, the Duc of Guise and the Cardinal of Lorraine, the most formidable of her mother's five brothers. They were staking their claim to her, and through her to any child she might bear.

Outside Notre Dame, banners emblazoned with the arms of Scotland and England as well as the arms of France, were flying in the breeze. Through his wife, Francois was making claim to these other kingdoms, a presumption that caused great resentment to the English ambassador at the French court, and, when he sent the news to Elizabeth Tudor, even greater fury in her.

In the nave of Notre Dame, Mary felt safe, for her uncles reminded her again of her mother. They had the same tall bodies and long, proud noses, and similar inflections in their voices.

'I wish mother could have been here today,' she whispered to the Cardinal, who said, soothingly, 'She is with you in spirit, my dear.'

He knew, but his niece did not, that Mary of Guise was too grievously ill to travel and could not live much longer.

All the women of the court except Mary were wearing mourning gowns of black. Only she was in her customary white, and was dismayed when her mother-in-law leaned past the Cardinal and hissed, 'You should be wearing black today like every other woman here.'

Mary stared into the angry, jealous face and said, 'But at my wedding you accused me of being improperly dressed because I wore white. You said it was the colour of mourning.'

Catherine gave an exasperated splutter and her eyes went up to the narrow walk along the top of the cathedral pillars where she knew a seat had been placed for Nostradamus to observe everything that went on below and report to her later. Since his prediction about Henry's death, she hadn't made a move without asking his advice first.

At their private audience later that night she asked him, 'What did you see for the new king, my son Francois?'

He pursed his lips. 'He is a fruitless vine that withers without grace, but there are others of his blood to take the honourable place.'

'Do you mean I should look to my other sons?'

'This King's life will not be long,' he agreed and she impassively considered this cruel verdict for a few moments, without showing any signs of grief. She bore no particular affection for the snivelling boy, and she had other sons after all.

'And his wife, the Scottish queen?' she asked.

Nostradamus had hoped to avoid this question. 'I cannot be sure,' he equivocated, for Mary's beauty, her magnificent red hair and imposing height had deeply impressed him, but he knew better than to tell that to Catherine, whose jealousy of the girl was only too obvious.

She was determined to make him commit himself, however. 'Tell me what lies in future for her,' she demanded.

He looked at her bleakly and abandoned his usual way of giving predictions in verse.

'I see blood,' was all he said.

'BLOOD! Whose blood? Mine? Francois's blood?'

'Only blood, a great deal of blood.'

Ten

1560

'If the young queen does conceive a child, it certainly won't be his,' joked a young courtier, pointing at the back of the king as he passed by.

Catherine, the Queen Mother, overhearing this sally, reacted in fury, boxing the young man's ears and banishing him from court, but the jibe could not be ignored and again she summoned Doctor Pare.

'Do something about my son and his wife. I don't know which one is to blame but they have shown no sign of having a child. Prove your competence by solving this problem,' she ordered.

There was little doubt in Pare's mind about which of the pair was to blame. The young Queen was growing in beauty and high spirits every day and if Francois did not mature soon, it was inevitable that she would have to find a father for her child somewhere else. Catherine was well aware of that too.

Pare put the young man on a course of strengthening medicines and aphrodisiacs, but the only result was that Francois grew even more keen on hunting and hawking. To please the Queen Mother, the doctor also prescribed medicines for Mary so that her nights were disturbed by erotic dreams and she found herself surveying the men of the court in a way that disturbed her.

It was when she was in this highly heightened state that the Scotsman of the green doublet turned up again in the French court.

She saw him at an open air ball when couples were dancing on the sward outside the palace of Fontainebleu one hot summer night. His doublet was blue and gold this time, but the effect he had on her as he trod a measure with Mary Beaton was like a stab in the heart.

'What is that Scotsman doing here in France?' she whispered to Mary Fleming, pointing at him.

'You mean Jamie Hepburn?'

'Yes, he's the Earl of Bothwell, isn't he? He was here with my mother but she doubted his devotion to our religion.'

'I don't expect he is devoted to any religion,' said Fleming gaily. 'He's a Border reiver from Crichton Castle who thinks he's above the law. He's on the run because he stole a lot of gold that Elizabeth of England was sending up to the Protestant lords in Scotland. They sent five thousand men after him but never caught him – or got back the money. I'll find out what he's up to here if you're curious.'

Mary herself danced with Bothwell. She could not help herself. It was as if she were drawn into his orbit by an irresistible force. He was not as tall she was but the six-inch difference in their heights did not seem to intimidate him in any way and he danced as if he were bigger, stronger and far more important. Amazingly she felt that too.

She introduced him to Francois, who promptly invited him to join them in a hunt next day and in the morning she was so excited, she could hardly eat before they rode out. Bothwell was mounted on a dappled grey horse with a fearsome reputation for unseating riders, but its cavorting and bucking only made him exultant. Francois was a good horseman but Bothwell was better.

Mary was still starry-eyed with admiration that evening when Fleming brought back gossip about the new arrival. 'You were asking about Bothwell. He's on the run again, this time from a Norwegian admiral. Apparently he went to Denmark and met a woman called Anna Rustung. Her father, the admiral, is Royal Consul there. She has a large dowry, so he coaxed her into running away with him.'

'Is she here now?' asked Mary

'No, he left her in Flanders, but he's going back to collect her. He's got her dowry though and some people doubt she'll ever see him again.'

'How awful,' said Mary in a shocked voice.

Fleming laughed. 'He's probably spent the dowry already.'

'That's villainous!' Mary thought it shocking that a man who looked so courtly and behaved with such grace could be a black-hearted villain.

'But he is a villain. People say he's under the influence of his uncle, who dabbles in the black arts and he's been a devil with women too, ever since he was young. There's talk that he contracted a hand-fasting marriage with one of the Buccleuch women who's a witch and much older than him, so he was probably not in a position to marry anybody when he ran off with the Norwegian,' Fleming told the Queen.

'How do you know all this?' Mary asked.

'My mother sends me news and she never has a good word to say about Bothwell, I'm afraid.'

A villain, a seducer, a thief, perhaps even a necromancer ... Mary thought about the man all night and he still held a fascination for her. She had no chance to investigate him further, however, because when she and Francois went hunting next day, Bothwell was nowhere to be seen.

In a light tone she asked her husband if the Scottish lord had taken farewell of him. 'Yes and I gave him a purse of 600 crowns,' he said.

'What for?'

'Because he confided in me that he's in money trouble,' said Francois.

So Fleming was right. The mysterious earl had vanished with her husband's money too and no one knew where he'd turn up next.

Apart from trying to make love with her unsatisfactory husband, Mary's life was idyllic. Many men fell in love with her, but she was warned by her uncles to be cautious. Francois' mother, who was ostensibly ruling as his Regent because he was not yet of age, would exact a terrible vengeance if his wife was suspected of

88

cuckolding him.

She and Francois were good friends, though he was still incapable of consummating the marriage. They enjoyed playing music together, dancing and learning to write poetry under the tutelage of France's most famous poet, Pierre Ronsard, who became a close friend of Mary's, and, if he had his way, would have been her lover.

Remembering how her mother was widowed while still a young woman, Mary often secretly speculated about which of the great lords of France she might take as a husband if her sickly husband died. Her Maries giggled and speculated with her, but none of them ever suggested a Scottish possible husband, and certainly not the Earl of Bothwell.

'Why is everyone so gloomy?' she asked gaily one day when she passed a group of her uncles' friends having a serious conversation in a corner of the great hall at Fontainebleu.

'Just politics. There's been rioting between Protestants and Catholics in Paris,' she was told, but the general air of despondency did not lift and eventually her uncle, the Cardinal of Lorraine, sought her out to say, 'Come and sit down with me, my dear, I have something to tell you.'

They sat in a window embrasure overlooking the formally laid out gardens and he took her hand as he said, 'Don't be too distressed. I know how much affection you have for your mother and she for you.'

Her heart gave a strange leap in her chest and

she stared at him with wide, terrified eyes. 'My mother? Is my mother ill? Is that what you are trying to tell me? Oh no, tell me no.'

He said nothing but still stared solemnly at her.

'Send a ship to fetch her, or I'll go to her if she isn't able to come to me,' cried Mary

He shook his head but stayed silent.

'Oh dear God, she's not dead? My darling mother isn't dead. She can't be dead. If she's dead, I'll kill myself. I can't believe I'll never see her again...' Mary began screaming hysterically, startling everybody and bringing people running towards them.

'Control yourself, please control yourself,' the Cardinal pleaded, but it was as if she had become deaf.

'I want my mother, I want my darling mother, she can't be dead. Tell me she's not dead!' she went on howling like a child, while tears poured from her eyes.

This was worse than he'd feared, though he'd known her reaction would be extreme when she heard of his sister's death from dropsy. He'd kept the news of the death from her for ten days, but knew the information would inevitably leak out, so she had to be told by someone close to her.

She horrified him by tearing at her hair and scratching her face. If she wasn't stopped, she'd do herself an injury. He grabbed her hands and one of her companions, Mary Seton, ran up to calm the writing girl. For her pains, she too was scratched.

Eventually they managed to hold her still and

Seton took her, keening like a banshee, to her chamber. As he watched, her uncle wondered if she was going out of her mind.

'I thought she was a young woman of good judgement, but today I see she has a lot of Stewart in her. They all lose their heads in a crisis,' he told his brother, the Duke of Guise.

'Indeed,' was the reply. 'And the Stewarts have another failing. At times of crisis, when they are faced with a choice, they always make the wrong one. It's their fatal flaw.'

While Mary stayed in seclusion for a month, mourning for her mother, France was in the grip of frenzied religious ferment and Francois was advised to leave Fontainebleu to seek safety and seclusion in the country.

He chose to go to Chenonceaux in the Loire, now vacated by Diane and taken over by his mother, who delighted in her usurpation of the beautiful chateau and its vast parks. There he pursued his favourite pastime and hunted continually till his mother announced one morning, 'No hunting today. We must leave here at once.'

Mary who loved Chenonceaux as much as Francois, asked in disappointment, 'Why? Where will we go?'

'Some people are plotting to kill your husband, so we'll go to Orleans where he can be more closely guarded,' her mother-in-law told her.

'But who wants to kill Francois?' Mary found it difficult to believe, because her husband never exercised any power.

Catherine stared balefully at her. 'Either your

uncles or the Huguenots want to kill him. Both are very dangerous.'

So to Orleans they went, passing through golden autumn country at a time when the grapes were being gathered, and the sun gilded their faces as they rode along. Mary was not to know that she would treasure the memory of her last luscious autumn in France for the rest of her life.

They were attending Mass in the chapel of the Jacobins at Orleans on a bitterly cold Sunday a few weeks later when Francois slumped down in a faint at his wife's side. She knelt beside him, trying to raise his head, so that he half returned to consciousness and pushed her roughly away.

'My head hurts, don't touch me,' he muttered.

She looked up and saw a strange expression on her mother-in-law's face. Was it fear or a horrible kind of anticipation?

Whatever Catherine was thinking, she scared Mary, who remembered gossip about what the astrologer had told Francois's mother. When he said her son would die young, her reply had been, 'I have other sons.'

There were even some who said that she was not above poisoning him to make way for a more healthy successor, with no beautiful wife.

Francois was carried to bed and two local doctors were summoned. They diagnosed earache.

'Has he been out in the cold weather?' one of them asked and Mary said, 'We hunted all day yesterday when the weather was bitter.'

'That could cause his illness. He'll recover in

time,' was the reply.

All next day and the day after, she sat by his bed, trying to divert him with cheerful chatter and playing his favourite tunes on her lute. Her old affection for him returned when she saw how feeble he was and she held his hand, whispering endearments. She enjoyed nursing sick people.

'You're my dearest friend. We've hardly spent a day apart since I first arrived from Scotland,' she told him, but he only smiled feebly and went on complaining about the pain. The doctors were summoned again and this time they discovered a large swelling had risen behind his left ear.

'We'll have to cut it out,' they said. Apparently Francois was suffering from mastoiditis, an illness that claimed the lives of many children, and which the doctors had failed to diagnose.

Catherine turned on them and ordered, 'Do whatever is necessary. You must save my son.'

Remembering her ferocity towards the unfortunate Montmorency, they panicked and began to try every cure they knew or had ever heard about on the poor young man, but his condition continued to deteriorate and the pain was terrible.

'No one outside must know how ill he is,' Catherine ordered her courtiers and for two weeks they managed to keep the prying ambassadors from other countries at bay, but the usual cast of plotters gathered – Mary's Guise uncles among them – as the doctors bled, cupped, dosed and re-dosed the feverish king.

His wife and mother took turns sitting with him, and when they were excluded from the sickroom, they visited all the chapels and churches of Orleans frantically praying for his survival.

To no avail.

When the swelling behind his ear was lanced, the agony of the operation proved the last straw for Francois. Like his father, he suffered an inflammation of the brain and merciful death claimed him fifteen days after he first became ill. He was a few days short of his sixteenth birthday.

For Mary, it was as if the sun had gone in and would never shine again. She had barely recovered from mourning her mother when once again she was plunged into inconsolable grief. She refused to come out of her darkened chamber for many days and her desolation scared her uncles, who found it difficult to believe she cared so much for the unappetizing boy with his perpetually running nose and ugly skin rashes.

Her plain-speaking grandmother, Antoinette of Guise, who was not famed for tact, found the girl lying in bed, clad all in black with a handkerchief at her eyes.

'Pull yourself together. This is self-indulgent weakness. People think you're going mad, and if that gets about you'll find it hard to marry a good man the second time,' she said.

Mary turned on her like a tigress, 'But I loved Francois! He was my friend. I must be cursed to lose my dear husband and my beloved mother at almost the same time. Everything and everyone I love is taken away from me.'

'Be sensible. He was a weakling and he'd never have given you a child. You're only seventeen and still a virgin. Your uncles are already looking for a better husband for you.'

'I don't want another husband, no matter how great he may be.'

'Then will I tell them to put you in a nunnery? Is that what you want? There'll be no trouble marrying you off. There are plenty of candidates. Maybe even Don Carlos.'

A messenger from her mother-in-law arrived and told Mary, 'Her Majesty the Queen Mother demands that you return the crown jewels immediately.' Mary sat up at last and stared angrily at him. It was the same man who had taken away Diane's jewels. Fury galvanized her.

'But my husband is only just dead. He's not even buried yet.'

'The crown jewels must be returned immediately. You are no longer Queen. The new king is young Charles and his mother is ruling for him,' was the unbending reply.

Outraged, Mary said, 'She did the same thing to Diane. She's nothing more than a grasping merchant's daughter. Give her the jewel box and its keys. I have no need of French jewels for I have plenty of my own.'

She emerged from seclusion for Francois' state funeral when his embalmed heart was buried in the abbey of St Denis outside Paris. Even during the ceremony, she heard people speculating about whom she might marry next. Names were suggested in hushed whispers – the Emperor of Austria; Don Carlos; the kings of Denmark and

Sweden; an English Lord, Henry Darnley, who also had a claim to Elizabeth Tudor's throne; even Francois's own brother, Charles, the new King of France.

'I don't want to marry Charles,' she told her uncle the Duke of Guise, when he put that suggestion to her.

'But it would be very easy to arrange. A papal dispensation is needed but will meet with no opposition. The marriage with Francois was never consummated. You're still a virgin, aren't you?' he said.

'How do you know that? I never told you. Whose word do you have for it? Anyway I don't like Charles. I never did.'

Fortunately, Charles did not want to marry her either and his mother was especially against the match. 'I don't care if her Guise uncles get a papal dispensation for non-consummation. She went around for almost a year in loose gowns saying she was pregnant. How can they explain that away?' snapped Catherine, who badly wanted to be rid of Mary though she tried to hide her feelings under a veneer of concern.

Antoinette was well aware of the danger of antagonizing a Medici and, when the funeral was over, told her granddaughter, 'Get ready to leave this place. I'll tell your women to pack everything you need.'

Mary looked round her luxuriously furnished chamber and asked, 'Everything? That'll take days.'

'Only take the things that are most precious to you. We must leave here at once.'

'But I've lived in this court and with these people for fourteen years. Why must I leave in a hurry and where will I go?' Mary asked. Her life was falling down around her.

'Your uncles want us to travel round the Guise properties. Only there will you be safe among friends.'

'But my friends are here. I hardly know my Guise relatives. Besides, I'm too unwell to travel.'

Mary's protests were ignored and Antoinette leaned forward to stare into the girl's face. 'You've no choice. If you don't leave here, you won't only be unwell, you will be dead.'

'Who'll kill me?' Mary looked shocked.

'The Medici woman will organize it. These Italians are good any getting rid of enemies. It hasn't been safe to break bread with an Italian since your grandfather's time.'

'You mean since the Borgias. But my mother-in-law isn't a Borgia.'

'She's worse and she hates you. You're too beautiful, and too good a marriage prospect. She's afraid for her own power. Don't argue Marie, do as your uncles say. Once you are away from this court, you'll be able to pick your next husband without interference or hindrance. The Medici woman has already turned the King of Spain against you as a bride for his son.'

'I would have liked to go to Spain. Francois's sister Elisabeth is there, married to Carlos's father, and she's my friend.'

'You think so? Then you're wrong. Her mother has made her a traitor towards you. She was told to persuade Philip to refuse to consider you as a bride for his son. And she's succeeded, I'm afraid.'

'That's not possible. Elisabeth and I have always been very close, like sisters. We both wept when she had to go away after she married Philip. I miss her still and I know she misses me.'

'Letters between her and her mother have been intercepted. Believe me, she is no longer your friend. Her mother poisoned her mind because she's afraid that you and our family would become too powerful if you marry the Spanish heir.'

Mary was reluctant to believe in the deceit of her childhood friend but accepted it eventually. 'It doesn't matter if they don't want me to marry into Spain. Don Carlos is mad. He pushed his last wife down the stairs and killed her,' she said.

Antoinette agreed, 'Yes, he's rumoured to be wicked, but in marriages like yours, there's little room for choice. You'd have been well-guarded if you'd gone to Spain. There are other candidates for your hand, though not perhaps as prestigious as Carlos. Don't tell anyone what we plan, but be assured it's for your own good.'

'Will I have a choice in picking the man I marry?' asked Mary.

'Of course, my dear. Your feelings will be consulted. But you must either marry quickly or go back to Scotland. It's not safe for you to stay in France.'

For the best part of a year Mary and her Guise entourage travelled from one chateau to another, while her family weighed the advantages and disadvantages of possible husbands.

Week followed week and month followed month, while Mary maintained her grieving status, and gloried in the fact that ambassadors and envoys from all over Europe sought her out wherever she was.

News of the enthusiastic receptions the widowed young queen received in various parts of the country infuriated Catherine, and when Francois's brother was crowned as King Charles IX at Rheims, the Guises decided it was safer if Mary did not appear at the ceremony. They spread the news that she was unwell, and still too grief stricken to attend. In fact this was partly true, for she was on the verge of a nervous collapse, and showing signs of the intermittent depressions that were to plague her life and which had plagued her father's.

In her lowest days, she found solace in writing poetry, and her supporters circulated a poem of mourning she composed for her dead husband. It was passed from hand to hand and exclaimed over for its elegance and accomplishment.

'In my sad song, a melancholy air,
I shall look deep and long, a loss beyond compare.
And with bitter tears, I'll pass my best years...

Deep in my eyes and heart, a portrait has its place,
Which shows the world my hurt in the

pallor of my face,
Pale as when violets fade, true love's
becoming shade.'

When her uncle the Cardinal of Lorraine read
it, he decided the mourning ritual had gone on
long enough.

'It has been decided that it will be best for you
to go back to Scotland,' he told his pallid niece,
whose inability to recover her spirits was
beginning to annoy him.

'But I love France. I don't want to leave here.
I can hardly remember Scotland and when I do,
it always seems to be cold and raining,' she said
dejectedly.

He frowned. 'You're Scotland's Queen. It's
time you went back and took over your responsibility. Your mother ruled it effectively for
years. Now it's your turn.'

Privately he thought there was not much
chance of his niece making as good a job of
containing the unruly Scots as his sister had
done. Perhaps not enough care had been taken to
teach statecraft to the girl – concentrating
instead on womanly pursuits like poetry and
music-making, but no one had expected Francois to die so soon. Mary had been a useful tool
for the Guise family in the French court, but now
her usefulness was over, and it did not look as if
another good marriage was coming her way.

She shivered as she thought about Scotland. 'Is
there no alternative?' she asked.

'My brothers and I have been negotiating with
your half-brothers and other Scottish men of

influence and they're pleased to welcome you home as their ruler,' he said, though he knew that the word 'pleased' was an exaggeration. 'Will tolerate' was closer to the truth.

'But they are Protestants, aren't they? What about my religion?'

'I've a guarantee that you'll be allowed to practise your religion in peace.'

He did not say that she would only be allowed to celebrate Mass in her private apartments and never in public. She'd find out soon enough. What must be done was to get her and her court onto a boat and ship her across to Scotland.

Mary knew that she was a failure in her uncles' eyes. All the marriage proposals that came up for her either withered in the bud or were vetoed for various reasons. It never occurred to her that she might stay unmarried, like Elizabeth of England. There were still plenty of suitors baying at her door and she badly wanted to be a wife, she needed a man beside her.

At last, the beautiful Queen of Scotland and her court boarded two galleys at Calais and headed for Scotland.

The French royal family saw her off with a round of festivities, flattery and insincere protestations of eternal love and friendship. Her Guise relations bade farewell to her also, with varying degrees of sincerity. Before she boarded her ship, the Cardinal arrived to give her his good wishes, but when he was on the point of leaving he said in a casual way, 'Why don't you leave your jewels in France? Crossing the sea is dangerous, after all.'

Mary had a magnificent jewel collection including a long string of twenty-four flawless black pearls as big as grapes, of which she was intensely proud.

'But if the ship sinks, I'll sink with it as well as the jewels and then it won't matter, will it?' she said.

He tried more blandishments but she argued, 'I'm a queen and my subjects in Scotland will expect me to be adorned like a queen,' she told him.

'Take the lesser jewels then. They won't know the difference.'

'They're not savages. Why should I not take my jewels with me?'

'Because the English queen hasn't guaranteed you a safe passage. She won't give you a passport to cross the North Sea. Her fleet might catch up with you.'

'I arrived in France without a passport from the English, and I'm sure I can return to my kingdom without one from Elizabeth,' snapped Mary.

Her uncle pursed his lips, 'But if she knew how many valuable jewels you're taking with you, she'd make a point of capturing your ship. Her fleet is sailed by pirates.'

'Can't my Scottish escort see them off?'

'That man Hepburn, Earl of Bothwell, is the Scottish Lord High Admiral. If he learns about your jewels, he's capable of stealing them himself.'

Mary remembered Bothwell only too well and

said nothing to that, but instead asked her uncle, 'If I don't take my jewels, what will I do with them?'

He put on a serious face. 'Leave them with me. Your own kin are the only people you can truly trust, Marie.'

Disillusionment hit her like a blow. She could not believe that her family, those who had been close to her all her life, coveted her property. The lure of her jewels was too much even for them. *Is there anyone in the entire world that I can trust?* she wondered.

'I'll take my jewels with me to Scotland. Pray for my safe journey,' she said firmly.

As she embarked, she seemed to be looking forward to her new life with keen enthusiasm, but her secret thoughts were hidden and she only gave a hint of what she really felt when the ship was casting off.

As her beloved France fell away, she rushed to the edge of the deck and gripping the wooden rail, cried out in an anguished voice, 'Adieu France, Adieu. I may never see you again.'

Eleven

1561

Ghostly trails of sea mist swirled round two royal galleys in the Forth estuary and followed them like wraiths as they headed for the port of Leith. Shivering in the clammy air, Mary stood on the promenade deck of the largest ship and clutched the collar of a fur-lined black cloak to her neck.

Her gown too was black, for she was still in mourning for Francois, but its slashed sleeves were lined with cloth of gold and she was gloriously bejewelled, because she wanted to make a magnificent impact when she landed in her kingdom.

The ship's captain approached and saluted her as he said, 'We dock in an hour, Your Majesty. I regret I can do nothing about the weather. It's not usually like this in August, even in Scotland.'

She smiled. 'But the rest of the voyage has been very tranquil and you made the crossing in record time. I expected to be at sea for at least a week, because when I went to France as a baby it took ten days and everyone was sick except me.'

He was pleased. 'And we avoided the English, though they've been on our tail for four days.'

'I've seen their little baques, nothing like as imposing as ours. Perhaps what people say about the English fleet isn't true,' said Mary.

'We're safe from them now. They won't follow us into the Forth,' he replied and went off to urge one last effort out of the exhausted oarsmen.

He was under no delusions about the power of the English navy and wondered why they'd paid so little attention to the French galleys. Perhaps the wily Queen Elizabeth felt it better to let Mary languish in Scotland instead of France, where she might become the focus of plotting against the English throne.

The mist was even thicker on land than at sea and few people were lingering on the dock side when Nathan and Esther walked along the paved quay on their way to her father's warehouse.

When he saw her shivering, he stopped, tenderly draped a long woollen shawl over her head and tied it under her chin. 'You need a good covering to keep you warm, little bird,' he told her.

She smiled up at him and said, 'Don't worry, Nathan, we're nearly there.' They'd left Dunfermline the previous day and made their way overnight with a friendly carter to Leith docks. The fog was almost impenetrable when they alighted from his cart in the morning, but Esther knew the port well and picked a way along, keeping close to the walls of the houses lining the wharf, for she did not want to take a false step and fall into the water.

'I hope my father is in his warehouse, I need to rest,' she said, and Nathan told her, 'It'd take a Biblical storm to keep your father from his place of business.'

He was right. His father-in-law was bustling about, barking out orders and watching as his workmen opened boxes of multicoloured threads that dazzled the eye, even on such a bleak day.

'Dear daughter, dear son,' he cried when he saw them in the doorway and rushed forward to pull them inside, talking all the time. 'Does your mother know you're coming, Esther?'

'No, I've brought her home for a little while. She's not been well and needs rest,' said Nathan, solicitously helping his wife to a seat on a stout crate. Her father anxiously bent forward and stared into her face. 'What ails my little girl? All that tramping up and down the country is bad for you. You need a deep feather bed at night and a good fireside during the day.'

She laughed. 'I like tramping the country with Nathan, father, and we always have good places to stay in. We've done it long enough to know the best lodgings and they know us.'

'But do you eat properly? You're very thin. Your mother and sister will be horrified to see you.'

'They can feed her up,' said Nathan, 'The reason she needs rest is because she lost a baby last week.'

'Another one?' mourned her father. 'Oh poor Esther. Your sister has five and another is due at the end of the year.'

Nathan squeezed Esther's hand and knew that she was counting the number of stillbirths she had endured. Four. Most of short duration, only a couple of months' gestation, but they had been optimistic about the last one, which she carried for three months, the longest so far. Both grieved when she lost it. Nathan wanted to stop trying for a child, but she so longed for a baby that the sequence of hope and disappointment would go on.

Mr Leverson snapped his fingers at a man standing by and ordered him to go to the alehouse and fetch two pints of porter for his daughter and her husband. 'Porter is good for you,' he said firmly, when she tried objecting.

The King's Wark alehouse was next door and after a few moments, a serving maid came in with brimming pewter mugs in her hands. 'Have you come to see the French galleys arriving?' she asked.

'What's special about French ships? They come in every day,' said old Leverson.

'Not great galleys like these,' said the girl with a flounce. 'They're bringing Queen Mary back home.'

Nathan's face lit up. 'You mean the young queen who went away to France? Is she really coming back?'

'Yes. A pilot boat's come to tell us Queen Mary will land here. Her galley's tying up outside our inn now. No great lords have come down from Edinburgh so they can't be expecting her. We're all very excited.'

107

Esther looked at her husband and said, 'Go and watch, my dear. I know how you worship the young queen.' She'd often heard Nathan talk about seeing the baby Mary and appreciated the grip she had on his imagination.

Mist from the sea, mingled with smoke from fires in the hearths of Leith, made Nathan cough and choke as he ran along the quay to where a massive galley was being tied up to huge iron bollards. He stood with his neck cloth over his mouth and watched a gangplank being lowered and then – at last – the Queen emerged, with a man bearing a burning torch to show her the way down to the quay.

She was unmistakably a queen, as tall as a warrior, with luxuriant hair glowing like fire beneath a cap of white filigree lace edged with huge pearls. Round her neck was a narrow ruff that did not conceal many rich necklaces of glittering emeralds and diamonds that flashed eerily in the gloom. The queen whom Nathan had seen as a child had grown into a magnificent woman, taller than the average man, more dignified and beautiful than any fairy queen in the stories that his father used to tell him when he was a little boy. In the flickering light of torches held up by her retainers, he admired the paleness of her skin, the imperiousness of her long nose, the flashing of her eyes and the sweet curve of her lips as she cried out her thanks. He felt he was looking at a goddess come down from the heavens.

His legs went weak and he sank to his knees as she passed him. She took his collapse as a gallant's obeisance and smiled graciously.

'Welcome home, Your Majesty,' he managed to say. They were the first words she heard from any subject when she set foot again in Scotland.

There was no one else to greet her because her arrival was unexpected. The last stretch of her voyage up the Forth estuary had been covered more quickly than estimated, and there were rumours in Edinburgh that she would make landfall in Aberdeen. Many ambitious place seekers were already halfway there when she came ashore in Leith.

Her sophisticated French followers looked around the empty and unimpressive port with expressions of scorn and horror as they silently wondered, 'Is this how the Scots greet their Queen?'

A man came running out of the King's Wark to usher Mary inside, while a few drinkers were roughly evicted from the tap room.

Some of them were already drunk and a few were foreign sailors who had no idea what was happening and tried to object as the landlord pushed and shoved them out, but the sight of Mary's men at arms changed their minds about fighting and they scuttled off to another drinking den.

Wine was offered to the Queen and her ladies. They accepted and the serving girl ran outside to tell people craning their necks at the door, 'She's huge, like a giantess, but she speaks a guid Scots tongue. I can understand every word she says.'

A Leith burgess came running into the confusion, crying out, 'Our Queen can't be entertained in a low alehouse. Bring her to my house. My wife and daughters will prepare a proper meal.'

'Who's he?' Nathan asked the serving maid, who said indignantly, 'What does he mean low alehouse! That's Andrew Lamb and he has a great idea of himself. He imports wine and keeps a good table so she'll be fed well enough, but I hope it costs him plenty.'

In Lamb's house, Mary and her companions were abundantly plied with food and by the time they had finished, a clutch of flustered Edinburgh dignitaries, and a contingent of Scottish lords led by the Earl of Argyll, had arrived to escort her to the Palace of Holyrood, a mile and a half up the hill from Leith. They brought with them a few spavined and broken-winded horses, which were all they could round up in a hurry, and the poor look of the royal procession caused even more offence among the people from France.

Mary, however, did not seem to notice the poverty of her reception and enchanted everyone within her orbit with her brilliant gaiety and dazzling smiles. She burst upon her people with such a glorious impact that even though the muffling fog persisted, it seemed to those who saw her as if the sun were shining through.

Word that Mary Stewart had returned to her kingdom spread through Edinburgh like a raging fire and by late afternoon a huge crowd was gathering in the forecourt of Holyrood Palace. Among them were Nathan and his father-in-law, for old Leverson was so anxious to see the

110

Queen that he surprised Nathan with his deter-
mination and ability to climb the hill out of
Leith. His prosperous-looking belly did not
impede him at all.

They stood side by side against the wall of the
palace gatehouse and stared up at the lighted
north wing windows where people told them the
Queen had her apartments. Every would-be
musician in the city had also come down the
Canongate to serenade her and, as evening fell,
bagpipers, drummers, viol and lute players, plus
hoarse-voiced ballad singers, raised a caco-
phony of noise. Nathan winced at the tuneless
din but it was impossible not to be cheered by
their genuine joyfulness.

Mary was musical too and though she noticed
the wrong notes and bad timing, she felt the
universal joy and as darkness set in, she ordered
that the palace's great gates be thrown open so
she could stand on the drawbridge with her
hands widespread to thank her people. They
cheered till the heavens echoed with the din and
she continued waving and trying to tell them
how much she appreciated the welcome they
were giving her.

Nathan was bewitched and bedazzled by her.
On the walk back to Leith, he said in a dreamy
voice to his father-in-law, 'She's every inch a
queen. There's not a lady in the land to match
her.'

Mr Leverson was more reflective. 'I feel sorry
for her. Poor young woman, she's not yet nineteen years old and can't have much knowledge
of the world. They greeted her with joy tonight

111

but she'll need more than beauty and charm to keep herself safe on the throne. The great lords will try to control her, and religious bigots will harry the life out of her.'

Nathan sadly agreed, 'I suppose you're right. Let's hope she has good advice and good friends.'

'But who can she trust? How can she tell her friends from her enemies? Men in search of power are always plausible. Let's hope she wins loyalty from somebody but when power is up for seizing, it's difficult for a young woman to know the false from the true. It's time she finds herself another husband,' said practical old Leverson.

Mary had her fair share of the mercurial Stewart temperament, capable of going from depression to elation and back again in a very short time. When deep depression seized her, she fell ill, prostrated with raging fevers that no medicines could relieve till they burned out. Dr Pare, who treated her in France, privately thought that when she enjoyed a fulfilled sexual life, the recurrent fevers would disappear, because they stemmed from frustration.

On her first night back in Scotland, she stood at the window of her Holyrood chamber and felt a familiar wave of terror sweeping over her.

She tightened her hands into fists and fought its onset. 'I must keep hold of myself,' she thought, but there was no one to whom she could confide her fears. Even the Maries would not understand her terrible disquiet because they were exhilarated about returning to their families, and to the potential marriages that were being organized for them. But no one was organizing a marriage for her. She'd have to make that decision for herself.

She turned on her heel and surveyed the room where she would sleep. From the attitude of the people who showed her into it, she knew she was expected to be overcome with admiration for the glory of the palace, its decoration and furniture, but in fact she found it insufficient.

The painted beams of the ceiling were colourful enough but the furniture was rough hewn, and though the bed hangings were of cloth of gold, they were dusty, fraying and none too clean. For someone accustomed to the luxuries of the French court, the Scottish royal palace was a distinct disappointment. *If this is the most glorious house in my kingdom, what are the others like?* she thought.

She was well aware that her arrival at Holyrood had been demeaning and unsuitable for a ruler. In France, she rode prancing jennets, now she was mounted on broken-winded and ungroomed hacks. Her schooling was French and there was no denying she'd been imbued with the snobbery of a superior culture and brought up to regard the Scots as savages. French undergraduates at the University of Paris joked that students of the Scots College were completely uncultured and even had tails. They were said to be only good at fighting and getting drunk.

'Yet I'm part Scots and I don't have a tail,' she reprimanded herself.

She remembered being told how her grand-

113

father James IV spoke Gaelic to his wild subjects from the Highlands and they loved him for it. As far as she was concerned, her native language was French, however, and she would always think in French, though she could make a passable attempt at speaking the Scots tongue in which she had been specially tutored but still found rough and guttural.

A rush of rage filled her and flushed her cheeks when she thought how eagerly her Guise uncles had cast her off into this wild nation. Thank God she'd brought a large number of her French friends and servants with her. It was important to keep them as near as possible. She'd look out for a special place where they could recreate a corner of beloved France, like the sanctuaries of Fontainebleu and Chenonceaux where the French royal family enjoyed life away from Paris. She must find a retreat where she could live a French life, and celebrate a Roman Catholic Mass without antagonizing anyone.

Twelve

'Our young Queen's arrived!'

The servant girl was breathless when she burst into John Knox's writing room in his lodgings in Edinburgh's Netherbow.

He put down his pen and stared at her. 'Has she now?' he said and though his tone was laconic, she could tell he was deeply interested by the way his eyes flashed.

'She's down in Holyrood. They've brought her up from Leith. Folk who saw the procession are saying she has a great collection of French men and women in glorious clothes with her.'

'That's the French for ye,' said John Knox scornfully. He had no time for them after having nearly died when he'd been forced to work as a galley slave on a French vessel after the garrison of St Andrew's Castle capitulated after Beaton's murder.

'Are you going down to see her, master?' asked the girl.

'Certainly not. Look out of the window. It's a miserable day. She's brought a great fog with her. Maybe it's an omen of some sort. I just hope she sticks by her bargain and doesn't go around flaunting her Popery all over the place.'

'And if she does, she'll have you on her back,' thought the maid as she hurried from the room and went off to collect more gossip from the neighbours about the Queen and her entourage.

In spite of his pretended indifference, however, Knox was excited by the news and in a little while left the house to seek out more information in the tall houses that lined the High Street.

Everyone he met agreed that the best thing to do was affect uninterest in the new arrival but to watch every move she made. There were plenty of spying eyes among the servants at Holyrood to make sure they missed nothing.

* * *

115

In spite of continuing foggy weather, the Queen displayed herself every day to the citizens of Edinburgh, riding up and down the High Street between Holyrood and the castle at the head of a cavalcade of richly clad noblemen and women.

She was greeted with cheers, which she acknowledged with a flourish of her whip, and tongues wagged about her beauty, her flashing smile and the skill she showed on a horse now that she was properly mounted. When she galloped up Arthur's Seat, the craggy-sided hill that rose behind her palace, she rode astride.

This was considered to be an act of dreadful boldness by the conventional matrons of the city who, if they ventured into the streets, either walked on wooden pattens or had themselves carried in sedan chairs. The idea of riding a horse at all, far less astride, was shocking to them.

Most men, however, admired the beautiful girl and the alehouses that lined the streets of the Old Town rang with comments, some very ribald, about her. Though Knox pretended to have no interest in her, even he yielded to curiosity in the end and happened to be at his doorway one morning when she rode past.

He was shocked by the impact she had on him, and blinked as if to drive out the image of the tall, red-haired girl. The woman is a temptress, a Jezebel, an enticer of men, he thought angrily. Her mother, with whom he had had many audiences and many arguments, was a handsome, haughty woman, but the daughter was more than handsome. She was charismatic and he was as

116

attracted to her as a moth is to a flame, and hated himself because of the way he felt.

After his first sight of her, clutching his black robes around him, he strode up to the Church of St Giles where he sat with his head in his hands, praying to be released from the desires of the flesh and trying to concentrate on maintaining the Protestant church in Scotland even though the head of state was a Papist.

On her third day in Scotland, Mary went early in the morning to the palace chapel and no sooner had the door closed behind her than a ragged man ran up the Canongate to tell Knox, 'She's in the chapel hearing a Mass.'

The preacher clapped his hands together in satisfaction. Good! She'd stepped out of line, she'd given him ammunition and a reason to inveigh against her.

The next day was Sunday and he mounted the pulpit looking even more than usually austere, with his long beard carefully combed and spread out over his black cassocked chest. The church was packed and he stood silent in the pulpit for a while, looking down at the expectant faces staring back at him.

Then he launched into an outrageous attack on Mary, calling her a Papist, a loose woman and a betrayer of her promise not to celebrate Mass in Scotland. His voice rang out like a trumpet blast and echoed down from the ancient stone walls while his congregation sat silent, impressed by his fervent fluency. He was preaching against Mary so violently because of the effect she had on him, as well as because of her persistence in being a practising Roman Catholic.

Reports of his sermon were retailed to the Queen within half on hour of the words leaving his lips, and she went white as she listened.

'How can he say such wicked things about me?' she asked her half-brother Lord James Stewart, who was sitting down to dinner with her.

'He's only rabble rousing. He likes to excite his congregation,' said James lightly. He knew Knox well, but no one was entirely sure which side of the religious conflict he himself really favoured, for he ran with the hare and hunted with the hounds.

'But he doesn't know me. We've never met. How dare he say I'm a loose woman?' Mary was on the verge of tears.

'I suggest you invite him to a meeting and try to reason with him. Tell him you only want to celebrate Mass in private and have no intention of flaunting or encouraging Catholicism in public,' suggested her brother.

Though he was reluctant to admit it, John Knox was excited when he was shown into the presence of the young Queen. She sat at a needlework table by a long window and laid down her work when he stepped into the room. Her greeting was gracious, but she was nervous and wasted no time in getting to the point, charging him with unfairness in his Sunday sermon.

When he was face to face with her, it was almost a comfort to realize that her beauty was not flawless, for she had a slight cast in one eye: not as ferocious a squint as her father's, but a cast nonetheless.

Mary was unaware that she was being weighed up as a woman more than as a queen.

'What you said about me in your sermon was very unfair and untrue. Why did you blacken me so?' she charged him.

He equivocated. 'What I said was not personal. You signed an agreement not to bring Catholicism to Scotland, yet you heard Mass.'

'But I have no intention of interfering with the worship of my subjects, and it is unfair if you try to interfere with mine. I want to celebrate my beliefs in private. Surely that's not a sin?'

When he would not commit himself to agreeing with her, she became agitated and her hands shook as she accused him of pursuing a vendetta against her. 'You did the same with my mother. You attacked her in that book you wrote, the one about the *Monstrous Regimen of Women*. Don't tell me that you don't include me in your attack. My regimen doesn't suit you either, does it?' she said, her voice rising.

He pursed his lips prudishly. 'Your mother was pursuing a hard policy against Scottish Protestants when I wrote my book. If you agree to let us worship as we please, I have no fight with you. You must not openly support the Roman Catholic religion, that's all.'

By now she was losing control. 'You drove my poor mother to her death! You plunged Scotland into chaos!' she gasped. The pain of her mother's death, only a year ago, was still too painful to think about and she burst into tears.

Unnerved by her weeping, he withdrew and

later arranged with Lord James that Mary be allowed to celebrate Mass privately but not in public. This she accepted, but knew that John Knox was her enemy and it was necessary to watch him carefully.

I am surrounded by enemies. Whom can I trust? she wondered again.

Her dilemma was worse because her Guise uncles had warned her before she left France that James, this half-brother, was in the pay of the English. While they gave her that unsettling information, they did not suggest any other person in Scotland who was equally powerful and willing to help her, but sent her off like a twig on the tide with their youngest brother, the irresponsible Elboeuf, another possible inform-ant, in her party. They thought they'd seen the back of her and it still rankled that their biggest concern was for her jewels. At least her Scottish half-brothers and sisters were not casting covetous glances on her property. Should she trust her father's blood more than her mother's?

She wished with all her heart that the clock could be turned back a year and that Francois were still alive. In retrospect, her life then seem-ed idyllic. Even the weather was better. Ever since she'd come to Scotland, she'd been cold and shivering, but in France, she'd be hunting, or dancing, or listening to music; real music, elegant music, not the unbelievable racket that had welcomed her to her kingdom on the first night she arrived.

If she did not have some lightness in her life, she knew there was a danger that she might slip into one of her deep sadnesses. Running to the chamber door, she threw it open and called for her Marys – they had reverted to their Scots names since they had come back – and put on her brightest face as she told them, 'Let's organize a masque. Summon up my friends. We'll dance and laugh and play music. I don't care what that black-robed preacher says about me.'

Thirteen

As the weeks passed, Esther's health improved and she even put on weight, because her mother and sister pressed sugar sweetmeats on her.

Every time Nathan saw his sister-in-law, he felt a surge of relief that he had not been coerced into marrying her, for she was even fatter than before. After she married Stern, she'd shaved off her black hair and now possessed a wig of extreme luxuriance that made her look like a man in disguise.

Because Nathan loved Esther's long, soft and silky brown hair, he'd asked her not to shave it off but she always bound it up in a scarf when they went out among other people.

He sat beside her in the Leverson kitchen and held her hand when he said that he must go out on the road again soon.

'But Esther's still very weak,' protested her mother.

'I'll go on my own, and leave her with you till winter comes,' he said.

'No you won't,' said Esther. 'I've seen how women in the villages look at you when you pass by. I'm not allowing you to walk the roads alone!'

He laughed. 'I've no eyes for anyone but you and you know it. But we're using up our money. It won't last forever.'

Mr Leverson looked up sharply. 'But your father Ezra is a rich man. He has gold in Amsterdam.'

'Yes, and he's still alive so he's spending it himself,' said Nathan.

'How old is he?' asked Esther's mother.

'I think he must be about seventy.'

They threw up their hands and exclaimed at that. For a man to live so long was a great achievement.

'Why don't you take your pack round Edinburgh for a while? All the finest ladies of the land are in the city now because the Queen is here. Offer them my newest silks from France. The last order that came in was very fine. None of the Edinburgh sellers have anything as good,' said practical Mr Leverson.

'And people say that the young Queen never sits without a piece of sewing in her hands. Why don't you try to sell to her?' suggested Esther's mother, and Esther laughed. 'That's a challenge, my dear, sell silk to your heroine.'

It was a delight to Nathan to sit in his father-in-law's warehouse and lovingly pass skeins of silk and lengths of lace through his hands.

'Look at this red. Isn't it glorious? And the Valenciennes lace is crusted like ice. Only a fine lady could wear that,' said Leverson reverently holding up samples of his goods.

Nathan filled his pack with choice pieces and paid the old man for what he'd taken, though Mr Leverson protested and said, 'Pay when it's sold.'

'No. It's best to pay now. That'll make me more determined to sell,' said Nathan and passed over his money before he shouldered his pack and set off to climb the hill to Edinburgh.

At Holyrood he met his first disappointment. 'The Queen and her ladies have gone away,' said a friendly guard who was lounging at the gatehouse.

'Where have they gone?' asked Nathan, hoping it was only as far as the castle at the other end of the High Street.

'I heard she wants to go to Linlithgow because she was born there, and after that Stirling, where her mother kept her in the castle for a long time before she sent her to France.'

Nathan nodded and shifted the pack higher on his shoulders. He thought, *She's on horseback and I'm on foot. If I want to meet up with her, it's Stirling for me.*

It took three days to get to the castle, and when he got there, he was surprised to find people hauling what looked like blackened and burned spars of wood out of the main gate and throwing them down into the moat.

'What's happened?' he enquired and was told, 'The Queen's bedchamber went on fire last night. We're cleaning it out.'

'Was she in it at the time?'

'She was and she's lucky to be alive. Her brother thinks somebody put a candle to her bed hangings while she was asleep. The room was burned out.'

'But she's safe?' Nathan was worried.

'Oh yes, she woke up in time and rode off this morning. I don't think she wants to spend another night here and I don't blame her,' said his informant.

'Who'd want to kill her?' asked Nathan.

The castle guard looked at him in wonder at his naivety. 'Any number of folk want her out of the way, starting with her own half-brothers and going on to the English. She's lucky to have survived this long, if you ask me.'

'Did she head back to Edinburgh?' Nathan asked.

'No, she's a plucky one. She wants to see her people, so she went on to Dundee and then she's going to the palace her grandfather built at Falkland.'

It was autumn again and the weather was fine, so Nathan sang as he trudged along on his way to Falkland. His route took him through the heartland of Fife that was unknown to him, for Ezra had always stayed on the same roads and followed a well-trodden path through villages where he was known and welcomed from Stirling to Speyside, then back down to Leith from Aberdeen by the coastal road.

It was a pleasure to be walking in unfamiliar country and he stared around, admiring thick stands of ancient trees and prosperous-looking farms and mills tucked away in the clearings between them. This was the royal hunting ground, where Stewart kings had come for centuries to hunt and hawk.

Though his pack was heavy, he made no attempt to lighten it by selling goods on the way. He was keeping the best for Mary.

He reached Falkland before the Queen and stood gazing up at the façade of the palace with open-mouthed admiration. It even put Holyrood in the shade, for it did not have the grimness of the other royal castles. Its gatehouse, flanked by two rounded towers and topped by castellated walkways, opened straight on to the main street and seemed to beckon passers-by to come inside. Along the walls of the main building, lines of windows glittered in the sunlight, and tops of trees peeped over the top of a long retaining wall, which meant there was a garden and a park within.

Slowly he lowered his pack to the ground and wiped his brow with the back of his hand while he kept on staring at the beautiful place. An old woman passing by said, 'Admiring Falkland, are you, lad?'

'Indeed I am,' he told her.

She had a kindly face and her eyes almost disappeared in a network of wrinkles when she smiled.

'You're a pedlar, aren't you? What have you for sale today?'

'Yes, I'm a smous. I sell silks and laces, needles and pins, buttons and lace...'

'You'll do a good trade here then. There's a lot of grand folk in town because the Queen's coming down from Dundee and they all want to meet her.'

'I'd like to see her too.'

'You shouldn't have a problem. They say she's very open with her people and goes out among them like her grandfather did. I remember him because I was a little girl when he started building this palace, but he died at Flodden, poor soul.'

'He did a good thing here,' said Nathan appreciatively.

'Yes, we're proud of our palace. Won't you let me see what's in your pack or are you not wanting to sell anything? What's your name, by the way?'

He laughed. 'I'm Nathan and I want to sell all right, but I've come to show my things to the Queen and I don't want people picking out the best before she sees what I've got.'

'Oh la!' the old woman laughed too, in a kindly way. 'If it's her money you're after, you'll have to stay the night because she's not arriving till tomorrow. Have you a place to sleep?'

'I can sleep anywhere, under a hedge if necessary.'

'I've a stable with a big hayloft but don't keep a horse any more since my man died. You can sleep there if you like. I won't charge you anything if you let me see your stock before you show it to young Mary. I'm the local gown maker and always have a use for fine materials,

126

you see.'

They liked each other, so he took her hand and said, 'You've made a bargain. Let's get out of this sun and I'll give you a sight of what I have for sale.'

In the back courtyard of her house on the other side of the road from the palace, he unlaced his pack and spread it open on the paving stones. She bent over it and clicked her tongue appreciatively as she carefully handled the precious things. 'Lovely, very fine. I knew the moment I saw you that you weren't a cheap jack. If you've anything left after the ladies of the court pick over your treasures, I'll buy it all from you. By the way, how do you plan to get to the Queen? They're not just going to let you walk into the palace and sit down beside her.'

'No they're not, are they? I'll have to think of some way though, because I promised my wife I'd sell to Queen Mary.'

'My daughter cooks in the palace kitchen. I could ask her to get you inside,' suggested Nathan's new friend.

When Mary's cavalcade came clattering up the main street before noon next morning, she cantered her horse under the rounded gateway arch, and was greeted by a cheering group of servants from the kitchens. Among them was Nathan.

The royal party feasted for hours, and as the sun was setting, Nathan slipped into the inner courtyard of the palace and sat with his open pack beneath a sheltering tree. Soon Mary

Seton's eye was caught by his colourful display.

'Look at this,' she called out and some ladies came over to exclaim in admiration, before Mary Fleming asked Nathan, 'How did you get in? We don't see pedlars very often.'

'I was passing and thought the Queen might like to see my wares. I hear she loves sewing,' was his smiling reply.

'Cheeky fellow!' exclaimed Fleming and put her hand to her mouth to call out 'Marie, Your Highness, look at this.'

Wonder of wonders, the Queen herself came over the grass, with her long skirt making a wonderful swishing sound as she moved. The terror and depression that had caused her to flee from Stirling had been lifted by the great reception she had received in Dundee and by this pleasant sojourn in a palace so beautiful that it made her think she was back in France.

'What is it?' she asked. Without speaking, Fleming pointed down at Nathan's pack.

'Ooh, how lovely. What fine colours, what perfect lace,' exclaimed Mary and bent down to pick up a skein of thread that seemed to shimmer like a peacock's tail.

'And look at those buttons. They're made of fine mother of pearl,' cried Mary Seton, lifting a twist of buttons from the pack.

'And those are gold!' added Mary Fleming.

'Are you selling these fine things?' asked the Queen, straightening up.

Nathan nodded. He wished he could give her all he carried, but he and Esther must live for a long time on whatever they made from this load, because it had not been cheap to buy.

'How much do you want for this and this and this...?' The Queen was lifting up buttons and threads, packets of needles and fine pins. He itemized the pieces and gave her a price, at which she nodded and said to one of the male attendants who joined them, 'Give him the money.'

The man protested, 'But how did he get in?'

'I don't care how he got in. His goods are high quality. I want these things because they're better than anything outside France.'

Now that the Queen was buying, other ladies joined in and before very long, Nathan's pack was empty – though he took care to keep aside a skein of fine silk to give to Libby.

When he walked out of the palace gate that night, his pack swung empty by his side and in a calfskin purse tied securely around his waist there was enough gold to pay for Leverson's stock four times over.

He knew what he was going to do with some of his profit. He'd buy a pony cart with a neat canvas roof so that Esther could ride with him around his route. Perhaps if she had an easier life and did not have to walk so many miles, she might at last manage to have her longed-for child.

Fourteen

'I don't want to leave. I wish I could stay here forever.' There were tears in the Queen's eyes as she drew on velvet gloves and prepared to mount her horse in the courtyard of Falkland Palace after a stay of two weeks.

The Keeper's daughter, Mary Beaton, smiled and said, 'My father would be happy to hear that.'

'Tell him. Every day has been a delight in this beautiful place. I haven't felt so at peace or safe since I left France.'

Beautiful Mary Fleming laughed and said, 'I don't know about being safe. What about the way you risk breaking your neck by riding flat out through the forest.'

The Queen laughed back, 'You just don't like hunting, Fleming! I've had some wonderful days out, the best since Francois died.'

'You can come back whenever you choose. My father may be the Keeper, but this palace belongs to you,' said Beaton.

They rode away, lovely young women in a tight, chattering group. As she looked back over her shoulder at the palace, Mary Stewart feared that she was leaving tranquillity for chaos and confusion.

She was right.

As usual, her court was in a ferment, and Holyrood Palace awash with whispers. She could not understand why people got themselves into such states, for it seemed that no Scot was ever happy unless he was fighting with another – with the combatants changing as quickly as the fickle weather.

It would take someone as old and wise as Solomon to pick a way through the intrigues and I'm only nineteen and not wise at all, she thought sadly.

Apparently, there had been an outbreak of fighting in Edinburgh's High Street and the chief battlers were the Earl of Arran against Lord Bothwell.

'Not that man again,' she groaned when she heard his name. 'What has he been doing this time?'

'Arran's mistress, a woman called Alison, lives in the High Street, and Bothwell and your half-brother Lord John Stewart broke into her house and tried to abduct her to annoy him. The town guard was called out, the bells were rung, and they were fighting around the town cross and the Tron for hours,' Mary's secretary, Maitland of Lethington, told her.

'Who won?' Mary asked.

'Neither. Bothwell was arrested and is shut up in Edinburgh Castle. Arran's gone mad and is in St Andrews Castle. He's babbling about marrying you – by abduction if necessary, so Lord James took him away and shut him up.'

'What will be done with them?'

'Arran will stay shut away till he recovers his senses. Bothwell will be kept in the castle for a while, but he'll have to be let out eventually and sent down to quell the fighting in the Borderland. It's the best place for him.'

Mary asked, 'He wasn't conspiring to abduct me too, was he?'

'No, but if he thought he could, he'd probably try,' said Maitland.

The idea of being abducted by the dangerous man in the green doublet did not upset her as much as Maitland imagined.

Four months later, she was guest of honour at the wedding feast of her favourite half-brother Lord John Stewart, one of the fighters against Arran, to Lady Janet Hepburn, sister of the terrible Bothwell, in her family stronghold Crichton Castle, which was fifteen miles south of Edinburgh.

The celebration was boycotted by the Queen's senior half-brother Lord James Stewart, who nursed a life long-hatred for the bride's marauding brother, so Janet was particularly pleased when Mary arrived at the celebrations.

'Thank you for attending my wedding. I thought you might not come because of the trouble my brother's been in,' she said to the Queen.

'None of us can be held responsible for our relatives. Anyway, I don't see him here. Didn't they let him out of the castle to attend your wedding?'

Janet flushed and said, 'Haven't you heard? He's out. He escaped three days ago and is on the run again. I expect he'll be in Hermitage Castle by now.'

'Escaped? From the castle?' Mary asked in astonishment. That stronghold was reckoned to be impossible to get away from because the Castle Rock was so steep and rugged that it was impossible to climb. Was there anything the man would not try?

'Yes. Apparently he let himself down the rock on a rope. I don't know if the guards were paid to look the other way or if his enemies allowed him to get away because they prefer him to be occupied down in his own lands rather than making trouble in Edinburgh.' The subject obviously embarrassed the bride.

'I love weddings and everyone is marrying – except me!' said Mary, tactfully changing the subject.

'You could marry tomorrow if you chose. Many powerful men want to marry you,' replied Janet.

'Mad men like Arran or Don Carlos. And the Queen of England thinks I should marry her lover, the Earl of Leicester.'

'Leicester? She wants you to marry him?'

'Yes. It's an insult. She and her adviser, that man Cecil, obviously think I'm stupid enough to consider the idea.'

'Surely not!'

'Of course not. I'm not taking what she throws away. Besides, he's as bad as Don Carlos. His wife Amy Robsart fell down the stairs like Carlos's wife and broke her neck. It's said he organized it too. If I married him, Elizabeth would have a spy in my court and that's what she wants! I can't choose a husband from Scotland because that would turn all the other great lords against us, so I have to find a husband from a foreign land, and who is there? Elizabeth has the same problem. She plays her suitors against each other like deuces in a pack of cards, but she's more clever than me,' said Mary.

Janet found it hard to hide her pity as she looked at the magnificent Queen in luxurious clothes and priceless jewellery. In spite of her splendour, there was a yearning about Mary Stewart that touched the heart. She shook her head, 'No, she's not more clever but she has good advisers. Cecil would die for her and he has the most adroit mind in England.'

'I have good advisers too.'

'Some. Maitland of Lethington is a sensible man, but *he* has enemies and is careful not to antagonize them. Scotland is too small and too family-centred. It's like a honeycomb, each faction is joined to the one next to it.'

'But I don't know who is loyal to me and who is not.' Mary sounded anguished.

Janet had a strong survival instinct, like all the Hepburns. 'Watch and listen, Your Majesty. Make up your own mind. Sniff out bad people like a dog...'

'I'm not very good at sniffing,' said the Queen.

'Sniffing what?' asked Mary Beaton, who had joined them.

'Sniffing out a husband,' laughed the Queen. 'I've heard that you, my dear Marie, are about to be a bride. Is it true you're going to accept

Randolph, the English ambassador?'

Beaton went scarlet and said, 'I almost did but I've changed my mind. I refused him yesterday.'

Lord Thomas Randolph was the gallant and handsome English ambassador to the Scottish court, who had had been courting Beaton for several months, plying her with gifts and compliments, and she'd seemed well-disposed towards him.

'That's a pity. He's a fine-looking fellow and very good company. I like him, even if he is English! Why did you turn him down?' asked the Queen.

'Because it's not right for me to marry him,' Beaton said shortly. She was not prepared to tell the whole story, but when Randolph had seen that she was prepared to accept his proposal, he had asked her to spy on the Queen for him.

In that instant she changed her mind.

'You want me to spy on my lady?' she asked in a cold voice.

He equivocated. 'Not spy exactly, just tell me anything interesting she does, where she goes and what she says about my Queen.'

Beaton's pretty face was scarlet with indignation as she turned on him. 'I would never do anything as low as that. It's disgraceful that you've asked me. Is that how your Queen receives her information? By seducing friends? Have you been pretending to make love to me in order to turn me into a cheat?'

Protestations from him were useless. Their courtship ended.

The Queen saw that she was upset by the

135

mention of Randolph and said soothingly, 'He must have deceived you in some way. I'm sorry we're not going to have another wedding soon, but I have hopes of Fleming and secretary Maitland. They seem very close, too.'

'Her family think he's a good match, but he's older than her and not very romantic,' said Beaton doubtfully.

'She's full of gaiety though. She'll brighten him up if they make a match of it,' said Mary, but Beaton was not so sure.

The Queen did love weddings, and there were many among her courtiers that year. On every occasion she gave the bride a beautiful gown and sat at the banqueting table, smiling and congratulating the couple, and every time she yearned more and more to be married herself.

It was to tall, quiet Mary Seton that she revealed her feelings after the wedding at Crichton Castle.

'I've been married but know nothing of what goes on between a man and a woman. Sometimes I wonder if I'm capable of loving. The thought of it terrifies me because I remember how the eyes of the court followed me all the time when I was married to Francois. They speculated whether it was him or me who was to blame that I didn't produce a child. I don't know either, really.'

'When you pick another husband, make sure he's lusty, but you seem happy enough now. Why are you so in such a hurry to marry again?' asked Seton, who had no desire to find a husband herself. The other Maries often joked that she would make a perfect nun.

'It's true. I am happy at the moment,' said the Queen. She was the focus of a court filled with young people, who went hunting, hawking, dancing, flirting, making music, and acting in masques with her. She particularly enjoyed dressing up as a young gallant and rampaging with her friends up and down Edinburgh's High Street.

No one recognized her because she made a plausible youth and it was a delight for her to know how shocked the prim, churchgoing townspeople, who crowded into St Giles every Sunday to listen to John Knox preach, would be if they realized the true identity of the lad who strode along the street with a feather in his hat and a poignard at his side.

One day, when she was masquerading as a young man, she deliberately jostled black-clad Knox and enjoyed the look of dislike he cast at her.

'If he knew who I really was, he'd have dropped dead with shock,' she said to her new friend, the musician David Rizzio.

He giggled as she told him the story. 'Ooh, you should have gone up and propositioned him. He might have accepted. That would be SO amusing,' he said.

She laughed too. Rizzio's preference for making love with men was so blatant and outrageous that he made her feel daring by listening to him. She patted him on his head, for he was almost twelve inches shorter than herself, and said, 'Naughty boy,' in the same tone of voice she used when talking to her lapdogs.

He responded as a dog would by licking her hand, and that sent them both off into peals of laughter.

Rizzio had recently attached himself to her court after arriving in Edinburgh as a musician in the entourage of the ambassador from the court of Savoy, who came to make a marriage offer to Mary from a Savoyard prince. She did not consider him as a husband, but accepted the services of Rizzio, whose sweet singing voice filled a gap in her choir.

He was small, swarthy and ill-favoured, with a straggling little beard and a flaring nose, but, not only was he a good singer who also performed well on the lute, he was also happy to spend hours playing cards as he entertained her with his outrageous talk, mostly conducted in French.

James, her upright Stewart half-brother, disapproved of her new friend, but did not fear him gaining political influence, and noticed with relief that since Rizzio had joined the court, the Queen was not so prone to periods of depression. He was prepared to put up with the little man as a court jester, a fool, paid to perform and keep her amused.

Strangely, it was Rizzio who first swallowed the bait that Elizabeth and Cecil craftily prepared for Mary. He went to bed with Lord Darnley before she did.

Fifteen

A week after his sister's wedding, fugitive James Hepburn, fourth Earl of Bothwell, stood on the roof of his castle at Crichton and stared across to the shining waters of the River Forth. His eyes traced the ragged outline of Edinburgh, marking the towers of the castle from which he had made his escape and the four-branched spire of St Giles where Knox was probably preaching intolerance and hellfire to the mealy-mouthed burghers of the city.

He'd met the man once and thought him a canting hypocrite. All the arguing about religion left Bothwell cold, though he was a convinced Protestant; but that did not mean he went along with everything that Knox said. Mainly he rejected the idea of a Pope and greedy priests.

He turned and looked to the east where the Bass Rock rose spectre-like out of the North Sea. Crichton was his proudest possession. He had been born there and hoped to die there, but knew that because of his propensity for getting into fights, it was probable he'd die somewhere else.

'Remember to take me home,' he always counselled his men before an affray.

The castle was like an eagle's nest, perched

high and impregnable above the flat lands of the Lothians, and backed by the steep slope of Soutra Hill. Behind him, and unseen because of the hills, lay wild country, where he had both territorial friends and enemies but which was also the home of the woman he loved best, Janet Beton, the Witch of Branxholme.

Moving like an athlete, he ran down the steep, dark stairs from the roof to the inner courtyard, his buckskin boots making no noise on the stone steps. 'Bring my horse,' he shouted when he emerged into the daylight.

His favourite black stallion was waiting and he vaulted into the saddle, gathering up the reins in one hand and brandishing 'onwards' with the other. His bodyguard rushed joyously to mount as well. They relished his escapades and had been languishing unemployed during the months he was in prison.

'To Hawick!' he shouted as he went clattering over the drawbridge. He was going to Branxholme to see Janet, his first and most lasting love.

She was wife to Sir William Scott of Buccleuch, and more than twenty years older than Bothwell, but was the most tantalizing and fascinating woman he'd ever met. They had not been physical lovers for some years but were bonded by something even stronger. She was his soulmate.

A hundred yards from the castle gate stood ancient Crichton Church, and something made him stop, turning in the saddle to stare up the path to its arched door, remembering wor-

140

shipping there with his mother, Agnes Sinclair, who had been hiding him in her house at Morham outside Haddington since his escape from Edinburgh Castle.

The affection between them was strong and he resented the cruel way she was disdained, and later divorced, by his father. It was because of the love he felt for her that he was so drawn to women, he thought.

She was a devoted Catholic but he resisted her efforts to win him back to her church. As he looked at Crichton Church door, however, he could almost hear her soft Highland voice, saying, 'Go in Jamie, go in and say a little prayer.'

He dismounted and walked over the burial yard, smiling as always at the grimacing stone heads lined along the roof edge. The heavily studded door swung open at a push and he saw the church was deserted, but light through the stained glass window dappled the stone floor. He walked towards the altar and made an involuntary genuflection as if his mother were walking beside him. Then he said his prayer and felt strangely refreshed when he returned to the outside world.

At Branxholme, Janet was not surprised to see him. 'My Jamie, I heard you climbed down the castle rock,' she said with a laugh, as she cupped his face in both hands and stared into his eyes.

'My page Paris bribed the guards, or they would have cut the rope,' he told her.

She kissed his lips and he swelled with pride at her approval. She'd had that effect on him since he was sixteen years old and she first seduced him.

She took him into her chamber and ordered food and wine. While they ate, she gave advice. 'They're chasing you, aren't they? Go to Hermitage. It's the most secure place you possess. I'll get my folk to supply you with provisions. A well-stocked garrison can hold out in Hermitage for months, if not for years. One of the good things your father did was to persuade the Queen Mother to give it to him, even if he had to sleep with her to get it.'

'I'm on my way there now,' he agreed, 'but that bastard Moray is after me. I might have to move on to France again.'

'Moray?' she questioned, doubtful about the name.

'Queen Mary has made her half-brother James Stewart the Earl of Moray and it's gone to his head. He's the most important man in Scotland now and God help anyone who challenges him. He's never forgiven me for stealing the money the English were sending up to him four years ago. He ran with both sides then and still does. Thank God I've never taken any English money,' he told her.

'Except what you stole,' she laughed. 'It delights me to think of you dressing up as a kitchen maid and working under James Stewart's nose in the kitchen at Haddington while his men were looking for you when you took that money.'

He leaned back in his chair and laughed too. 'I hid in the kitchens of your friends, the Cockburns at Sandybed. I've ordered that a yearly payment should be made to them forever because of their help,' he said.

'Forever is a long time,' she said, suddenly solemn, leaning forward and taking his hand, stroking it gently with her forefinger, 'Isn't it time you were married and began fathering children? You're nearly thirty.'

'You and I are married. We married years ago,' he reminded her.

'We hand fasted when you were young but then I married Scott, the man my family wanted for me. You're not bound to me. Where is that Anna girl? You brought her to Scotland, didn't you? What have you done with her?'

'I sent her home. She stayed for three years and I was sick of her.'

'But she let you spend her dowry, all those guilders! She was beautiful too.'

He nodded and said, 'Her dowry was 40,000 silver dollars. I needed money at the time and I hope to be able to pay it back one day. She's empty-headed and prattles of nothing all the time.'

'I don't know what sort of woman would hold you.'

'You have done.'

'And others have tried but you're difficult to please. I don't think your father should have sent you to Paris to be educated. The only thing the university did for you was to give you dangerous ideas.'

'I relished Paris. I relished learning too, but not forever, because I longed for Scotland and for action.'

'You've been born too late. You belong to the

143

days of single combat, knightly rules and chivalry, like James IV, and look what happened to him.'

'I believe that I've the right to protect my lands and my interests against all enemies and that I will prevail,' he said stoutly.

She sighed. 'You've more enemies than even you realize. Arran has gone quite mad and is raving that you intended to abduct – and perhaps even murder – the Queen. The whole of Edinburgh is talking about it and the Queen is furious.'

'That's nonsense. No one in their right mind will believe him,' Bothwell replied.

'It suits some people to believe and persuade others as well. You should marry and quieten down for a while. Your sister's married to John Stewart, isn't she? She could find you a bride with a good dowry.'

'You witch,' he said fondly, but not really in jest. He thought she really was a witch, for she had about her the same aura of enchantment as his mother's brother, who was reputed to be a necromancer and often talked of the black arts. They were people whom it was better to have on your side than against you.

Janet was still pondering the question of his marriage. 'The Gordons have a beautiful daughter of marrying age, and she's said to be clever and witty too. Perhaps she would suit you?'

'As long as you don't try to marry me off to a Douglas or an Elliot,' he joked, for those families were his most bitter enemies.

'Tell me about the young Queen,' asked Janet.

'Everyone thinks she's a great beauty and very accomplished, and that's how she appears to me, but what's your opinion?'

He frowned. 'Her height and that beautiful copper-coloured hair make her stand out, but there's a slight cast in one of her eyes that gives her the look of a cat.'

'A cast in the eye can be tantalizing,' said Janet.

'Perhaps, but she's not very clever. She talks well and with confidence, but I'm not sure she thinks deeply. She temporizes and reacts impulsively. Moray twists her round his finger.'

'All the Stewarts have been impulsive. It ruins them.'

'She needs someone to help her, someone strong. There's something that makes me feel sorry for her, though she looks magnificent and is always dripping with precious stones, rings and pearl necklaces. She's very French – not Scots at all.'

Janet sat forward. 'She's made an impression on you, I can see. Perhaps you should marry *her*!'

'And get a dagger in my back one dark night? Any man who marries her will have Mar and Moray and Morton and Arran and all the Hamiltons and Douglases in Scotland ranged up against him.'

'But you like a fight.'

'I like a fight with a fair chance of winning. The Queen will have to find another husband. It won't be me.'

Refreshed after the break at Branxholme,

Bothwell and his group of heavily armed men kept up a breakneck pace all the way to Langholm, and when they stopped to eat in the town, a friend of his came to warn him about rumours that Moray intended to put him to the horn for plotting to abduct the Queen. If he was made an outlaw, any man who encountered him could kill him with impunity, which would suit the Elliots and Douglases very well.

His friend, a local lawyer, warned him solemnly, 'All the Elliots in the Borders will be out looking for you if Moray persuades the Queen to put you to the horn.'

'How do you know this?'

'A contact in Edinburgh sends me news. Apparently Moray is using Arran's ravings against you and he's persuaded the Queen to believe them. Leave the country till it all dies down.'

'Janet says I should get married. You say I should run away to France. I'm going to the Hermitage. I won't be driven out of my own country by the lies of a madman. Why should I want to kill or harm Mary Stewart? There are plenty of others, including her own half-brothers, who have more to gain from her death than me.'

'Jamie,' said his friend leaning forward. 'Your enemies – and you have plenty of those – will grab any chance to harm you.'

'They'll have to catch me first,' cried Bothwell, jumping to his feet and shouting to his men to get back on their horses and follow him to Liddesdale.

His heart always rose with pride of possession

when he breasted the last hill overlooking the valley of Rulewater and he saw his huge fortress lying in the green valley below.

The first thing to be done when he got down there was hoist his flag, with its bridled horse crest, to show that Jamie Hepburn was back.

Hermitage had withstood many sieges and was not a welcoming-looking place. It sat in the middle of a vast clear space, with a fast-flowing river running along its southern curtain wall. Built of reddish and grey stone, with walls at least forty feet high and a protected walk around the roof, it was capable of providing sanctuary for 600 men, and looked impregnable, menacing and huge.

There were no windows, only narrow slits along the third storey for men to aim arrows through, and one small entrance, just wide enough to admit a single horse at a time.

Inside there were no comfortable rooms where women or children could spend their leisure, no hidden gardens or green spaces. It appealed to the rough, aggressive side of Bothwell's nature because it was a place for a brigand.

It had a murky history too. Legends associated with it were all evil. Black magic had been practised there; defeated lords were sheathed in molten lead, boiled alive, or thrown in the river and held down till they drowned. Ghosts walked the fortifications at night. *I'll join them one day*, Bothwell thought, as he stared down at Hermitage Castle from the hill top.

He did not have long to enjoy his fortress. The danger from his surrounding enemies grew so strong that he soon realized he must follow his lawyer friend's advice and get out of Scotland if he wanted to stay alive.

In haste, he rode to Coldingham, where his newly married sister was living, and she lent him enough money to buy a passage on a ship sailing out of Leith, but storms drove it ashore on Holy Island, where he was captured by the English, taken to Berwick and then to London. There he was shut up in the Tower.

When news of his incarceration reached Scotland, his enemies were vastly relieved, for they could then make free with his possessions. With luck, he'd be out of circulation for years, they reckoned.

Sixteen

1563

'You're growing quite plump,' Nathan teased Esther after they had been living in Leith for over a year.

She pirouetted and said, 'I thought you liked me fat?'

'You're far from fat, but I'm happy when you're well.'

'I'm very well. Perhaps soon we might try for another baby?'

He shook his head. 'Not yet. We've plenty of

time. I want you to be fully recovered first.'

'But my sister has so many. Perhaps we could borrow one from her?'

He shook his head. 'Any of your sister's giant children would look like a cuckoo in a nest if it travelled round with us. We'll have a baby of our own in time, but I want you to have a rest now. That's why I've stayed in Leith and not gone back on the road.'

She put an arm round his neck and said, 'You're a good, kind man, Nathan, and you're selling so much to the court that the Queen is your best customer. She always asks for her special smous when she needs sewing threads. You're famous.'

It was true. When she saw him selling his wares in the Canongate, Mary recognized him and reined in her horse to tell him to take his pack down to Holyrood and show her what he had for sale. Again she bought liberally.

Slowly Nathan and Esther were growing rich, but every now and again he longed to be out on the road, especially when the weather was fine or the seasons were changing. He missed flowers in the hedgerows and merry shouts from people working in the fields.

'I've a plan,' he told her. 'There's a box of money to take over to Amsterdam. I heard a little while ago that my father is totally blind now, but he'll be able to give me advice about buying a house there.'

Her eyes lit up. 'My father often talks about Amsterdam too. He left there when he was a young boy and hasn't been back, but he'll not go again because sailing makes him sick.'

'When summer comes and the sea is smooth, we'll go,' said Nathan.

It was strange how much at home he felt as he sailed into the harbour at Amsterdam a month later. More than thirty years had passed since he had last seen the city, but the smells of the quayside, and the rumble of voices speaking a language that he was surprised to realize he still understood, delighted him. He seized his wife's hand to help her ashore, and said in delight, 'I remember everything. I know my way around without even asking the way.'

Hiring a porter to carry their bundles and his precious chest of gold, he hurried her along till they came to Jodenbreestart, which was lined by tall houses with elegantly plastered fronts and jutting out hoists from the top stories to load and unload goods on to boats in the canal below.

'Does your family live in a house like this?' asked Esther, round-eyed. She'd been born and grown up in humble circumstances in Leith because her father did not believe in putting on a show of wealth. It was safer, he said, to appear to be poor when you were an alien in a foreign land, especially in savage Scotland.

'They didn't at one time, but over the years we've been saving money and my father sent news a while ago that he'd bought one of the merchant houses next door to where we used to live. He's doing well. When he stopped travelling he began lending money and acting as a banker to small businessmen like himself,' Nathan told her.

She was not disappointed by Ezra's home. The smooth white walls were decorated with pale blue curves and curlicues and its image shimmered like a vision of delight in the still water of the canal that ran past it. 'It's beautiful,' she gasped.

Nathan too was delighted with the house, which had business premises on the ground floor and living quarters with long elegant windows above. On the window ledges, scarlet geraniums grew in earthenware pots and long tendrils of flowers trailed down towards the roadway. Over the entrance hung a wrought iron bracket, from which three brass balls swung.

They were not expected because Nathan wanted to give his parents a surprise. Holding Esther's hand, he pushed his way through a small crowd of men inside the office door and tears rose in his eyes when he saw his father seated behind a tall desk with an attentive clerk leaning over his shoulder.

Ezra looked ancient. His beard and his hair were long and very white against his unrelievedly black clothes. His lined face was like yellow crinkled parchment, but his fingers were never still because, although he was blind, he knew every coin by its shape and counted out his sums on an abacus.

Nathan stood in front of the desk with tears running down his cheeks, while the clerk and other men in the room stared silently at him. The sudden lapse in conversation made Ezra ask, 'What's wrong?'

'Father,' said Nathan, 'my wife and I have

151

come to see you.'

The old man gave a cry of delight and lurched forward with both arms extended, upsetting a bottle of ink as he did so, but he did not care.

The celebrations for their return went on for several days, with a throng of relatives and happy neighbours crowding into the elegant first floor room while serving maids ran around with plates of food and ewers of wine.

Esther's head swam as she tried to remember the names of all the people she met, people who squeezed her hands, paid her compliments, and, she knew, looked surreptitiously down at her belly to see if she was pregnant. No one asked why she had no children and she guessed that Nathan's parents had warned them that the subject was not to be talked about.

It soon became obvious that neither Ezra nor Miriam were as fragile as they liked to pretend. Ezra's mind was razor sharp, and he was served by devoted employees who revered him.

He'd launched himself as a money lender and was doing well. 'If you give me free rein with your gold, and if I'm granted a few more years of life, I'll make you a rich man before I die,' he told his son.

'I'd really like to buy a house soon. Esther is not as sturdy as her fat sister and life on the road tires her. Sadly, none of the children she's carried has lived, but she wants a baby so much that she'll go on trying for a while yet.'

'You could join me in the counting house,' said Ezra.

'What would a good house cost?' Nathan

asked.

Ezra said something to his clerk who muttered into his ear.

'You have a good sum already but you'll need a little more. You've been very successful on the road, and another couple of years should do it,' he told his son.

'I've Queen Mary to thank for that. She's my best customer and tells the court ladies about me. Esther's father still buys the best quality goods and that's what they like.'

Ezra laughed. 'It's right that you sell to the Queen! I remember how dazzled you were with her when she was a baby. You and she must be fated to cross each other's paths.'

'I think we are. She fascinates me because she's like someone from a fairy tale, as tall as a giant and straight as an aspen tree.'

'It sounds as if you're in love with her.'

But Nathan shook his head. 'No, I'm not. She dazzles me, she draws me like a moth to a candle, but I don't think of her as a woman somehow. It's as if she'd melt into the air if I tried to touch her. I like admiring her from a distance...'

'Perhaps she has that effect on other people too. That may be why she hasn't found a man to marry yet,' said Ezra.

'It isn't easy. The people around her only jostle for riches and power,' said Nathan.

'Someone will turn up. Fate will put a husband in her way, and her future will depend on what sort of a man he is,' said Ezra.

Sailing back to Leith a few weeks later, Nathan

saw the yearning look on his wife's face and put his hand over hers as he asked, 'Are you longing to be back in Scotland, my dearest?'

She shook her head, 'No, I'm sorry to leave Amsterdam – I like its cleanness, I like the houses, I like the lovely blue and white dishes in your mother's kitchen – and I love the canals. Your mother told me that in the winter they freeze over and everyone goes skating. That must be such fun.'

'We'll live there one day, I promise. I've asked my father to look for a house that I can buy for you when we get a little more money together.'

Seventeen

1564

'It can't be true, it can't be true! All the people I love best are taken from me!' Mary began weeping hysterically when a mud-splashed messenger brought the news to Holyrood that her favourite half-brother John, husband of Jane Hepburn, was dead.

'What happened? Was he killed?' she demanded as her ladies rushed around pouring out a soothing cordial for her to drink.

'No. He was holding a justice court in Inverness when he died of an ailment in his lungs.'

'Cursed Inverness! The place is inhospitable in

winter and in summer. Does his wife know?'

'Yes. She's at their castle in Dunbar with her sons.'

'And they're only infants. I must go to her.'

It was bleak January, a bad time of the year to travel, and Mary's progress was so slow that it was a week after her half-brother's death before she reached Dunbar Castle, where she clutched a weeping Jane in her arms.

'How cruel is fate. He was so young, only a year older than I am. Of all my relatives he was the one who didn't harbour resentment against me for being on the throne that he might have filled himself,' she told Jane, who nodded and said through racking sobs, 'He loved you as his sister and he was always loyal.'

They were having supper together, talking about the dead man, when there was a commotion outside the chamber door which was thrown open to reveal a bare-headed man in dark clothes and a battered-looking breast plate.

Jane stood up, gasped and exclaimed, 'Jamie, what are you doing here? I thought you were in prison in London!'

Mary was astonished too. 'Lord Bothwell!'

'I was in the Tower and it took a lot of talking to get out, but Percy and I did a deal and he brought me to Alnwick. I was there when I heard about John,' he said, walking into the room and shaking himself like a dog so that drops of the rain that had soaked him spattered over the surprised women.

'You must have talked to good effect,' said Mary tartly, remembering that this was the man who had been accused of plotting to kill her.

He grinned and his face changed, becoming almost engaging. 'I talked to Elizabeth Tudor too,' he told her.

He'd almost said by accident, 'I talked to the Queen,' before he remembered Mary's insistence that she was the rightful Queen of England and not the Tudor woman.

She clasped her hands together and exclaimed, 'You've talked to my cousin? I wish I could. I've never even seen her. What is she like?'

He held out his hands to the fire to warm them and said. 'She's very – colourful, very painted.' It would have been more politically aware, he thought, if Mary had wanted to know how he'd managed to persuade Elizabeth to let him return to the north. He'd wondered about that himself and guessed it was because he had more potential to make trouble for her enemies at home than in London.

'Painted?' Mary questioned.

'Her face. She paints it white with lead and her hair is shaved back to give her a high forehead. She's like a painted doll but very majestic looking.'

He did not say she was also very majestic sounding and did not suffer fools gladly.

'People say I'm majestic looking too,' said Mary, drawing herself up to her full height.

'Indeed you are,' he agreed and he was telling the truth. With the firelight casting highlights on her wonderful hair she looked truly beautiful. How much would it take to seduce her, he wondered? Not a great deal, he guessed.

He moved towards her and boldly took her hand. At first she was surprised and stiffened, but in seconds he saw her soften. 'She's not a match for you,' he said softly, then turned back to his sister and hugged her tight. She was the one who was suffering a great loss, after all.

That night, when the women retired to bed, he sat by the fire with his boots off and considered what he should do. He knew that if he showed his face in Edinburgh, his enemies would fall on him and plot to have him tried for treason. Now that Percy had looked the other way and let him ride away from Alnwick, should he take refuge in Crichton or Hermitage or steer clear of Scotland completely?

Though he longed to go home, he decided to head for France, which always was a safe refuge for him when he was in trouble. The political chaos of his native land changed like the tide. Before long, the great lords would fall out among themselves again and he'd be able to return and take up his rightful place.

When the last log in the hearth crashed down among the ashes in a shower of sparks, he stood up and looked at the doors opening off the chamber. One led to his sister's room, one to a corridor and the room where he would sleep, but behind the third lay the beautiful Queen.

He remembered how her hand had relaxed into his. She was ripe for the picking, but though she was dangerous fruit, he'd never drawn back from a challenge.

Stepping quietly on his sock feet, he went over and opened her door. A serving woman lay on a thin mattress on the floor by the bed, which had its curtains drawn. He bent over, shook her and motioned with his thumb to tell her to go away. Without speaking she sat up, blinked, clutched her wrapper to herself and hurried off, closing the door behind her.

He lifted an edge of the curtain and saw Mary, deeply asleep, lying on one side with her face sunk in the pillow and her hair flowing down her back. Gently he lifted a long tress. The only light came from another dying fire and showed the magnificent colour. He laid it down and brushed a hand across her cheek. She stirred and stared up at him. To her credit, she did not scream or protest, only looked up without fear.

'Marie,' he said using the French form of her name.

She lay still, staring up at him, wondering if he really was an assassin as Moray claimed.

'Marie,' he said again, very softly.

She moved across the mattress to make a space for him and he lay down beside her. He knew he could seduce her, but a sense of caution, unusual for him, held him back. He stroked her face and heard her breathing quicken. She was willing. Neither or them spoke for a few moments till he asked softly, 'Are you a virgin?' He remembered the stories about her marriage to Francois.

'I think so,' she whispered back.

'It wouldn't be right,' he said wearily and sat up in the bed.

Suddenly he felt dog-tired, too tired to think of making love. Dragging himself up, he staggered to the door and disappeared.

158

Mary lay wide awake, raging with fury and burning with desire. The terrible Bothwell had her in his power and turned away. He'd rejected a queen, he'd rejected *her*. He'd led her on and walked away. She felt as foolish as a silly serving girl.

'I should have him hung!' she told herself as she wept, but she knew there was no way she could confide this story to anyone. It was a secret between them.

By the time she appeared next morning he was nowhere to be seen and Jane said he'd ridden off early – and did not add that he'd borrowed money from her again. He'd gone to the harbour and was on a boat for the Low Countries already.

Eighteen

Margaret Douglas, Countess of Lennox, was a dangerous woman. Plain-faced like her mother Margaret Tudor, she burned with frustrated dynastic ambition, which she concentrated on her two sons, especially on the oldest, Henry, Lord Darnley.

When she looked at him, she glowed with pride and wonderment at how she had managed to produce such a magnificent example of humanity.

By the time he reached the age of eighteen, he was over six feet tall and golden-haired, an

Adonis, she thought, overlooking the weakness of his mouth and the petulance of his nature.

Her husband, Lord Lennox, whom she considered to be her social inferior, was bullied without mercy, and harried from pillar to post. He ran around doing her bidding and obeying her every whim.

'We ought to get some preference for Henry. He should go to court and catch Elizabeth Tudor's eye. He's not been there since he was a lad and she likes handsome young men,' she told Lennox one morning as they sat at a meal in their fairly modest home, Temple Newsome in Yorkshire.

He looked up, caught unawares, and asked, 'Surely you're not thinking he might be a suitor for her hand?'

'By rights he's very suitable but she's suspicious of us. She's too well aware that our son's claim to the throne is better than hers,' said the proud mother.

'You've said so often enough. She exiled you from the court for it,' Lennox reminded her.

'She's jealous. She's only a bastard and I'm the granddaughter of Henry VII. My mother was his daughter after all. If anything happens to Mary Stewart, our Henry will be in the direct line of succession for the Scottish throne too,' she reminded her husband, who had heard her on the subject many times before.

Her mother Margaret had married Archibald Douglas as her second husband after her first, James IV of Scotland, died at Flodden, but the second marriage had been declared invalid, which made Margaret Lennox a bastard too, a fact she preferred to forget.

'Perhaps, instead of presenting him at the English court, you should send him to the Scottish one. The Queen of Scotland might marry him,' said Henry's father.

His wife looked sharply at him. 'That's exactly what I've been thinking. She needs a husband and she's not a crafty, scheming minx like the woman down here. Let's send him to Scotland.'

'You'd be well advised to get Elizabeth's agreement first,' he said cautiously. He was afraid that his wife might try the Queen's patience and tolerance too far. She was lucky to be allowed to return to court the last time she caused offence.

Elizabeth Tudor was a shrewd judge of character. When Darnley's proud parents presented him at court, she cast her eye over him and was not impressed. A vain, spoiled, capricious youth was what she saw. Impassively she listened to the boy's mother whispering in her ear that she wanted to send him to Scotland in the hope he would attract some favour from Mary Stewart. The prospect of marriage was not mentioned.

'Send him north by all means,' Elizabeth said caustically and Lady Lennox almost burst with delight that the Queen had fallen into her trap. Of course Elizabeth had done nothing of the sort. She and her adviser Cecil were intensely interested in any suitor for Mary Stewart's hand and Darnley fitted their bill because he was so obviously ineffectual.

'Lady Lennox wants to send that baby-faced

son of hers to Edinburgh. I think she hopes he'll marry my cousin there,' Elizabeth told Cecil.

He smiled as he said, 'Mary Stewart might be desperate enough to do it.'

'Yes, the boy's a popinjay.'

'And we wouldn't want her to marry a man of power or sagacity, would we? Darnley would be more of a disadvantage for her than an advantage.'

'But there's a snag. What if they combine their claims to my throne? Isn't that dangerous?' she asked.

'The problem would only arise if they produce a child, which might have a double claim,' said Cecil.

'I'll worry about that when it happens,' said Elizabeth.

They'd both been irritated when Mary turned down the Leicester marriage proposal, though she'd recently recanted and made it known that she might be prepared to look more kindly on him as a marriage prospect if he were offered again. Elizabeth refused to sanction the idea a second time around however so, once again, the Scottish Queen was without a suitor and dangling Darnley before her was a fortuitous idea.

Graciously Elizabeth made no objection to Darnley travelling north and even went so far as to tell his mother that he was travelling with her blessing. She gave him a passport and a gift of a purse of golden coins so he could present himself in the proper style at Holyrood.

The Queen's magnanimity surprised Lady

Lennox, who wondered what game Elizabeth was playing but couldn't quite work it out. After all her son was perfect, wasn't he?

Nineteen

1565

In early February, nineteen-year-old Lord Darnley and his father arrived in Edinburgh but were disappointed to find that Mary was not in town. She'd gone hunting in Fife and was living in Wemyss Castle, near her beloved Falkland and its game-filled forests.

Darnley arrived armed with copious advice from his mother, who had gone to the trouble to find out the names of the Scottish Queen's closest confidantes and told him not to delay in making the acquaintance of David Rizzio, an Italian musician.

'Why should I waste time with a low-born troubadour?' he asked disdainfully.

'Because he has her ear more than anyone else in that court. She's even made him her secretary. He'll foster your suit if you treat him properly,' he was told.

'She's made an Italian singer her secretary? What sort of place is that Scottish court?' he asked in disbelief.

'She's a trivial-minded one who likes to be

entertained and her court's a hotbed of intrigue. All the Scottish lords hate each other. She doesn't trust any of them. Flatter Rizzio and make sure you're on the winning side,' she advised him.

It was easy to find Rizzio, who was well known among the young bloods of the town, and Darnley tracked him down to a tavern at the bottom of the Canongate where the Italian held court. He swaggered in, glorious in a scarlet silk waistcoat embroidered with silver and golden thread and crusted with pearls.

He was so tall that the feather in his bonnet touched the roof beams, and there was a united squeal of delight when the crowd in the tap room saw him.

'What have we here?' cried a short, dark-haired fellow in a blue and yellow doublet decorated with golden buttons the size of pigeon's eggs.

'Which of you is David Rizzio?' asked the stranger and the little man made an exaggerated bow as he said, 'At your pleasure, sire.'

'I'm Lord Henry Darnley and I've been told to seek you out because you're the most powerful man in Scotland.'

Rizzio giggled like a girl but did not dispute this. He waved an arm and told the landlord to fill a tankard of wine for the newcomer and they settled down to drink and gamble. They gambled on anything, the turn of a dice or the throwing of a knuckle bone. No skill was involved, gambling was the thrill.

By the time darkness fell, Darnley had lost his

boots, his fur-lined cloak, and finally the magnificent waistcoat which cost his father a year's rent from twenty farms on his Yorkshire estates. He took it off with reluctance and handed it to Rizzio, who fingered it with appreciation.

'This is a fine thing. The Queen loves good stitching. She'll appreciate it,' he said.

Darnley was drunk and always incautious. 'You won it. Give it to her. I want to marry her,' he said.

'And you want me to say it's from you?' asked Rizzio.

'Yes, that would help.'

The Italian draped the beautiful thing over his arm and said, 'No. I'll give it to the landlord to pay his bill. We owe him a fair sum by now and since you've lost, you're the one who must pay it. Hey!' he called to the landlord, whose jaw dropped when he saw what was being offered in payment of the wine they'd drunk.

'Whose is this?' he asked suspiciously, fearful of being charged with stealing it.

'It's Lord Darnley's. He's going to be the King soon. Put it in your window to show the quality of the people who drink here,' said Rizzio.

The waistcoat was displayed in a small window overlooking the street, opposite the gatehouse of Holyrood Palace. The landlord would have been astonished to know that it would stay there for the next 400 years.

When they emerged from the tavern it was after midnight and the street was carpeted in a thin covering of snow. Rizzio took hold of Darnley, who was sliding around in his bare feet

165

and hurried him into the palace and his own bed. As an unwanted gift, he gave Darnley the pox.

'I regret that our meeting did not happen two days ago,' said Darnley gallantly to the Queen when he helped her down from her horse in the courtyard of Wemyss Castle.

She laughed and asked, 'Why? What's the significance of the date?'

'Two days ago was the feast of St Valentine, the day for lovers, and I'm in love with you,' he told her.

'Bold boy,' she said and tapped him lightly with her whip but liked his effrontery, and even more she liked his looks. How delightful to be standing beside a man who was taller than herself, how pleasant to be able to look up to him and not to have to bend her neck as she usually did.

She'd seen him before because he once paid a short visit to the French court before Francois died, but then he was a callow boy. Now he had grown into adulthood and she looked at him with admiration as he walked beside her into the castle hall. His hair was butter yellow and curling, his skin fresh and clean, his carriage elegant and his clothes magnificent, with the slashed sleeves of his scarlet doublet displaying cloth of gold inside.

No one could be more different to most men in her court. If they were not dressed in black, they were as rough as peasants in the fields – like that Bothwell in his muddy boots and a torn leather

166

jerkin. She still cringed inside when she remembered their last encounter.

Darnley was putting himself out to be entertaining and she found herself laughing at his sallies, though most of them poked fun at the people around about them.

'Let's sit by the fire and share a cup of wine,' he said, drawing her towards the huge fireplace, but she shook her head. 'No, I'm tired and dirty. I must change my clothes before I chat with you, but I'll see you after Mass.'

His face became solemn. 'Madam, can I accompany you to chapel?'

She stared at him. 'Are you a believer in the Catholic faith?'

'Indeed I am, but in England my family are obliged to hide it. We hear Mass in private, though.'

It was true that his mother kept a priest in the house in Yorkshire, but she was not a regular attender in chapel. Nor was he, because he had no religious belief at all, but everyone knew that Mary Stewart clung to the old faith with fanatical zeal.

His fate, and hers, was sealed at that moment. In an instant she decided that this was a possible candidate for her hand in marriage.

Her decision was typically Stewart, rashly taken on the spur of the moment and not thought out at all.

Next day, Darnley felt as if his mother was at his elbow, urging him on to gallantries. He found a clump of snowdrops and jumped off his horse to

167

present them to the Queen from bended knee. When he saw her eyes sparkle with delight, he knew he was making headway.

On the third night, he kissed her in the shadow of the inglenook and the night after that he went to her bed and was surprised to discover she was still a virgin.

Twenty-two, a widow, and still virginal till he took her! There was nothing to stop him marrying her now and becoming King of Scotland. Always eager to pass on information to anyone who would listen, he wanted to tell his mother about this success but, for once, knew better than to give more than a hint in the letters he sent home.

Cecil had spies inside Mary's entourage and nothing anyone did or said went unnoticed by Elizabeth's agents, who read every word Darnley wrote.

'She's taken the bait. I never cease to be amazed by your wiliness. It's working out exactly as you predicted,' rejoiced the English Queen to Cecil.

'I know human nature,' he replied.

'I wonder if we're not being a little too clever. What if he turns out to be more capable than he looks?' Elizabeth asked.

'There's no fear of that. He'll bring her nothing but trouble.'

'But what if she realizes that he's a hollow man before she marries him?'

'She'll have to be driven towards it. You must send an angry message to Scotland ordering him and his father to return home. That'll stiffen their backs and antagonize her. She's capable of marrying him to defy you.'

When they returned to Holyrood, Mary and Darnley made no attempt to hide the fact that they were lovers. Their continual spoken endearments and the way it seemed impossible for them to keep their hands off each other scandalized people in the court, but not Rizzio, who urged them on with Boccaccio-style ribaldry.

When he had Mary's ear, he told her how lucky she was to have a young and vigorous lover. 'Elizabeth Tudor is burning with jealousy. That's why she's sending those messages telling him and his father to go home at once. She's trying to stop you marrying him. You have a young and vigorous partner and she has no one. She's peculiar if you ask me,' Rizzio assured her.

'People are saying he's too young for me. He's only nineteen,' Mary told him.

'What rubbish. You're both young – you're just twenty-two. Though he's nineteen, he's more experienced than his years. You're perfectly matched, believe me,' Rizzio replied.

Other criticisms of Darnley came to the Queen's ears. Her wiser councillors complained that he was stupid, but she made excuses for that. 'You're being too critical. When he seems to fail in understanding, it's because of his youth. He'll learn as he grows older,' she told them.

Rizzio agreed with her, delighted to be advancing the cause of one he regarded as his own protégé. If Darnley and Mary married, his own prospects would be even more golden.

To do him justice, he was not acting entirely out of self-interest, for he was genuinely fond of Mary and pleased to see her blooming into fulfilled womanhood at last. The desolating depressions that often laid her low for days at a time disappeared and laughter echoed through the corridors of the gloomy old palace. Even the grey city of Edinburgh seemed bathed in a softer, kinder light and the rain stopped falling.

The Queen's purpose to marry Darnley faltered a little when she received a letter from her uncle the Cardinal of Lorraine, expressing his amazement that she should even contemplate uniting herself with such a callow youth.

When she read it, she gave an exclamation of annoyance and said to Rizzio, 'Listen to this Davie! My uncle says that Lord Darnley is an *amiable idiot* and wonders why I want to marry him.'

'Who would he marry you to instead?' asked Rizzio sharply.

Mary fingered the string of black pearls round her neck and remembered how the Cardinal had wanted her to leave them behind in France. Any advice that came from her Guise uncles probably had an ulterior motive.

'I'll pay no heed to him,' she said, and that decision became stronger when letters arrived from her mother-in-law Catherine de Medici and her brother-in-law Charles IX, complimenting her on her choice of a bridegroom. She failed to discern the note of sarcasm in Catherine's letter.

'At least she knows you're doing the right thing,' Rizzio reassured her.

If Darnley had not become ill while staying with the Queen at Stirling Castle, the affair between them might well have petered out in spite of Rizzio's urging, but Mary's young lover caught a bad dose of what looked like measles, and, being the spoilt child that he was, he acted as if he were on his death bed, groaning and moaning and demanding constant attention.

One of the things that made her love the pathetic Francois was that he was constantly in need of care, for she enjoyed the role of nurse. She delighted in ensuring that her patient was kept comfortable and reassured, and because she had suffered from measles when small, it was safe for her to spend all day with Darnley, mopping his brow and holding potions to his lips. He lapped up both medicine and attention. By the time he recovered, Mary was completely infatuated with him.

'It seems I'll have to leave you soon,' he told her when another furious message arrived from Elizabeth ordering him and his father to return to England at once.

'Why?' she asked.

'Because Elizabeth Tudor has thrown my mother in the Tower to make sure I do as I'm told.'

'I'm your Queen now and you do not have to leave my kingdom. You're my subject, not hers. We'll marry and I'll make you King. Elizabeth Tudor will have to bite back her threats then because both of us have legitimate claims to the throne she's falsely occupying,' she told him.

Of course he accepted her proposal.

Twenty

On a fine day in June Nathan was among the crowd that clustered round Edinburgh's Mercat Cross by the side of St Giles Cathedral, watching as a royal herald, resplendent in a brightly patterned jerkin and scarlet tights, climbed on to the stone plinth and solemnly rang a hand bell.

'Hear ye, hear ye, hear ye...' he yelled and the crowd went silent, staring attentively. 'Hear ye that her Majesty Queen Mary of Scotland today announces that Henry Lord Darnley, Earl of Ross and Duke of Albany, is created King of Scotland.'

The words rang round the people like a growing flame and they exclaimed to each other, *He's our King, she's made him King, she's gone mad ... King of Scotland ... and he's a papist ... She can't foist an English Catholic on us ... What's Knox going to say about this?'*

Knox had plenty to say. His furious words thundered out of the church beside the Mercat Cross, and they were words intended to inflame the passions of the populace. He even went so far as to call the Queen a 'whore'.

But nothing stopped her. She made her lover

King of a reluctant people and next day the banns of marriage were called in Holyrood chapel as well as in the chapel of Edinburgh Castle, but not in St Giles. That night there were riots in Edinburgh's High Street and an angry mob clustered outside Holyrood calling out insults to their Queen.

Nathan stood at the bottom of the Canongate once more and felt heartsick as he listened to the slurs being heaped on Mary. Disconsolate, he turned to walk slowly back to Leith and when he entered the Leverson family kitchen, Esther ran towards him and took his hands, 'Whatever's happened? You look shocked,' she asked.

'I am shocked. The Queen is going to marry that long streak of nothing that she's made Duke of Albany, wherever that is.'

'Oh my dear, it doesn't matter. She's young and he's young. They'll be all right and have children to carry on the line. It's natural.'

'It does matter, Esther. I've seen him with her the last time I sold her silks and he's rude and capricious. She doesn't know what she's taking on. It'll end in tears, believe me.'

Esther's father agreed. 'There's a lot of talk about young Darnley. He goes whoring in the High Street and drinks with the wrong people. He never pays his bills either and insults servants and people he considers beneath him. He's a bad one.'

'Does it matter who she marries? It won't affect people like us,' said Esther's mother, but Esther shook her head. 'It matters to Nathan. He worships the Queen and hates to think of anything bad happening to her.'

'Then let's hope that she's right and we're wrong,' said Mr Leverson.

Since returning to Scotland, Mary's personal retinue had grown in size and several new young women from prominent Scottish families joined her in her favourite pursuits of dancing, music making and hunting. She lavished gifts on them and was generous to a fault, but even her closest friends were surprised by her lavish expenditure on Darnley.

He rode the finest horses, wore gilded armour even when he was nowhere near a jousting field, sparkled with priceless jewels and had so many luxurious cloaks, doublets, breeches and boots that an army of tailors and shoemakers were kept busy catering for him alone.

Mary Seton, the most practical and level-headed of the Queen's confidantes, raised her eyebrows at the vast expenditure and said to Fleming, 'I suspect our friend Lord Darnley has always been a pampered boy, but he's now in such a state of indulgence that if the Queen doesn't marry him, he'll never be able to return to ordinary life. His tailoring bills are enormous.'

'I heard that his breeches makers are paid extra to pad his leggings with horsehair because he thinks his legs are too thin and he wants a more manly backside,' Fleming said disapprovingly.

'The quicker the marriage takes place the better, if you ask me. The sooner she has him tied to her, the sooner she'll start to see through him,' Seton said.

'I hope you're right,' said Fleming doubtfully.

Listening to this exchange was a recent addition to their circle, a pretty dark-haired girl called Mary Hamilton, whose eyes went from face to face as they talked, but she said nothing herself.

'What's your opinion, Hamilton? Your brother goes hawking with Darnley. What does he think of him?' Seton asked.

The girl shrugged. 'I don't know. He doesn't say.' Her expression was glum and her face very white as if she were unwell.

Fleming was more forthright. 'If the Queen doesn't get the marriage over soon, there'll be serious riots in Edinburgh. Knox is stirring up people against her every day. Once she's married, the excitement will die down. She and her new husband will be able to spend their time hunting and hawking and Maitland can get on with running Scotland.'

'Ssh, that's treasonable talk,' warned Seton, holding her fingers to her lips.

They'd been with Mary for too long for her not to sense their feelings and later that night she called them together to announce that since the banns had been called, she was free to marry at any time.

'And I've decided that it will be tonight!' she said with a laugh.

'Tonight? When, where?' asked Mary Seton in astonishment.

'You're surprised, but everything has been arranged. My lord and I will marry in the chapel

175

here in the palace at four o'clock tomorrow morning.'

'A strange hour,' said Seton slowly and Mary nodded. 'That's because no one will be expecting it. There'll be no mobs howling up and down the High Street at this wedding. Once the people find out, everything will be over. When the people hear that I'm married, they'll stop complaining. The mob loves a celebration, and they love me too. Even Knox hasn't been able to change that.'

'But what about a wedding gown?' asked young Mary Hamilton, who was fond of fine clothes.

'I'll marry in black but change after the ceremony. I want to come out like a butterfly from its chrysalis.'

They knew that she had purchased sixty gowns in the last few weeks, so many and so luscious and full-skirted that her ladies found it difficult to store them.

'What about a banquet?' was another question.

'I've given orders for that too. We'll have a wedding breakfast after the ceremony and a banquet tomorrow night. Rizzio is writing a special masque for the occasion.'

Early in the morning of twenty-ninth July, just as dawn was breaking, Mary, escorted by Darnley's father, a beaming Lord Lennox, descended from her chamber on the second floor of the palace and walked along to the chapel, which was brilliantly lit with hundreds of candles that made the beautiful stained glass windows glitter and glow. Because of her height and the un-

176

mitigated black of her clothes, for even her head was covered with a black hood, she seemed to rise like a stark pillar out of the floor as she stood in front of the priest and took her vows.

The bridegroom was not dressed simply. He glittered and glowed with gold and silver thread embroidery on scarlet and royal blue. Long loops of necklets and chains of precious metals and valuable jewels, all gifts from the jewellery-loving Queen, hung round his neck. More than one witness to the ceremony caustically wondered what he had given her in exchange.

After they took their vows, the couple exchanged rings and doubters were relieved to see that the one Darnley slid on to Mary's finger contained an enormous diamond. In the pause after the rings were exchanged, a joyous voice rang out. 'God be praised, the marriage cannot be broken,' it cried. The voice was Rizzio's.

Henry Darnley was now King of Scotland by marriage as well as by proclamation.

As she proceeded down the aisle and her trumpeters sounded a glorious carillon, Mary noticed that many of the people invited to witness her marriage had not turned up. Chief among the absentees was her half-brother the Earl of Moray, the most powerful man in the realm.

'What does it matter! He'll come round in the end. He has no alternative,' she said to Darnley.

In her bedchamber, each of her closest friends took a pin out of her mourning robe and when it fell to the ground, a beautiful flowing gown of primrose silk festooned with loops of flowers and a high starched ruff of magnificent lace rising behind her head was revealed. She was indeed the butterfly emerging from its chrysalis that she'd promised to be. She stood before them laughing and exulting in their surprise.

The wedding breakfast consisted of sixty courses of exotic dishes – boar's heads, roast fowl of every sort from tiny song birds to swans, barons of beef and suckling pigs. Darnley sat beside her, shouting out in jollification and making puerile jokes like a rumbustious boy.

As he showed off, he looked around at the surrounding faces to see who was not laughing with him, and if he noticed the glum countenance of Mary Hamilton, he paid her no attention.

The celebrations continued with music and the performance of Rizzio's masque about the jealousy of the pagan goddess of the hunt Diana when Mary was taken away from her by love. The four Marys appeared in the play as white-clad nymphs. Another grand banquet followed, with even more expensive dishes, some coated in sheets of beaten gold or silver. Enough food was wasted to feed the poor of Edinburgh for a week.

Gradually the diners became aware that masses of people thronging into the end of the Canongate were yelling insults about the Queen and her new husband. Suddenly grave-faced, Mary stood up and said to Darnley, 'Come, we must go out to them.'

He shrank back, visibly reluctant. 'They might kill us,' he said.

'Of course they won't. I'm their Queen. Come with me and let us show ourselves.'

He had no alternative but to go, though he took care to walk behind his wife as they stepped into the courtyard.

Mary behaved magnificently. Putting on her most glorious smile and holding out her hands towards the yelling faces beyond the gate, she literally charmed them into silence. 'Rejoice with me, my people. Be happy for me. Today I have married the man I love. We'll rule over you in peace for many years, I hope. Be happy for me and share my joy.'

The din died away and only a few voices continued to be raised in accusation. Little by little, the protesters drifted off, but before the crowd dispersed completely, the Queen ordered her treasurer to open her coffers and, with wide-armed gestures, she threw a rain of coins of all denominations over the closed gates into the crowd.

Nathan was not among them. He was too sad and disappointed to watch his Queen on what she imagined was her happiest day.

'I think it's time for us to go back on the road,' he told Esther next morning.

Twenty-One

Like an avenging angel, John Knox climbed into the pulpit at St Giles and launched into a denunciation of the royal marriage, though Darnley was sitting in the congregation listening to him. As his words rang out, the audience sat transfixed, not raising one murmur when he called the Queen 'a Jezebel harlot'.

Scotland, he said, was being ruled by an immoral woman and a boy. The Protestant religion was in danger because the Queen and her callow consort were set on bringing back Roman Catholicism.

While he was in full flow, Darnley gave a great shout, standing up and cursing the preacher. Knox stared him down, and scarlet-faced he stormed out of the church with his entourage following him, pushing people away as they went.

Knox only paused to let them go, then started all over again with his denunciations. When the service finally ended, people spilled out on to the pavement and stood around discussing what they had heard, most of them agreeing with Knox and very few with a good word to say for Darnley.

They disliked his arrogance and the way he

was inclined to draw his dagger on anyone who thwarted him, even over the most minor things. They disliked the way he got drunk in taverns and refused to pay the reckoning, or swept people out of his way to the danger of their lives when he and his unruly entourage charged up the High Street. No good would come to Scotland now that the Queen was married to such a man, people said.

After most of the congregation left St Giles, the great lords of Scotland stayed on and clustered round grim-faced James Stewart, Earl of Moray, the man whom everyone was beginning to believe should have been their ruler.

'What can we do? Already the royal mint is making coins with that baby-faced boy's head on them,' said the Earl of Argyll.

'And his name is to appear before mine on all state documents,' said Moray bitterly. 'She's made him her chief adviser but he's not capable of advising himself when to take a piss.'

Maitland of Lethington was equally disgruntled. 'The Queen wants me to give him advice,' he said.

'You'd be busy night and day if you did that and even then there's no guarantee that he's going to listen to you. I never met a more pig-headed young fool,' jeered Argyll.

Moray cut through the complaints by saying, 'The point is, how can we curb him? We must think of a way.'

As it happened, they did not have to do anything, because Mary took affairs in hand herself by banning Knox from preaching for a fortnight.

181

Then she summoned Moray to appear before her to explain his boycott of her wedding. If he did not turn up, she threatened he would be put to the horn. He ignored her orders.

Meanwhile Elizabeth and Cecil were observing the goings on in Edinburgh with secret satisfaction. Lennox's lands in England were confiscated and Lady Lennox was imprisoned in the Tower. To add fuel to the flames, Elizabeth sent £10,000 to Moray to assist him in what she hoped would be a rebellion against Mary and Darnley.

'Lord James has defied my summons. He and his supporters are massing in Stirling. We must raise an army and ride against them,' said Mary when news came of the gathering of her opponents.

'It's a pity that Bothwell isn't here. He's the only man who could lead our troops effectively,' said Lord Ruthven, Darnley's uncle, who owned Huntingtower in Perthshire.

Mary disliked Ruthven, a sinister man who dabbled in witchcraft, but knew he was correct about Bothwell's capacity on the field. She sent a message to France telling him to come home and promising that all his crimes would be forgiven if he did so. It took her an effort to call him back because she heard from informants that, in France, he had been overheard to say, 'If you add the Queen of Scotland and the Queen of England together you will not have the makings of one honest woman.'

'Till Bothwell arrives, I'll lead my own troops, and my husband will ride beside me,' she said boldly to Ruthven.

Darnley jumped to his feet at this, withdrew a rapier he wore at his side and made a few flashing moves with it. 'We'll drive them off the field.' he boasted while the others watched with the tolerance they would have shown towards a playful child.

'This whole business is a farce,' said Maitland of Lethington to his new wife Mary Fleming when they discussed the Queen's decision.

Next day Mary and Darnley, the latter resplendent in golden armour, set out at the head of an army to capture Moray. They followed him to Linlithgow and then went on to Stirling.

When he heard they were close on his tail, he fled to Dumfries and sent a message to Elizabeth asking for more money. Behaving as if they were on a glorious hunt, Mary and Darnley followed, stopping off at Ruthven's Huntingtower and then at Lochmaben Castle, where they were entertained to a grand banquet.

During this martial ride out there were no actual battles and people started to refer to it as The Chaseabout Raid. Mary's reputation was enhanced, however, by her willingness to pursue her enemies and even John Knox, who took the precaution of leaving Edinburgh till things died down, praised her for riding at the head of her troops like a true warrior.

Everyone was growing tired of the pointless expedition when the Queen's contingent eventually pitched camp in a wooded valley a few miles outside Dumfries. While they were settling down for the night, a lookout shouted that a group carrying a flag of truce could be seen approaching along the river bank.

Five men came riding towards the waiting Queen. They looked like reivers in steel helmets, but one of Mary's supporters noticed a dirty tabard bearing the device of a bridled horse.

'It's Bothwell!' he called out.

Mary's heart leapt in her chest and a strange faintness came over her. 'Is it really?' she asked breathlessly.

The captain of her guard did not have time to reply because the man in the tabard rode right up to her and took off his helmet, revealing his fox-coloured hair. Bothwell was as rough-looking as ever but still retained his peculiar aura of maleness that both repelled and attracted her.

'Your servant, Majesty,' he said courteously.

'Lord Bothwell,' she replied icily.

'I received your summons but require your assurance there are no charges outstanding against me,' he said.

'I give you my word, and as an *honest* woman, I'll keep it,' she replied and felt annoyed when he laughed.

That night they stayed in the provost's house at Dumfries and talked into the early morning, discussing tactics and the best way to deal with Moray, whom Mary wanted to punish as a traitor. 'I hate him. He's my half-brother but he betrays me at every turn. He wants my throne. He wants to kill me and for that I want him dead,' she said vengefully.

Bothwell shook his head. 'He's on the run now but he's worth more to you alive than dead. He has a big following among the Protestant lords and if you killed him, they'd rise against you. Rope him in and count yourself lucky you're alive to do it. If he'd been less fastidious he could have killed you long ago.'

Darnley, who by this time was half drunk and lying over the table, said, 'Before he killed her, he'd have to kill me.'

'That wouldn't worry him or take him long,' said Bothwell scornfully, before turning to the Queen and gesturing with his thumb towards her husband as he asked, 'What possessed you to marry that baby-faced chick?'

Rizzio was waiting in the great hall when the royal party from the futile Chaseabout Raid clattered into the courtyard of Holyrood Palace on their return to Edinburgh.

Ignoring Darnley, he rushed up to Mary and grasped both her hands as he welcomed her in French.

She responded in the same language and told him how pleased she was to see him again, which was true, for she relished his sophistication after days of riding around parts of Scotland that were still primitive. The people there could be living 200 years ago and their dialects were so thick and impenetrable that they might as well have been speaking Chinese.

The Marys clustered round her, exclaiming about her mud-spattered and torn riding clothes. They wanted to bear her away and restore her to royal magnificence, so she went gratefully. The last three weeks with Darnley had been trying

185

and she was growing disillusioned with his childish, capricious behaviour. Bothwell's scornful comment stuck in her mind.

When she was dressed in her usual magnificence, with her precious pearls round her neck and her fingers sparkling with rings, she summoned Rizzio to come with his lute.

While pet dogs frolicked at her feet and a line of servants bore in sweetmeats and a pitcher of wine, she said to him, 'Play for me, sing to me, talk to me. It's such a relief to be home, Davie.'

His sharp dark eyes stared at her. 'Does your husband not entertain you?'

'Of course he does, but he's so young. He's not interested in the things that interest me. Only when we're out hunting or hawking is he a good companion.'

'And I hate hunting but I entertain you at home,' Rizzio said with a laugh.

She took his hand. 'Yes, you do. Tell me the news of the court, who is about to marry, who is in love and who is out of love? You always know.'

'First tell me about *your* triumph. Moray ran away, didn't he? Elizabeth Tudor's money didn't arrive in time.'

'He ran in front of us all the way to Dumfries and then backed down when he saw Bothwell. We've come to an arrangement. He and the rebel lords will accept my husband as king if he signs a covenant promising not to bring Catholicism back to Scotland.'

'I don't suppose he'll make any trouble about that. His religious convictions are not as strong

186

as yours,' was Rizzio's comment.

She defended Darnley. 'But he's a true believer, Davie. He's of our faith.'

'Is he?' Rizzio was not so sure, but he'd observed Darnley in different circumstances than Mary.

She saw his misgivings. 'He behaved well in the field but was put out when Bothwell turned up.'

'I heard the ruffian earl is back. He can run most of the other lords off the field.'

'I've put him in charge of my forces,' said Mary shortly.

'And forgiven his sins?' asked Rizzio because he knew how angry she'd been when she heard about him saying that she and Elizabeth Tudor together did not make one honest woman.

'I had to. He's effective at least. He was loyal to my mother and I hope he's loyal to me. Darnley doesn't like him, though.'

Rizzio laughed, 'I wouldn't expect him to. You'll have to keep them apart.'

'I know. I've told Darnley that Bothwell is in charge of my forces and you are to be my chief adviser. The business of ruling bores him and he's not mature enough to have power yet – so I'm having a stamp made with his signature, and when it's necessary for his name to be on documents, you'll print it with the stamp.'

'He won't like that!' Rizzio was genuinely surprised at this deliberate insult to Darnley.

'He's very displeased. He screamed and shouted and said you were usurping him. He wants to be given the crown matrimonial, but I'm not prepared to have him crowned yet, so he's complaining that he's king in name only.'

Rizzio nodded. 'You're right to withhold the crown from him. If he had it, he could take over the kingdom if you died.'

Their eyes met and they knew they were thinking the same thing. Darnley with the crown matrimonial would be a menace, capable of killing Mary to get his hands on absolute power.

Over the next few weeks, the Queen and her sulking husband patched up their differences, and seemed to enjoy each other's company again, especially when she dressed up as a boy and sallied out with him and his noisy gang of followers to the city's taverns. These expeditions made her feel very daring, and, strangely, they stimulated her and Darnley sexually. After one of those nights, she realized she was pregnant, but when she told him the good news, his reaction was disappointing, for he only pouted and made no comment.

She was seeing him now in a less infatuated light, and was more drawn to the company of Rizzio. Their closeness annoyed Darnley and late one evening, after drinking heavily, he ran into Mary's bed chamber shouting, 'Where is he? Where's the Italian bastard who's cuckolding me?'

Mary, in nightclothes and a long wrapper, stood in the middle of the floor and defied him, telling him to leave. 'Get out of my chamber!' she ordered.

'I will not. I know that Italian is here. Bring

him out.' Like a madman he rumpled up the bed, throwing pillows onto the floor and ripping down the curtains. With no one to protect her, she lifted the ewer off the wash table and broke it over his head, making him reel back, putting a hand to a bleeding cut on his brow.

'Are you trying to kill me?' he asked.

'I will if I have to. Get out!' She menaced him with a broken shard of pottery and he backed away, but his eyes glittered evilly, like the eyes of a cornered animal.

'*Get out*!' she hissed again and pushed him to the door. He left, shouting threats, and she barred the secret stairway between their rooms after him.

Next morning he spread the story that Rizzio had been in bed with his wife and was seen making a getaway from Mary's room.

She treated this story with scorn. 'He made it up to justify the way he behaved,' she said, but was worried in case the parentage of her unborn child might be questioned. In spite of her protestations, many people believed Darnley's story and no one could be sure of the truth.

'Where's Mary Hamilton? I haven't seen her for some time.' Mary looked around her sewing circle enquiringly and was surprised to see the other women dropping their eyes so as not to meet hers.

'She's indisposed,' said Mary Beaton shortly.

'Indisposed? What does that mean? How ill is she to avoid waiting on me for weeks?'

'She's in labour.' The stark statement came

from Fleming, who paid no attention to Mary Seton who was trying to hush her.

'In labour? At this moment? Here, in Holyrood?'

'She's probably delivered it by now. She had her first pains last night,' Beaton said.

'She's not married, is she?'

Seton put down her sewing and said, 'She's not yet eighteen. When she discovered she was with child, she didn't go home because her family would be shamed. Even to herself she pretended it wasn't happening.'

'She should have talked to me. Diane de Poitiers gave me a book of remedies to deal with situations like hers,' said Mary, shaking her head.

Silence met this remark as she stared from face to face. 'Who's the father? Can he be persuaded to marry her?'

'No one knows who he is,' said Fleming firmly, as if putting an end to the conversation.

Mary, however, was not prepared to give up the topic. Pregnant and sensitive to every movement in her womb, she sent a messenger to the attic rooms where her ladies lodged to find out news of Hamilton.

A scared-looking servant came back and curtsied in front of the Queen, twittering like a sparrow when asked, 'Did you find Mary Hamilton?'

'Her mother came and took her away, Your Majesty.'

'And the baby?'

'Yes. It was a little girl.'

'Were they both well?'

'Yes'm, the babe was very lusty but the poor lass was raving a bit. When her mother dragged her off she was screaming and carrying on. She wanted to see the father and her mother took her away to quieten her.'

All her life Mary had been afraid of sinking into one of her depressions and not coming out again. *Was mental disturbance a possible result of childbirth?* she wondered, with a chill of fear.

'Where did she go?' she asked.

'To Hamilton house in the High Street.'

'I hope they won't harm her,' said Mary and sent for Rizzio, telling him to send a messenger to the Hamiltons' town house and enquire about young Mary. 'I'm concerned for her. She's an innocent young thing,' she said.

He shuffled his feet and asked, 'Are you sure you want to do this?'

'Of course. I care about all my women. If she's in trouble I want to help. I might be able to force the father to marry her.'

'What if he isn't a position to do that?'

'Then he must make provision for her and the child. My father and grandfather made provision for plenty, as you well know. Send someone to enquire.'

Next morning Rizzio entered her chamber at breakfast time and sat beside her at the table. 'Young Mary Hamilton's baby is dead,' he said solemnly.

Mary put down her knife and stared at him in horror. 'But the serving woman said it was well and lusty. How did it die?'

191

He shook his head sadly. 'Madam, she drowned it.'

'What?' Mary jumped up, knocking over her stool.

'She took a horse early this morning and rode to Duddingston Loch on the other side of the Crag. An old hermit on the hillside saw her lay the infant in the water and hold it down. She's been arrested by the magistrates but she's not denying it. The poor girl has lost her mind,' he said.

Mary was stricken, 'Oh, poor girl, poor baby. The magistrates must treat her with clemency. She didn't know what she was doing,'

Rizzio gestured to the servants in the room to leave them, saying, 'Allez! We must speak privately.'

When they were alone he took her hands in his and said, 'Be strong, my Queen.'

She stared at him, wondering what he meant. 'I feel for the girl. I'm having a child myself...'

'It's not that. Some people have known for a long time about Mary Hamilton's baby.'

'I thought she was unwell but I didn't realize she was with child. She was so quiet and shy it was hard to notice her.'

'She was noticed by some people, and by one in particular,' he said.

'I felt the other Marys kept her away from me.'

'That was because she talked too much about the father of her child. They were afraid that she'd tell you.'

Mary's face hardened. 'What are you saying?'

'I'm telling you that the child you carry in

192

your womb and Mary Hamilton's child share a father.'

'NO! It isn't Darnley!' Mary raised both hands above her head and shook her closed fists in angry passion.

Rizzio could not keep satisfaction out of his voice. 'She says he promised to marry her when he got rid of you. She's a simple-minded girl.'

All pity cast aside, Mary became a fury. 'She's a harlot. And a murderer. She'll hang for this. How did she think she could take my man away from me? She has insulted me. I hope she burns in hell.'

Next day the city magistrates heard the case and pronounced the death penalty for infanticide on eighteen-year-old Mary Hamilton. She was to be hung from the gibbet at the bottom of the Canongate.

Distraught, her father and mother sought an audience with the Queen, who refused to see them, saying, 'The law must take its course. If an ordinary serving wench drowned her child, the magistrates would hang her. Because she's a noblewoman, it is the same. I cannot interfere.'

Weeping, the other Marys also tried to intercede but met with no success. Pleas that the girl was innocent and naive cut no ice with the Queen. 'She seduced my husband, she's an adulteress,' was her only response.

The only person who did not intercede for young Mary Hamilton was Darnley, who took himself off to the Ettrick Forest to hunt, and his wife had no opportunity to task him with infidelity.

On the morning of the execution, Mary Seton went into the Queen's room and knelt by the bedside with her hands folded in prayer. 'Please, my Queen, show mercy to the poor girl who is to die this morning. It will only take an order from you to save her life.'

'I cannot interfere with the administration of justice,' said Mary coldly.

'But she's half-demented. The law should not hang demented people.'

'It is going to hang this one,' said the Queen coldly and Mary Seton stood up, knowing there was no hope. When she looked into Mary's face, she saw something that had never been there before. The old softness was gone forever and a steel-like quality replaced it.

Worse was to come. 'I intend to watch the hanging,' announced Mary.

'Oh no,' moaned gentle Seton. She loved the Queen but this was trying her love to its limit. What had happened to the tender-hearted girl who refused to watch Montmorency's beheading?

'Tell my women to join me in the large room in the north end tower. It has a window that overlooks the gibbet. I'll watch from there and I expect them and you to be with me.'

Towering over the others, face set as hard as stone, she stood in the window and stared down on to the gibbet, never moving her eyes when the shivering girl was led up to the platform and a knotted rope was dropped over her head.

Mary Hamilton looked like a child in a long

white gown with her flaxen hair falling down her back like a waterfall. As a black-clad minister of the Protestant church asked for God's forgiveness on her behalf, she looked around distractedly, making it obvious she was out of her mind. The women beside the Queen sobbed and more than one hated her for refusing to save the girl, and for the way she seemed to be relishing the terrible scene.

Mary kept on staring and did not flinch or seem to hear their sobbing when a trap door fell away beneath the girl's bare feet and she swung to and fro, kicking and jerking like a toy on a string.

That night a new song was being sung in Edinburgh's taverns. Plaintive and catching, it was a lament for the dead girl.

'Last night there were four Marys, tonight there'll be but three. There's Mary Seaton and Mary Beaton and Mary Carmichael and me...

Oh often have I dressed my Queen and put on her braw silk gown. But all the thanks I've got tonight is to be hanged in Edinbro town.'

'That's one piece of music I won't dare to play before the Queen,' said David Rizzio.

Darnley returned a week later, and Mary's people noticed that her attitude towards him had changed. Tolerance was gone. He and she no longer went out in rollicking night-time expeditions and they spent as little time as possible in each other's company. Even more, she took care to shut him out of the business of ruling and Rizzio stamped his signature on all important papers without consulting him.

Darnley burned at the insult, but knew he was on dangerous ground, and could not confront Mary, confining himself to complaining to who-ever would listen, especially his wife's enemies. He was particularly bitter against Rizzio, who he knew had told Mary the name of the father of Hamilton's baby.

Twenty-Two

Life on the road was good for Nathan and Esther. He delighted at the feel of rough ground beneath his feet, and the cries of pleasure that arose when old customers saw him again. As he hefted his pack into farmhouses and ministers' manses, merchants' houses, cottages and the homes of small shopkeepers, he rejoiced to be greeted with cries of, 'We've missed you, smous. It's good to see you back.'

It did not matter that the sales he made were less than those to the royal court and in the big mansions of the city. He felt young and free again. His muscles tightened, his skin browned, and his teeth shone white in his face when he smiled, which he did often.

Esther was happy too, travelling along behind him in their little pony cart and letting the sum-mer sunshine beat down on her uncovered hair. Her sorrows of the past about losing longed-for babies were cast aside, and they made their way through the golden Scottish autumn land while the last of the harvest was being gathered in.

When they were greeted in the morning by drifting wraiths of November mist over the trees, they knew it was time to go back to Leith. Esther watched her husband methodically packing their goods into the cart and put a hand on his back as she said, 'Winter's coming my dear, but we've had a good summer.'

He looked over his shoulder at her and smiled, 'The best thing for me is how well you look.'

She giggled. 'I'm very well – very well indeed.'

He straightened up, with the pony's bridle hanging from his hand. 'Very well?' he queried.

'Yes, indeed. I have never felt so well in my whole life.'

He held out his arms and she walked into them, leaning her face on his chest as he asked, 'Has it happened? We didn't mean it to happen so soon, did we?'

'It's happened, I'm sure it's happened. There's no sickness this time but I know.'

'Oh my dearest,' he cried and, clasping each other tightly, they danced round and round like children.

'We'll have our baby this time, I'm sure of it,' cried Esther when they collapsed laughing on the grass.

That night they met up with a group of travelling musicians who were going from village to village playing music at harvest celebrations. In a big barn on a farm outside Perth, they sat on straw and listened to a fiddler who could switch his mood from jollity to melancholy with the flick of his bow. As his last piece he played a simple little song and the women of his party sang the words, *'Last night there were four Marys...'*

Nathan's face went solemn as he listened and when the piece finished he called out, 'Is that a new song?'

The fiddler nodded and said, 'Folk say that the Queen's secretary, the Italian man, wrote it.'

'Is what it says true? Has one of the Queen's women been hung?'

'So they say. There's a lot of talk about it in Edinburgh. That's where I first heard the song.'

'Which Mary was it?' Nathan knew them all.

The man shrugged, 'Don't ask me. It was a young one who had a baby and drowned it. So they hung her.'

The women around them made tongue clicking noises, for the disposing of unwanted or sickly babies was nothing unusual, and most poor people felt pity for the mother involved.

'You sang that the Queen wouldn't save her. Is that true too?' asked Nathan.

'All I know is what the song says. The man who taught me the words said the Queen was mad with jealousy because the father of the child was her husband, that beardless popinjay she's married to.'

Esther saw the effect this information had on her husband and clutched his hand in comfort. 'Perhaps it's only gossip, or just a sad song,' she whispered.

When they reached Leith however, her family were full of the story about Mary Hamilton being hung and the Queen watching from the palace window.

'But Queen Mary has always been such a gentle lady,' mourned Nathan.

'She was angry because the girl had Darnley's baby and she has no child herself,' said Esther's fat sister smugly.

Twenty-Three

1566

Mary Stewart was well aware of her tendency to drop into melancholy and fought hard against it, but there were times when misery engulfed her and she had no alternative but to take to her bed and stay there till the sadness passed.

Her mother had warned her against allowing the malaise to take her over. 'Your father was the same and melancholy killed him. He lay down in Falkland and died. He didn't even want to see you, his newborn daughter. He let melancholy rule his mind,' she was told many times.

After Hamilton's death, the Queen was on the verge of breakdown, unable to eat or sleep. The child she was carrying in her womb was no longer a source of joy, for it was Darnley's and when she looked at the smug face of her husband, she wondered what had possessed her to marry him.

She no longer even thought him handsome and only saw a lean beanpole with a self-satisfied face and a childishly spoiled mouth. His mind was as mediocre as his face too, and all he talked about was his resentment at not being crowned King of Scotland.

When she sat in her chamber listening to his ranting, she turned her face away to hide her expression. Darnley was oblivious to her growing dislike for him, but Rizzio saw the effect he had on her and often took her hand, comforting her with soft words when her husband swept out of the room.

'I've made a terrible mistake!' she mourned to him but he shook his head. 'You're the Queen and it's within your right to withhold power from him. Everyone knows he's a fool and no one listens to him any more.'

'Why did I marry him?' she groaned for the hundredth time.

'You needed a man and he was available. Anybody you married would bring you trouble. I've never heard of a country with so many troublemakers contending for positions. These are men who are prepared to cheat their own shadows. I don't know what Signor Macchiavelli would make of Scotland but I suspect it might outmanoeuvre even him.'

Mary's sadness was not lifted by the news of a new spate of weddings among her entourage. First Jane Bothwell, the widow of her favourite brother Lord John Stewart, came to say she was remarrying.

Mary stared bleakly at her and said, 'But your husband is only recently dead.'

'Last year,' said Jane with a meekness she did not feel.

'Only months. Why do you rush in and out of marriages like a panicked sheep?'

Jane said nothing and Mary went on, 'Who's the new husband?'

'The Master of Caithness.'

Mary was rude. 'Another ruffian, like your brother.'

'My brother too is marrying,' said Lady Jane.

The Queen showed surprise. 'Who is brave enough to marry him?' she asked. From time to time she saw Bothwell around the Palace but had heard nothing about this marriage.

'Jean Gordon, the daughter of the Earl of Huntly. They're to be married in Greyfriars Church next month.'

'Huh, a Protestant service, of course. How old is the girl? I don't remember seeing her at court.'

'She doesn't come to Edinburgh often because she's very shy. She's only nineteen and very beautiful.'

'A beauty. Poor thing. How old is he?'

'Thirty-one this year. Lady Jean is happy to become Countess of Bothwell,' said Jane stiffly.

Though still angry about the night Bothwell climbed into her bed, it was important to Mary to appear gracious about this wedding. Because the couple were marrying in a Protestant church, she did not attend the service, though she sent the bride a lavish gift of twelve yards of cloth of silver and six yards of white taffeta to make a gown.

Darnley went to the ceremony on her behalf and reported back that the bride was a beauty and sweetly virginal, but the groom, who loved dressing grandly when the occasion demanded, looked like 'an ape in purple'. This sally made Mary laugh, the first time she'd showed amusement at anything her husband said for ages.

The marriage ceremony was followed by five days of feasting, dancing and jousting. Mary attended most events but was disturbed because she found it difficult to take her eyes off the groom, who was in his element, triumphing in the dancing as much as in the lists.

Damn him, thought Mary. He was so animal that he woke strange feelings in her and she found herself envying the blushing girl who shared his bed at night.

The way she watched him did not escape Bothwell's notice. 'She looks like a hungry wolf,' he thought.

The Queen's closest confidante during her pregnancy was 'dearest Davie'.

'I don't know what I'd do without you,' she said when they sat playing cards together.

'You have many friends,' he said consolingly.

'But none of them understand me as you do. I can't talk about my real feelings with them. The Marys are all married now – except Seton, and she is so holy that I shock her. Other people are impossible to trust. Some of them sympathize with HIM, and I'm not sure who sympathizes with me.'

Rizzio laid down a losing card though he had a better one in his hand, but this allowed her to win. 'He complains to everyone,' he said.

'And the lords encourage him for their own reasons. He's being used. You should have stopped me marrying him, Davie.'

'He seemed a good option at the time.'

'I know. I could get a divorce because we're cousins, but I'd find it difficult to marry again. There's not a nobleman in Scotland who can be trusted.'

Rizzio looked up at her and said, 'I know. An astrologer told me the other day to beware of the bastard, but there are so many bastards in this court, I don't know whom to fear most. I suspect he meant Moray, but you've exiled him from Scotland at the moment so I feel easier in my mind.'

'You're right. Moray is the one we both fear. But who can we trust?'

'Perhaps the ape in purple,' suggested Rizzio.

She stared back at him in surprise. Could he read her mind?

'Why?' she asked.

'He has no ambitions to seize your throne and he doesn't take English money like Moray did. He's a brigand, it's true, but brigandage is in his blood. It's better to have men like that on your side than against you.'

'He's only on my side because he hates Moray.'

'But he's not silken-tongued. If he's against someone, he shows it, and he's against almost everyone except his band of villains.'

The Queen shook her head sadly. 'Though he's loyal to the throne, I think he despises me. He certainly despises my husband. He spits on the floor when they pass each other. If Darnley had his way, he'd have him hung for it.'

'If Darnley had his way, the country would be in ruin and he'd be out hunting all the time. I heard the other day that he's sleeping with one of the Douglas women.'

Mary bristled. 'I don't care if he sleeps with the entire Douglas family, men and women. I hate him, but I have to pretend all is well between us, and you must do the same. I wish I could rid myself of him, but he is my child's father and I must keep him with me because of that. If I repudiate him, the baby might not be the legitimate heir. Sometimes I wish I weren't having this child, but since I am, I hope it doesn't resemble him. And I hope it's a boy. Any woman trying to rule this lawless country is doomed to disaster. My mother tried hard, but even she was thwarted in the end by Moray.'

'You'll feel differently about the baby when it's born,' said Rizzio gently.

'No, I might feel worse. I'm not a mothering sort of woman. I love little dogs and monkeys and pretty birds but I've never been drawn to children. I've never seen a newborn baby and don't particularly want to.'

'In that case, I'll bring you a puppy when the baby's born,' laughed Rizzio.

The next day was February ninth, and a bitter

wind was blowing through the streets of Edinburgh, bowling people along in front of it like ships at sea. Darnley and Rizzio played tennis together in the palace's closed court in the morning and were on good terms when they parted. Neither enquired of the other what plans they had for the rest of the day.

When evening fell, a group of the Queen's friends gathered in a small reception room next door to her bedroom. Though the still shrieking wind made the tapestries on the wall billow in and out as if someone were hidden behind them, a huge fire burned in the hearth and kept the room warm. Six people sat round the table laughing and talking as they enjoyed succulent roast beef, which was normally forbidden in Lent, but the pregnant Queen was advised to eat it by her French doctor Bourgoing, who was one of the guests.

Rizzio, resplendent in a fur-lined robe, a feathered bonnet and russet-coloured hose, sat at her side, and when the meal was finished, he took up his lute to play her favourite music. Halfway through the second piece, the tapestry curtain over the door to the stairway was roughly pulled aside and Darnley appeared.

Mary stared at him in surprise because he had not been invited to join the party. 'Have you eaten?' she asked.

'Yes, enough,' he said in a hurried way and it occurred to her that he was drunk. He walked around the table to where she and Rizzio sat together and squeezed himself between them. She moved along slightly and Darnley put out an arm, holding her hard round the waist.

She sat rigid and angry but said nothing. Then he kissed her roughly and while he was doing that, the door was thrown open again and Darnley's uncle Ruthven, who had always scared her, stood in the gap, looking like a devil in black armour. Mary had been told only a few days before that he was on his deathbed, but he must have risen from it to turn up now in Holyrood.

Her eyes went from him to her husband and suddenly she knew she'd been betrayed. 'What have you done?' she asked Darnley but there was no time for an answer because Ruthven was pointing at Rizzio. 'That man hath been in your chamber too long, Your Majesty,' he cried.

She tried to stand up but Darnley still held her down. 'He's done nothing wrong!' she shouted.

'He's offended your honour and your husband's honour,' was Ruthven's reply. Then he said to Darnley, 'Hold your wife.'

Mary was too quick and desperate, however. Escaping with effort from the arm round her waist, she ran to Rizzio and held his head protectively between her hands. 'Go away! Do not harm him,' she shouted.

As if on a signal, there was a sudden influx of men into the room, which was too small to hold them all. She recognized Morton, Mar, Ker of Fawdonside and several heavily armed Douglases, who yelled their family battle cry, 'A Douglas, a Douglas!' as they burst in. The terrible Ruthven was presiding over an assassination.

Candles were knocked off the table and dishes

smashed in pieces on the floor. The room would have been in darkness if the Queen's half-sister, Lady Argyll, had not had the presence of mind to grab a burning candle before it hit the floor. By its light she saw Mary being torn away from Rizzio by Ruthven and shoved back to Darnley who held on to her again. The Italian, knowing he was in mortal danger, clung frantically on to her skirts, imploring her to save him.

'Madame, save me, save my life!' he screamed and, as she bent down to hold him, a man called George Douglas, who was indeed a bastard as the astrologer had predicted, stabbed him over her shoulder with Darnley's dagger.

Horrified, she looked into the contorting face of her beloved friend and began to scream, 'Poor Davie, poor Davie, may God have mercy on your soul.'

His half-lifeless body was dragged away from her and stabbed again by Ker as the fingers of the hands that still clutched on to her skirt were bent back to loosen his hold. He was thrown out through the open doorway and down the stairs like a sack of straw. When he hit the ground, the assassins fell on him again, stabbing and gouging like madmen till he sustained 56 stab wounds.

The noise and screaming attracted Bothwell and his brother-in-law Huntly, who were dining in another part of the Palace. They came running to rescue the Queen but were met by a locked and barred door that they could not break down. Outside in the courtyard, the Provost of Edinburgh with the town guard stood staring up at the windows of the Queen's apartments and sent up a roar when Mary appeared at the window, with her hair wild and her bodice ripped so badly that her bare breasts could be seen. Hysterical, she called down, 'Help me, help me!'

Within seconds she had disappeared again because Ker of Fawdonside pulled her back and held a pistol to her belly, saying through gritted teeth, 'If you call out again, I'll cut you into collops.' She looked into his bloodshot eyes and realized he meant what he said, so slumped down on to the floor in a half-faint, but was conscious enough to hear her husband take her place at the window and call down to the townspeople that the Queen was safe and that they should all go home.

Gently, Lady Argyll helped her to her feet and told her Rizzio was dead. 'No more tears. Now is the time for revenge,' she whispered.

When they realized that there was nothing they could do inside the palace and that they too would be killed if the rebels caught them, Huntly and Bothwell ran into the palace zoo and escaped through the lions' cage. Fortunately for them, the animals had recently been fed and were too full and comatose to fall on a pair of fugitives.

They ran across the Queen's Park to Huntly's townhouse, where they waited for news, which soon arrived as a message from Lady Argyll, who told them the Queen was being held prisoner. Moray was on his way back to Edinburgh from exile in England and the rebels intended to keep Mary a prisoner for the rest of her life.

'Not if I have anything to do with it,' swore Bothwell when he read the note.

Mary spent a terrifying night. None of her women were allowed to join her and she lay sleepless, shaking with nerves and alone till dawn, her mind turning back continually to the sight of Rizzio dying at her feet. She knew she was in mortal danger, for it would be easy to kill her now and no one, neither Elizabeth of England nor her relatives in France, would do anything to revenge her killing other than making a few loud protestations. To survive, she must fall back on her own resources and fortunately she had a strong streak of self-preservation.

When food was brought to her in the morning, she was writhing in bed with both hands clutching her belly.

'My child is coming,' she groaned.

Darnley arrived to see if what she said was true, and she knew him so well it was easy to hoodwink him. 'I'm in labour. I'll lose our child if you don't find me a doctor. Help me,' she told him through realistic groans of agony.

He approached her tentatively, expecting to be upbraided for his part in the previous night's killing, but she managed that well too. 'Dear husband, you've been deceived. I know you had nothing to do with the killing of poor Davie. Help me now, help our child,' she sobbed. He took the bait.

'I'd no idea what they were going to do,' he lied, although he had actually signed a document agreeing to the murder of Rizzio days before it was carried out.

'I believe you, dear husband, and I know you'll help me now. Fetch my doctor and a midwife or this will end in another disaster,' she told him.

Her acting was so realistic that he did as she asked. Accompanying her doctor came her close friend, Lady Huntly, Bothwell's mother-in-law, whom Mary knew well and trusted totally.

As the doctor was examining her, she kept hold of Darnley's hand, assuring him that she believed him to be innocent of plotting against her. 'Who was behind it?' she asked, and Darnley, being a turncoat, told her the names of the conspirators, most of whom she knew anyway. He named her half-brother Moray as the mastermind though he had been still in England when the plot was hatched.

'The Italian was gaining too much influence over you,' Darnley explained as if that was sufficient justification for what had been done.

Her French doctor Bourgoing could tell she was faking a miscarriage as her only hope of escape from her captors, but he went along with her and shook his head solemnly as he warned Darnley that his wife was about to lose her child unless her conditions were improved. He gave her sedatives and before she fell asleep, she told Darnley to go back to the conspirators and assure them that she was prepared to forgive what had been done.

'Tell them I'm not bloodthirsty,' she said and stupid Darnley did not realize how greatly she was lying. He did as she asked and brought the men who had tried to kill her back into her presence. Apparently calm and chastened, she looked on them without a trace of anger or bitterness, though it took all her powers as an actress to keep up the pretence. She did it so well, they thought she accepted the situation as a fait accompli.

'We can do whatever we want with her. She's as stupid as her husband,' said Ker of Fawdonside dismissively.

'One thing we can't do is kill her though,' said George Douglas.

'Why not?' asked ruthless Ker.

'Because she's popular. You saw the crowd in the courtyard last night, didn't you? They'll storm the palace and tear us apart if we kill her. We'll keep her in custody and make her do what we want. When Moray comes back, he'll decide where to send her; probably Stirling because it's easier to guard than the castle here.'

Duplicitously, they acted their parts as effectively as Mary. Morton even went so far as to go down on his knees in front of her and when he stood up he realized that Rizzio's blood was still wetting the floorboards and his legs were stained with it. Trying to make little of the murder, he said, 'After all, what is the loss of a low-born man when the fate of lords and gentlemen like us is in the balance.'

Though burning with hatred inside, the Queen smiled and agreed with him.

Because it seemed that her life and the life of her child were in danger, Lady Huntly was permitted to tend to her and as she bent solicitously over the bed, she whispered, 'Take courage. Lord Bothwell will help you. He's waiting for you at Seton.'

Though it was less than twenty miles away, how to get to Seton, Mary wondered? Again she decided to use Darnley.

'If we stay here, we're both in danger,' she told him when they were alone, and he knew it was true because the rebels considered him a turncoat and would not hesitate to put him out of the way. He knew too much and Mary was his only protection.

'Organize horses for us. We have to leave Edinburgh,' she told him and, armed with one of her rings as a pledge of loyalty to her, he went to the stables to arrange for a pair of horses to be waiting for them in the palace burying ground that night.

But first they had to get out of the Queen's locked chamber, and she devised the plan of knotting bedsheets and blankets together to let them down to ground level. As she went hand over hand down the rope of sheets, she wondered if the baby inside her would ever see the light of day, and, if it did survive, would it be a braver person because of what she was going through?

Once on the ground they sneaked past tilted old gravestones to where the horses waited as arranged.

Typically Darnley had no appreciation of Mary's cunning or bravery and led the way out of the Queen's park at a gallop, keeping on galloping till they were ten miles from the city.

She rode behind him crying out, 'Slow down. It's dangerous for my baby to make me ride so fast.'

He did not slacken his pace, for he was mortally afraid, but only turned his head and shouted back, 'What matters if you lose this child? We can make another.'

I hate you Henry Darnley. I really hate you and I will revenge myself on you, she silently swore.

Dawn was breaking when they neared Seton Castle and through the frosty mist, three mounted figures rode towards them. The leader of the group was Bothwell, who galloped straight for the Queen and leaped from his horse to gently lift her out of the saddle. She clung to him, sinking her face into his shoulder and gasping with sobs, all the pent up terrors of the previous days gushing out of her.

'They killed my Davie, they killed my Davie!' she gasped and he held her close, his face stricken as he stroked her neck in the same way as he would soothe a terrified horse, 'Sssh, ssh, you're safe. I'll take care of you,' he told her.

Darnley saw them together and his face went as black as thunder.

Twenty-Four

Mary's medical attendants had confidence that she had survived her ordeal without any ill effects on her baby. It was growing fast and her nervous symptoms disappeared. She seemed more like the carefree girl who had first arrived from France than she had been for years.

As soon as she arranged for Rizzio's body to be recovered from a makeshift grave in Grey-friars churchyard and re-interred in a place of honour in the Holyrood burying ground, she seemed to stop grieving for him.

Only one man knew she was still burning with a desire for vengeance, and that was James Hepburn, Earl of Bothwell.

When he met her at Seton, he took her to Dunbar, where she stayed safe from her enemies while he gathered an army of five thousand spearmen to escort her back to Edinburgh. In Dunbar castle they spent hours together and for the first time, she had a man in whom she could confide.

She poured out her loathing of Darnley and he said, 'Bide your time. The opportunity will come to pay him back.'

She grabbed his hand and held it to her lips. 'Promise me, promise me that you will stay true,' she pleaded.

He felt something strange move in his heart, something which he had not expected and which he wished was not happening. 'I promise, truly I promise,' he told her.

After they parted, he walked on the castle battlements and paused, laying his forehead against the cold stone of the wall and closing his eyes.

'I don't want this,' he told himself.

He had been with many women, but until he had married his young wife less than a year ago, he only truly felt love for Janet, his witch lady. The marriage with Jean Gordon was dynastic and he needed her dowry, but to his surprise he began to love her and she loved him. The marriage was deepening into true happiness, but this latest development looked about to spoil it.

As if he were enchanted, he fell into a kind of love for the Queen. Was it possible to love two women at once, he wondered? In the past, he had viewed her as an opportunity for advancement, hoping that through her he could fill his coffers and extend his lands, but now that she needed his help and protection as a woman as well as a ruler, he was unmanned.

He raised his head and stared out over the cold grey sea. *Will I run away, take ship again and return to France?* he wondered. Mary was not a wise woman like Janet. If he abandoned her, someone else would champion her cause. But who? He probably was the only man who was truly altruistic in her defence, and perhaps the only one capable of defeating her enemies, for they were his enemies too and he had their measure.

'I'll take you back to Edinburgh. I'll make sure you're safe and that the city is yours again before I leave you,' he said abruptly when he hurried back to her chamber.

She looked up, eyes swimming. 'And then?' she asked.

'Then I'll go back to my wife,' he said.

'I don't want you to leave me,' she implored and rose to her feet, walking towards him with her arms held out. Half-knowing that he was being deliberately exploited, he walked into her embrace, and they shared a bed for the first time.

About midnight, alone in a tall tower, Janet Beton was consulting her astrological charts when she suddenly gasped and stood up, scattering papers on the floor. 'Oh Jamie, I don't know what you've done but it will be your doom,' she cried aloud and wrung her hands in anguish.

Magnificent in finely-chased armour under a flowing fur-lined cloak and with a pair of pistols prominent on her saddle pommel, Mary rode beside him next day at the head of his spearmen into Edinburgh, and when the news of her approach reached the city, Rizzio's killers fled to England.

Without resistance, she cantered up the High Street and into the castle, which she did not intend to leave till her child was born, for she could not bear the thought of going into labour in her old chamber at Holyrood next door to where Rizzio had been slaughtered and where his blood still stained the floor.

As she crossed the castle drawbridge, she turned in the saddle and called out to a watching crowd, 'Your Queen is back!'

They cheered.

Riding disconsolate behind her was her husband Darnley, whom she studiously ignored, and had ignored since they escaped from Holyrood. Before outsiders she pretended to trust him, assuring everyone that he was innocent of the killing of Rizzio, even though the other conspirators, angry at the way he had betrayed them and helped her to slip out of their grasp, sent written proof of his involvement in the plot to her.

She read the incriminating papers without emotion. 'He was misled,' she said.

'Is she stupid or very cunning?' Moray asked his fellow rebel lords. None of them was sure of the answer.

Twenty-Five

'You're precious. Till the day the baby is born you have to do nothing but eat and sleep. I want to see you as plump and happy as a roosting chicken,' Nathan teased his wife while they sat enjoying spring sunshine on a bench outside her father's house in Leith.

'Plump? As plump as my sister?' she teased back and he laughed. 'Well perhaps not, but plumper than you are at the moment.'

They held hands and allowed themselves to dream. Esther put one hand on her round little belly and said softly, 'Do you think it's a boy or a girl?'

'I don't care. I only want to hold it in my arms and kiss its little face.'

'So do I. We've waited such a long time, and been disappointed so often but this time it feels different. I felt it move today. It turned over inside me, like a little fish.'

He laughed. 'Let's give it a fishy name then. How about calling it Jonah who was swallowed by the whale?'

'And if it's a girl?'

'Sprat! We'll call her Sprat.'

'Oh, poor thing. We'd better hope for a boy. Can't you think of another name?'

'How about Minnow?'

They were happy and as much in love as ever. Because he was determined not to risk Esther's health, and because she refused to allow him to go back on the road without her, they stayed in Leith and Nathan returned to his old system of selling his goods to the aristocratic ladies of Edinburgh.

One day he returned home with an empty pack in high excitement. 'I saw the Queen again today. She bought everything I had to sell!'

Esther was surprised. 'Everything? She's going to be busy if she uses it all.'

'She has time on her hands. Like you, she's having a child. Her belly is very big.'

'As big as mine?' asked Esther.

218

'Bigger, but she's a giant of a woman and you're a sprat like your baby!' he said fondly.

'When is the Queen's baby due?' the Leverson women wanted to know.

'It looks as if it could come soon. She's in big, airy rooms in the castle looking out over the town, and all the way to the river Forth. The court is in a ferment of excitement, with people rushing about, and doctors coming and going.'

'Doctors?' Esther looked scared but her mother reassured her, 'You don't need doctors. The woman who delivered your sister's children will be here and you'll be well looked after. Besides, you're better with this child than you've ever been before. This time you'll have a healthy baby, I'm sure of it.' On the fifteenth of June, during a very hot spell of weather, Esther began having labour pains. The lying-in woman who had attended her sister's births took care to conceal concern from the sweating mother but told Esther's mother in a whisper that the birth could be imminent but there was no movement from the baby.

Mrs Leverson put her hands to her face and moaned, 'I cannot bear for her to have another disappointment,' she said.

'These things are out of our control,' said the midwife.

Labouring with Nathan by her side, Esther tried to concentrate on him desperately talking about the first thing that came into his head. His voice helped her fight the pains that racked her. She had never gone so long into a pregnancy before and the agonies that convulsed her were a dreadful revelation, but she did not want to upset him by betraying how she felt.

'Talk to me, talk more to me,' she whispered, clutching his hand so tightly that her fingernails made deep impressions in his palm.

'What about?' he asked.

'Talk to me about the Queen. Tell me what her chambers are like...'

'Very beautiful, with tapestries hanging round the walls. They show hunting scenes. There's a running deer on one with people on white horses chasing after it. All along the bottom are deep panels of spring flowers...'

'What kind of flowers?'

'Primroses and little purple irises, the kind you love.'

She sighed and said, 'How pretty.' He noticed that her lips were cracked and dry and paused to give her a sip of wine before he went on with the story.

'She has a parrot brought all the way from Africa.'

'A parrot! What is it like?'

'It's red and green and yellow and has wrinkled eyes like an old man. It's very wicked and screeches like a witch.'

'Is it in a cage?'

'No, it flies round the room. Her serving ladies bought it for her to brighten the waiting time.'

'And does it?'

'Yes, I think so. She laughs at it but her pet dogs hate it. They run round barking and trying to catch its tail.'

'How many little dogs are there?'

'About six, little things with curled tails. They bite people.'

'Did they bite you when you went there showing your silks?'

'One tried to but I pushed it away with my foot when the Queen wasn't looking.'

Esther tried to laugh but the chuckle died in her throat and became a moan. 'Oh, I think the baby's coming,' she cried.

The women delivered her child a few hours later. It was a beautiful little girl with curling black hair and chalk white skin...but it was dead.

Nathan held the pathetic scrap and wept bitterly. Esther could not be told for several hours because she was too ill to withstand the sorrow. When she eventually opened her eyes, and saw her husband sitting by the bed with his head in his hands, she knew what had happened.

'Dear Nathan, I'm so sorry. I'm no use to you. I can't give you a child,' she wept, but he threw himself across the bed and sobbed with her. 'I only want you, I only want you. You mustn't think for one minute that I'm disappointed about not having a child. My only wish is that you could have one because you want it so. But you have me, Esther, and you always will.'

A week before her child was due, Mary took to her bed, which was enormous and hung with curtains of blue velvet. She whiled away the waiting time with embroidery, playing cards with her ladies, going over the inventory of her precious jewellery and, a favourite pastime, making her will, changing it practically every day.

Because she was so alienated from her half-brothers in Scotland, her best treasures were left to relations in France, people with whom she grew up. She yearned to be back at Fontainebleu or Chenonceaux and wished her destiny had been different.

Before she left the French court, her mother-in-law Catherine maliciously passed on to her what Nostradamus predicted for her – *blood* – and now that word dominated her mind.

Will I die in a welter of birthing blood? she wondered, and fearfully asked Bourgoing if she was in danger.

He made a French sound of exasperation. 'Ttchh! What rubbish. You're a healthy woman. There are no danger signs that I can see. Don't allow fantasies to poison your mind.'

Reprimanded, she sank back among her pillows and determined not to think about Nostradamus again.

After a false start, labour began on June eighteenth and was difficult. Distressed at seeing the Queen in agony, her chief birthing attendant, the Countess of Atholl, who was reputed to be a witch, bent over the bed and said, 'I can cast a spell to take away the pain, if you're not afraid of black magic.'

Through gritted teeth Mary groaned, 'Try it, try it. God will forgive me.'

The room was cleared of everyone except Dr Bourgoing and two women. One was Lady Atholl and the other fat Lady Reres, who was to be the baby's wet nurse. Lady Reres was told to lie down beside the Queen and have the labour pains transferred to her while the Countess of Atholl intoned strange words and passed her hands over the bodies of the two women.

Almost at once Lady Reres began writhing in agony, but unfortunately Mary's pains did not lessen and they both suffered through the rest of the night. On the point of delivery, the Queen fainted and was not fully aware when her baby was born at ten o'clock in the morning.

Dr Bourgoing held it up to the watching women and said softly, 'Alas, a girl.'

The little body hung limply from his hand and showed no sign of life. He swung it to and fro but it made no sound.

Lady Atholl groaned, 'Is it dead?' Lady Reres got off the bed and took the apparently lifeless child from the doctor, opened its mouth with her finger and said, 'I think it is. Perhaps it's just as well. It should've been a boy. Scotland will never thole another Queen. And look at all that black hair. It could be Rizzio's in spite of what the Queen said.'

The doctor, putting his mouth to the baby's blue lips in an attempt to breathe life into it but there was no response and dejectedly he handed it back to Lady Argyll saying, 'I've failed! I must go outside for a moment and be alone. Let the Queen rest but call me when she wakens.'

Shoulders hunched, and disconsolate at losing such a precious charge, he walked out into a small courtyard by the castle ramparts, from where he stared towards the Forth. As he stood with his hands tucked into the ends of his sleeves, one of the Queen's dressers came running up gasping, 'Doctor, please come with me. A kitchen girl is labouring with child and if she's not helped she'll die.'

He was a good doctor who took his calling seriously and did not discriminate between rich and poor, so he ran after her to the vast kitchens where, in a squalid shed, a young girl was lying on the floor in a welter of blood.

'She's haemorrhaged. How long has she been like this?' he said, kneeling by the body.

'Since the child was born, two or three hours ago. The bleeding started afterwards and we couldn't stop it,' said a distraught woman standing by.

He held a hand to the girl's face and felt the coldness of the skin. 'I'm afraid the poor girl's dead. Where's her child?'

The dresser pointed to a rag-wrapped bundle lying under a three-legged stool and he lifted it, peeling back the meagre covering. The baby gave a loud cry and wriggled in his hands. It was a fine, healthy boy.

'Is there a father?' he asked.

The two women shook their heads. 'No one wanted it, not even the mother,' said the first woman.

He thought it bitterly unfair that the Queen, who needed a child so badly, had lost her baby and a dead kitchen girl was leaving behind an unwanted orphan.

He hurried back to the royal lying-in room by a back entrance, where he found her ladies

224

washing and tending to Mary who was now semi-conscious but still too ill to be told the sad news.

'How cruel! I've just been asked to look at one of the kitchen women who has given birth to a boy. That child is healthy but the mother died in a flux of blood and I was too late to save her,' Bourgoing blurted out to Lady Atholl.

She stared at him and exclaimed, 'A maid had a boy? Is it healthy?'

Her tone of voice alerted him to her implication and he replied, 'Yes, very. He's in the kitchens. No one seems to know what to do with him.'

'I know,' said the redoubtable Lady Atholl, and went out of the room at a run. As she passed through the outer chamber, anxious people asked, 'Is it born yet?' but she shook her head and said, 'Soon, soon.'

When she returned a few minutes later she was carrying a copper warming pan with a long wooden handle and used it to cut her way through the waiting crowd. 'Get out of my way,' she shouted and pushed her way into the Queen's chamber.

Once the door was safely closed, she laid the warming pan down on the bed and opened the lid. Inside lay a baby wrapped in a dirty cloth.

When the doctor lifted it out, it opened its mouth to yell and the sound alerted the crowd on the other side of the door, who set up a joyful shout. At the same time the Queen stirred and asked in a faltering voice, 'Is it over?'

Lady Reres bent over her saying, 'Yes, Your

225

Majesty. You have a fine son.'

As the doctor wrapped the bastard boy in a length of cloth of silver, the real child of Mary Stewart was put into a winding sheet of fine white silk and laid back in the warming pan, which Lady Atholl stuck under the bed to be sneaked out later.

When mother and little boy were settled, Lady Reres took the warming pan into the closet off the bed chamber, expecting to find the baby cold, but was surprised when it felt warm, though still comatose. With its long lashed eyes closed and dark curls clustering on its head, it looked like a doll.

'Poor wee thing, it's not dead yet,' she said and went in search of Lady Atholl. What to do? They decided that the most important thing was to keep the boy and ensure the substitution was a close secret. No one, apart from the two of them and Dr Bourgoing, must ever know, not even the Queen.

Practical Lady Atholl handled the situation. 'We'll keep it hidden till evening and if it's still alive, we'll arrange somewhere to take it,' she said, before going back to the kitchen to pay off the two friends of the dead mother, passing over a golden coin to each of them and saying, 'Get your boxes and leave now. Forget about the dead girl's baby. I'll give you positions in my castle at Blair Atholl and keep you for the rest of your lives provided you never tell a soul what happened here today. As far as you know, the servant girl's baby died with her.'

'Yes, of course it did,' they agreed.

226

There still was the problem of disposing of the extra child, alive or dead. Lady Reres suggested they announce that the Queen had given birth to twins, one of which died. The doctor refused to agree to that because it meant that the first baby would have to be killed if it was not already dead. To do that was against his principles, even for the sake of Mary.

'You and Lady Atholl must decide what to do. Don't tell me your decision, whatever it is,' he said.

When he left the ladies stared at each other over the warming pan. 'Mary Hamilton drowned her unwanted child,' said Lady Atholl in a meaningful tone.

'I can't commit murder,' whispered Lady Reres.

'If it's taken to the shore of the Nor' Loch and laid in the reeds it'll surely die there tonight.'

'But whoever lays it down will be a murderer.'

'I could send my steward. He's a man with no feelings,' said Lady Argyll.

'But he has a memory, hasn't he? We'll have to do it ourselves.'

'Mary Hamilton was hung for that.'

'But only because the child was hers. She was guilty of infanticide. We could simply lay it down and go back later to see if it has survived.'

Lady Reres began to weep. 'I can't do it. My conscience won't let me. I'm afraid of the wrath of God.'

Lady Atholl spat. 'Wrath of God! Wrath of the devil more like. I'll see to it. Just don't ask me how.'

227

'Believe me, I never want to know,' said Lady Reres with feeling.

The sun was setting and a beautiful rose pink light was reflected from the sky on to the waters of the Nor' Loch that spread along the base of rocky castle crag. People who had been out walking were heading for home, leaving only a few scavengers rummaging about among rubbish deposited on the shores of the loch.

Nathan sat on the driving box of the pony cart with his head on his fist staring up towards the castle. He was in misery, mourning for his dead baby but even more for the inconsolable grief of his poor wife. He'd tried to coax her out in the hope of cheering her up but she refused to move from her bed.

When the Queen was delivered of her baby earlier that morning, the birth had been greeted by a fusillade of cannon fire, which only deepened his sorrow.

He got down from the cart and walked slowly towards the loch. At the mouth of a dark narrow close leading downhill to the water, he saw a hurrying woman in a cloak of dark green velvet, which he noticed because of its quality.

Then he recognized her. *What's Lady Argyll doing walking out alone at this time of day?* he wondered.

He liked the woman, and, worried in case she would be harried by some drunken man, he hurried to catch up with her to ask, 'Can I help you, my lady?'

She stared at him with open hostility in her

eyes. Beneath her cloak she was carrying what looked like a bundle of rags and he wondered if she was throwing them away. It didn't seem likely.

Suddenly she recognized him and said, 'Oh, it's you, smous! I'm taking a walk. It's been a hard day. The Queen had her son this morning.'

At that moment, to her panic, she felt movement in the bundle she carried. The unwanted child was stirring! At any moment it might start to cry.

He smiled, unaware of her discomfort. 'I heard the cannons. I'm very pleased. Send my best wishes to Her Majesty. When she's well again, I'll bring her a length of fine taffeta to make a gown for the baby.'

Lady Argyll tightened her arms around the bundle and nodded abruptly, 'I'll tell her,' she said and tried to step past him but he walked with her, for he suddenly felt the need to talk about his own tragedy. 'My wife had a baby yesterday but sadly it was born dead,' he blurted out.

Lady Argyll stopped and said sympathetically, 'Oh, I'm sorry. I hope your wife is safe.'

'She's suffering. It's her sixth loss. And she wants a child so much.'

'She wants a child?' repeated Lady Argyll in a strange voice.

'Very badly,' said Nathan unhappily.

'Then she shall have one.' Lady Argyll threw open her cloak and showed him the white-wrapped bundle. 'One of my maids had this child today but died in labour. I'm on my way to take it to some nuns in the Dean village, but it'll have a better life with you, I'm sure.'

Nathan looked at her as if she'd gone mad.

'You're giving me a baby, Lady Argyll?'

'It'll be an act of mercy if you take it. You're a good man and prosperous too. If this child goes to the nuns, who knows how it will end up. Scrubbing floors probably.'

'Is it a boy or a girl?'

'A girl.' She pulled a corner of the wrapper down to show a little face. The dark eyelids were fluttering. It was indeed alive. That made her more determined to persuade him to take it so she could avoid committing mortal sin. In spite of her necromancy, a Catholic upbringing still dominated her thinking.

Nathan stared at the baby as if he'd never seen one before and almost held out his arms to grasp it, but something restrained him.

'Is this a trick? Are you being honest with me?' he asked.

She drew close to him, staring intently into his face. 'I'm offering you a newborn baby to fill the place of the one you lost. Tell me you want it,' she said, holding up the child.

Tears filled his eyes. He stretched out his arms but drew back again. 'I can't take a child that you might claim back some day,' he said.

'I assure you that will never happen. This is a secret between us and you must never tell anyone who gave you the child. Please take it.'

With only a moment's hesitation, he accepted the little bundle.

'Thank you,' he said.

In Leith he went straight to Esther's bedroom and laid the child on the counterpane beside her. They both stared at it as if it were made of pure gold.

'I've brought you a little girl,' he said simply.

Weeping, she touched its face. The eyelids fluttered and it sighed.

'How?' she whispered.

'Through a miracle.'

'But where has it come from?'

'The woman who gave it to me is a lady of the court, but you must ask no more questions.'

'Is it her own baby?'

'No, she's too old and she says it is the child of her maid. We mustn't question how she got it but I'm happy that she did. Don't worry, Esther. We've been given this child to love.'

Nathan told the rest of the family he had bought the baby from a kitchen maid who did not want it. A neighbouring woman, who was suckling a child of her own and had milk enough for two, was called in to feed the new arrival. She presumed the child was Esther's and that the skinny little mother could not produce enough milk herself.

Mrs Leverson shook her head every time she looked at her youngest daughter cuddling her daughter. 'The wet nurse said the little thing was starving. It hadn't been fed since it was born but apparently that's not a bad thing. It seems healthy enough now,' she said.

'She's perfect! She has a lovely face and she's so big, she's going to be tall,' exalted Esther.

231

Nathan examined the cloth around the child and found it was of the finest quality silk, the sort he sold to the Queen. *I must try to find out more about this,* he thought, but said nothing to the others.

Sharp Mr Leverson had his suspicions too and took Nathan aside to ask, 'Tell me the truth about that baby, please.'

'The nuns wanted a home for it,' Nathan said lamely.

'NUNS?' questioned Mr Leverson. 'What were you doing with nuns?'

'I've sold silks to them...' He stared levelly into his father-in-law's shrewd eyes and his meaning got through. Esther wants this child. By a miracle it has come our way. Do not question too much or it might disappear.

Mr Leverson stayed silent but next day returned to the subject and Nathan, swearing him to secrecy, told him how Lady Argyll had given him a child for Esther.

'Was it hers to give?' he asked.

'She said it is the child of a dead servant of hers.'

'Why should she be carrying it away?'

'I suspect she was going to drown it.'

'Is she capable of such an act?'

'People say she's a witch. She casts spells.'

'Mmm. What if she tries to get it back?'

'She knows I'm the Queen's smous but not where I live.'

'I think it would be best if you and Esther take your child to Amsterdam, at least for a while.'

'I think so too but before I go, I want to try to

find out more about it. It must have come from the Queen's household. Someone will know.'

He was thinking, *Lady Argyll is a close companion of the Queen. So close that she'd be present at the royal birth. But I mustn't imagine things.*

Next day, with his pack on his back, he walked to the castle and found old friends in the kitchens, drinking ale and making merry on account of the Queen giving birth to an heir.

Not rejoicing were a trio of sober-faced maids with black ribbons in their hair and he stopped to speak to them. 'You're not as happy as the others. What's wrong?' he asked.

The youngest said, 'Our friend died yesterday. They took her away to a pauper's grave today.'

'What happened?'

'She died giving birth.'

His heart gave a little skip. 'Did the baby die too?'

'No. It was taken away. The cook said it was dead, but I heard it yell. Then it disappeared. Just as well, I expect. None of us could have kept it,' said the oldest girl, the most affected of the three.

'Is there a father?'

'It could have been anyone really. She was a pretty girl and easily persuaded. We think it was one of the horsemen who came with the Queen from France, but he's taken himself off to Craig-millar.'

'Who took the baby girl then?'

One piped up, 'It wasn't a girl. It was a boy.'

He walked away crestfallen. A false trail, he

thought.

Hurrying back to Leith, he measured out twenty ells of fine taffeta as a present for the Queen and wrapped it up carefully, before returning to the castle the next day.

Bowing and scraping and showing his parcel, he was admitted into the chamber where the Marys were receiving congratulations on the Queen's behalf. To his relief, there was no sign of Lady Argyll.

His present was received with thanks. Leaving, he met up with a pair of royal bodyguards whom he knew from previous visits. They were half tipsy and very friendly.

'So you've come to hear about the next King, have you,' cried one, clapping him on the back.

'At least it's a man this time,' he said duplicitously.

'True. It doesn't matter who a king marries. Our children won't have to put up with a fool like Darnley,' said the other.

'Let's hope the new baby doesn't look like him,' added his friend.

'The women say it doesn't. It has black hair like Rizzio, and it's not long in the body. Both Darnley and the Queen are very long but Rizzio wasn't.'

Nathan pretended to be shocked. 'So you think it was his child? Is that why he was killed?'

The first guard chipped in. 'I don't think Rizzio had anything to do with it. I saw Lady Argyll running about with a warming pan. Maybe the Queen's baby died and she brought in another one.'

234

They stared at him and he nodded, solemnly drunk. 'My woman was in the Queen's closet washing up the mess. She's sure she heard the doctor saying the royal baby was dead but she's terrified of that witch Argyll. She thinks she'll kill her or put a spell on her if she lets out the truth.'

Nathan forced himself to laugh. 'Stories like that always come up when there's a royal birth,' he said.

'People love to gossip,' agreed the guards.

Head down and deep in thought, he walked back to Leith. It fitted too well. Could Lady Argyll have given the Queen's baby to Esther? He must never divulge his doubts to anyone, not even to the child herself. Like the guards, he feared Lady Argyll's familiarity with the black arts. The sooner he could take his wife and child away to Amsterdam, the better.

Twenty-Six

Pouting and spoiled, Henry Darnley hung around the court, but few people spoke to him, and when they did it was only in a perfunctory way. They made it obvious he was a spent power, a man of no influence.

The rebel lords with whom he had conspired against Rizzio disdained him because he'd betrayed them by babbling to the Queen, naming everyone involved. When he met them, they stared him down and one day, in a shadowy corridor, a dark figure hissed in his ear, 'Watch your back. Your end is coming.'

The lavish gifts that Mary had once poured out on him ceased. She still adopted a falsely sweet tone when she addressed him, but he found it difficult to have any conversation with her, and when he tried, she cut it short, pleading pressure of business in which he was not invited to share.

His only confidant was his father Lord Lennox, who followed him around like a dog. He also poured out his anger and frustration in letters to his mother, who was still Elizabeth's prisoner in the Tower.

'I am disdained by all. My wife is consorting with yet another man, the villain Bothwell this time. They're lovers, I'm sure, and he has first place in her council. The child she says is mine looks like that low-born Rizzio. It has a peasant face. When I went to see it, I walked away in disgust, but she ran after me and said that it is truly my son, and that is its bad fortune.'

Mary Beaton advised the Queen not to show so much open affection for Lord Bothwell.

Mary bristled and asked, 'Why should I not show my regard for him? He's the only man in Scotland I trust.'

'People are talking. They say you're lovers and your husband is going up and down the taverns of the High Street talking about being cuckolded.'

'I can't put a curb on Darnley's tongue.'

'But he gathers sympathy.'

'He needs all the sympathy he can get,' said Mary.

It pleased her to know that she and Bothwell were linked by gossip because she was infatuated with the man. It was if she were engulfed by an emotion against which she was powerless to struggle. Whenever he came into her presence, she felt her heartbeat quicken. Over and over again she relived the night they had spent together, though it had not been repeated.

She did not see much of him because he spent more time out of Edinburgh than in it. Constant fighting in the Borders kept him occupied – or so he said, though she jealously supposed he preferred to be with his young wife rather than her.

She must have him. Nothing and no one else would do. Common sense was cast aside till Beaton's warning cautioned her, and she decided to try to put a better face on her relations with Darnley, though her hatred of him deepened with every week that passed.

She sent a messenger to summon him out of whatever alehouse he was in and when he appeared, poured the full force of her charm onto him.

'Dear husband, we've been drifting apart. Now I'm recovered from the birth of our son, let's go on a hunting trip together. We both enjoy those,' she said.

He looked suspicious. 'Where will we go?' he asked.

'Tweedale. The deer are plentiful there this

year, I'm told. We both need exercise, we need to gallop with the wind in our faces.'

'When?' It was obvious that he would not put it past her to lure him into the forest and have him killed.

'Before our son's christening. Sit down with me now and let's talk as friends, the way we used to do.'

She even overcame her distaste for him sufficiently to sleep with him that night and partially allay the suspicions he had of her.

They rode south for a few days of unsatisfactory hunting, before ending up at Traquair House outside Peebles. The serene 400-year-old house looked kind and hospitable as they rode up to it and Lord John Stewart, the laird of Traquair, came out of the front door to greet them, with the excited women of his family flocking behind him.

He was a staunch supporter of the Queen and had been instrumental in helping her to escape from Holyrood after Rizzio was killed, so she was delighted to see him again.

Their first day's sport was good but Mary felt tired afterwards and at dinner that night, she told Darnley he should hunt without her the next day.

He had drunk a lot of wine and was truculent and suspicious. 'I want you to come with me,' he said. In truth he hated not having her beside him, because he was never sure what she was doing behind his back, or what she had arranged for him.

She whispered in his ear that she thought she might be pregnant again and was worried about becoming overtired in case she lost the child.

He leaned back in his seat and roared out, 'Carrying another child? Is it mine this time? Are you sure it's not Bothwell's? And if you are carrying, isn't it better to work a mare when it's in foal than letting it stand idle?'

Everyone at the table stared at him in horror, shocked by this discourtesy. Angry Lord John, who disdained the callow youth, asked him to apologize, but he was unrepentant.

'Why should I apologize? She's my wife and I can say what I like to her,' was his rude response. The Queen was furious and announced there and then that they would leave Traquair the next morning and return to Edinburgh.

They went in such a hurry that she left behind a bundle of half-finished embroideries which stayed in the old house for another 400 years.

As far as Mary was concerned, the hunting trip and the effort to heal the breach with Darnley was a disaster. She never went hunting with him again.

Twenty-Seven

After Rizzio's murder, Mary made his younger brother Joseph her secretary, but Joseph was a cautious fellow who had no intention of risking his life as David had done by being too close to the Queen.

He also believed in speaking his mind. 'Your Majesty,' he said one day, 'you are too trusting. Why have you taken the men who killed my brother back into your confidence? Not one of them has paid any penalty for what they did and they're all as powerful as ever, especially Moray, who never ceases undermining you. Yet you listen to him, and include him in your council.'

She stared into his earnest face. 'I've no alternative, Joseph. They're too powerful to overturn.'

'But you're the Queen! You have the ultimate power. Have you ever heard of the works of Machiavelli?'

She nodded, 'Your brother talked about him. He wrote *The Prince*, didn't he?'

'Have you read it?'

'I'm afraid not ... There are so many calls on my time.'

He sighed. 'Your cousin Elizabeth has read it, I'm sure.'

'How would his book help me?'

'He says princes should combine power with prudence, but act with audacity and ferocity when necessary.'

Mary sighed. 'Power with prudence. Audacity and ferocity. I like that. But my situation is difficult.'

'If you rooted out your enemies, the mass of the people would support you because you're much loved by your subjects.'

'But I'm only a woman.'

'So is your cousin and she doesn't listen to

traitors.'

'She has Cecil at her elbow.'

Joseph sighed, for he saw that the Queen had no idea what he was telling her and no notion of how to establish her own power apart from parading before the masses dressed like a Scottish goddess of war in armour and tartan. When it came to making decisions or doing something forceful, she took the easy way out.

At the beginning of October, Mary did take one bold decision, however. Urged on by Bothwell, she announced her intention of venturing into the Borderland, the resort of every sort of thief and villain, to preside over a court of justice at Jedburgh and try to bring some of her most unruly subjects into order.

She made Bothwell Lord Lieutenant of the Borderland, and he set out to round up as many lawbreakers as possible, especially his long-time enemies the Elliots and the Armstrongs. He intended to take them to Jedburgh jail to await the Queen's sentencing.

'I've never ventured into the lawless lands before. Will I be safe there?' Mary asked anxiously.

'I'll make sure you're as safe as you would be in your own chamber in Edinburgh Castle,' he boasted.

She looked at him with admiration. 'You're the only man in Scotland who can do that for me,' she told him.

The year was dying in style with purple heather

on the hillsides and trees glowing in brilliant shades of red, orange and gold as James Hepburn, Earl of Bothwell, galloped proudly along on his great war horse with his head held high. Wild country was where he felt most at home. The falsities of court life bored him.

Unlike the Queen, he had no taste for hunting for killing's sake. When he chased across country, there had to be a serious reason, either hunting for food or pursuing an enemy. His preferred quarry was human.

With 400 armed men riding behind him, he was fulfilling his destiny, and following the way of life of his ancestors from the beginning of time. His heart soared as his horse leapt walls and ditches and he knew that if he were to be locked up for long he would lose his reason. He had a recurring nightmare of being shut up in an oubliette, like a captured animal, with only a shaft of light shining down on him from above.

'God grant that never happens. Let me be killed outright rather than taken captive,' he prayed when he woke.

The Jedburgh expedition went well. Without warning, he and his men attacked isolated peel towers where malefactors hid out, and gathered in dozens of Armstrongs as well as many of their allies, the Johnstones of Nithsdale. His men roped them together with nooses round their necks and drove them along like sheep till they reached Hermitage Castle, that rose like a rock face from the emerald green sward along its river bank.

His personal standard flew from the roof, and,

as always, it gave him more satisfaction than the possession of any woman.

His shouting, swearing prisoners, who did not take kindly to capture, were driven through the castle's narrow doorway into the central courtyard and left to mill around with ropes still holding them together.

'Hey Bothwell, you bastard, what are you going to do with us?' yelled one of the Johnstones.

'What do you think? I could starve you to death, I might string you from the battlements, or take you down to Jedburgh to face the Queen's justice,' was his reply, and his captives set up a series of cat-calling, cursing a queen who had so little sense that she'd climb into bed with a man like him.

Bothwell only laughed. He had not finished his round-up yet. When the Queen and her lords arrived in Jedburgh he intended to have every serious evil-doer in the Borders lined up for her to fine, imprison or execute according to her fancy.

Chief among them were the Elliots, especially their leader Jock o' the Park, whose reputation was fearsome, because he terrorized the peaceable people of the district. Without warning, he was liable to fall on their towers and farms, clearing out everything of value, from hens and ducks to babies' cradles. There was nothing chivalrous or gentlemanly about Jock.

The next day, Bothwell and his men set off in search of him. His chief hideout was a peel tower at Witterhope Burn, a few miles to the north of Hermitage, and they fell upon him when he was rounding up a herd of stolen cattle belonging to a family at Larriston Castle on the far side of the Liddle Water.

As soon as Jock saw the proud figure on the huge charger, he knew who had come for him and why, so he turned and belted for home.

Bothwell took up the chase but Jock knew his way through the bogs and burns and had a good lead. His pursuer gained ground on him all the time, however, till there were only the two of them streaking along.

When Bothwell drew alongside his enemy, Jock yelled, 'If I surrender, will you spare my life?'

Bothwell hesitated. Jock had been a thorn in his flesh for years and it would be easy to kill him now, but if he got the villain to Jedburgh that would be an even bigger feather in his cap. In Jedburgh, Jock would be hung for his crimes anyway.

'All right, I'll take you to answer to the Queen's law,' he shouted back.

Jock knew that meant the gallows, so he jumped from his saddle and took off on foot, jumping from tussock to tussock over a treacherous bog. No horse could negotiate the terrain, so Bothwell jumped down too and pursued him. They were within a sword's length of each other when Bothwell slipped over a hidden tree stump and fell face down.

Instantly, Jock, who was more lightly dressed in a leather jerkin and steel bonnet than the heavily armoured earl, turned and struck the fallen man three times with his two handed sword, inflicting deep wounds in the shoulder, hand and forehead.

Before he fainted, Bothwell had time to strike back, hitting Elliot in the chest. It was a deep hit but not enough to prevent the other man taking to his heels and making his escape.

When Bothwell's men arrived they thought he was dead because he was lying crumpled, with his blood seeping into the boggy ground around him. Realizing he was still breathing, they made a makeshift stretcher from hazel tree branches and dragged him over the ground, all the way back to Hermitage.

When they reached its narrow entrance, however, they found it barred and a rain of missiles was chucked over the battlements onto their heads. The prisoners had overpowered the garrison and were holding the castle against its lord.

'It's a good thing the Lord Jamie doesnae ken he canna get intae his ain castle. The shame'd kill him,' said the sergeant of arms, a man who had fought alongside Bothwell for twenty years.

'If we don't get him inside soon he'll be dead anyway, and if the Elliots come back to attack us again, we'll be dead too,' said a spearman, looking down into the ghostly white face of their unconscious leader. If he lay much longer without treatment he would surely die.

The sergeant cupped a hand round his mouth to yell, 'What do you want? We're not going to let you out and you're not letting us in. Let's do a deal.'

The prisoners yelled back that they wanted

their freedom plus as much plunder as they could carry. There was no alternative but to accept.

Jeering, making obscene gestures and laughing raucously, Johnstones, Armstrongs and Douglases emerged from the castle carrying shields, spears and swords and hefting bundles over their shoulders. Bothwell's men watched stony-faced, knowing that the shaming story would have spread across the entire district by nightfall.

For several days, Bothwell hovered between life and death. The wound to his shoulder was serious, because Jock's sword had pierced his lung, and the slash across his face was horribly disfiguring. That scar would never disappear.

Without a woman to nurse him or medical men to treat him, he was cared for by rough soldiery, but they were devoted to him and spared no effort in their fight to keep him alive, though they almost lost the battle. In fact, on the third day, word went out that Jamie Hepburn was dead and when the news reached London and France, wise men shook their heads and said that the Queen of Scotland had lost the only trustworthy man in her kingdom.

One person who did not hear the rumours was Mary herself, for she was in transit between Edinburgh and Jedburgh, travelling slowly and stopping off along the way. When she reached Melrose, a local dignitary offered her condolences about the loss of a valuable supporter, but was cut off in mid-sentence by Mary Beaton, who did not want Mary to be devastated by rumours until Bothwell's death was confirmed.

They reached Jedburgh at last and a solidly built little tower house was rented for the Queen by the side of the main street leading up to the impressive abbey that stood on a hill staring south over the entrance to the town.

Jedburgh was the first sizeable town north of the border, and suffered a great deal from English incursions. Its history was full of stories about battles won and lost and as a result, it was a very patriotic place. Mary was cheered to the skies whenever she showed herself to the townspeople.

In the cramped rented house she had a small room on the first floor, while her ladies slept in the attic over her head.

'It's like a child's house,' she exulted, running up and down the twisting narrow stairs, making the Marys pleased to see her in such good health and spirits.

She enjoyed sitting in judgement in the courthouse beside the abbey's main gate and blithely made rulings fixing the prices of staple goods and prosecuting minor offenders, but the list of wrong doers was not long and she protested to an official, 'Bothwell told me this court would be crowded with law breakers, robbers and sheep stealers and that I'd have to harden my heart to hang most of them. Where are they?'

He shuffled his papers and said, 'They haven't turned up.'

'But he was bringing them in.'

'Lord Bothwell is lying wounded at Hermitage. They say he's gravely ill.'

'Wounded? When?'

'I don't know Your Majesty. I don't even know if he's still alive...'

He had no time to say any more because the Queen, face white and hands shaking, flew out of the courtroom and accosted Moray, who was waiting with her entourage.

'Why has no one told me Lord Bothwell is injured?'

'We feared upsetting you...'

'He is my Lord Lieutenant in the Borders. I rely on him. I must go to him. Where is Hermitage?'

'A long way off. At least thirty miles.'

Thirty miles would take six hours to cover even on good tracks, but this country was hard going. Eight hours was more likely.

Abbey bells tolled above her head. One – two – three – four – five – six – seven – eight – nine – ten – eleven – twelve. Noon. Too late. They could not set out today.

'Have the horses saddled by seven o'clock tomorrow morning. I'm riding to Hermitage,' she ordered.

Mary Beaton was frowning with worry the next day as she dressed the Queen in riding clothes. 'Put breeches on me. I'll ride astride,' Mary ordered. She felt easier in men's clothing. It made her feel happier and she often thought she should have been born a man, which was why she got such pleasure from pretending to be a young gallant.

'You shouldn't be going on this journey. It's a long way, the country's very wild and boggy, and you're not fully recovered from the prince's birth,' Beaton protested.

The Queen ignored her. Face set, she pushed her feet into leather top boots and buckled a broad belt around her waist. 'Knot the scarf tightly round my neck and bring my gloves,' she snapped.

Seton put a silver flask of whisky into the deep pocket of her riding coat and said, 'That'll warm you and you'll need it. Oh Madame, must you go?'

Mary pulled a close-fitting bonnet onto her head and said firmly, 'I must. I must see him. If he dies before I get there, I'll kill myself.'

The women were used to her histrionics and threats of suicide, but this scared them because it was said with a strange coldness of tone.

Seton hugged the Queen. 'May God protect you,' she sobbed.

Moray with five other lords waited at the door of the house and a groom held the reins of a fine chestnut stallion that was rolling its eyes and snorting excitedly. Its nervousness did not intimidate the Queen, who disdained sluggish horses. She placed her foot in the cupped hands of the groom and was thrown on to the saddle.

'Let's go!' she called and slapped the stallion on the shoulder with her riding stick. It leaped forward as if fired from a cannon and charged up the street with the others cantering behind it. The noise brought townspeople out of their beds and they threw back their shutters to peer out in alarm.

Mary rode thirty miles as if the devil was on

her tail, plunging across moors and bogs while her face became more and more spattered with mud. Anyone who fell behind was abandoned and she did not draw rein till the party began to descend the hills that loomed above the Liddle water.

In drizzling rain, under a purplish grey sky that presaged worse weather to come, Mary stopped and gazed along the valley to where a distant castle rose beside a river bank.

'That's it, that's the Hermitage,' said her guide, one of the few men who had managed to keep pace with her.

It was brooding and apparently deserted without a sign of life, not even a flag was flying. It scared her.

'It looks evil,' she said.

'It is evil,' said the guide solemnly, 'Terrible things have been done there. They say the devil rules within its walls.'

'The devil?' She looked at him questioningly.

'One of the old lords worshipped him and once you make room for the devil, he never leaves.'

She shivered, but squared her shoulders and said briskly, 'Such nonsense. God will rout the devil.'

'He hasn't till now,' was the guide's reply, but the Queen was heading for the castle with her followers streaming behind her.

When the garrison heard the noise of her cavalcade outside the castle walls, a guard stepped out of the door with a raised sword and demanded, 'Who comes?'

250

'The Queen to see Lord Bothwell,' shouted Mary.

She was first in the narrow doorway and jumped from the saddle shouting, 'Take me to him.'

Bothwell, sour-smelling and feeble, lay on a cot in the middle of a long passage. The place stank and was without any comforts: no tapestries lined the walls, no curtains shielded his bed from piercing draughts. He lay on his side with his face to the wall like a wounded soldier in a barrack room. His head and eyes were covered by bloodstained bandages like a sultan's turban and his bare feet protruded from the end of a checked plaid like the ones hill shepherds wore.

Although his men said he was too ill to be disturbed, Mary ran to him and knelt by the cot. The straw covering the floor smelt of urine. She put her head level with his and whispered, 'Oh Jamie, don't die, please don't die. Don't leave me. I love you.'

His shoulders heaved and he tried to turn, but the wound in his shoulder was open and suppurating so he slumped back.

'Is it Janet?' he asked.

'No, it's your Queen. Marie. I've come to nurse you.'

There was nothing she liked more than looking after sick people. It had made her think she loved Darnley and also formed the bond with her sickly first husband who was ill more often than he was well. She loved sitting by bedsides, holding hands and mopping brows, but this was not the sort of sick room she'd been in before.

'Go away,' groaned Bothwell.

'I've ridden from Jedburgh. They told me you were wounded and I had to come to you.'

'This isn't the place for you, it's not the place for women.'

She sat back on her heels, disregarding the filthy state of the floor on to which he had been peeing like a dog. 'Where are your wounds?' she asked.

He held out one hand and pointed at his bandaged head. 'Jock o' the Park did this. I should have killed the bastard when he was down.'

'Why didn't you?'

'I wanted to take him to your court of justice.'

She looked over her shoulder at the men standing by the door. 'Is there a doctor here?' Bothwell managed a hoarse laugh.

She got up and walked back to the watchers. 'He needs a doctor. Is he well enough to be moved?'

'Not yet, but he's growing stronger. Two days ago we thought he'd die but he's rallied since,' said his sergeant.

'I hope he's getting enough good food and drink.'

The sergeant said, 'We have meat. Lady Janet of Buccleuch sends cattle and sheep and we kill them as we need them. There's plenty of porter to drink, too.'

Mary felt jealousy at the mention of Bothwell's mistress. *I want to be the one who provides for him*, she thought.

'Bring him to Jedburgh where he can get better food and good wine,' she said but the sergeant shook his head. 'He can't ride and if we try to carry him out, the Elliots will kill him on the way.'

'Then I'll stay here and have proper provisions brought in.'

At this a chorus of protest broke out, both from the garrison and Mary's companions. 'That's impossible. This is no place for women. There are no private chambers...'

'It's only a huge barracks,' Moray told her. 'If you stay here you'll have compromised yourself for ever.'

She looked around at the rough walls and bare floors. There wasn't even a decent chair to sit on. Men in breastplates and leather jerkins squatted on the ground with pikes and spears stuck between their knees.

Her half-brother saw her hesitate. 'If we are to reach Jedburgh again before darkness falls, we must start back within the hour,' he reminded her.

She knew this was true, but ran back to the recumbent man and knelt by him again, whispering urgently, 'You're getting better. I'm going back to Jedburgh now but as soon as you're able, join me there. I love you. I want to marry you.'

Through cracked lips he croaked, 'You're married already and so am I.'

'Marriages can be ended. I want you by my side forever.'

He sank back on the cot and said nothing, but his mind was racing. Marriage to the Queen! Utter power and dominance. Scotland needed a

253

strong ruler and he might be the man. As if refilled with vigour, he felt strength flowing back into him. He'd live now because he had something huge to live for.

The garrison managed to feed the Queen and her party but there was no room for her to wash or change clothes, so, still muddied, and smelling of the urine from the floor, she kissed Bothwell's uninjured hand and made him swear to join her soon.

Two hours after she arrived, she exchanged an exhausted stallion for a strong horse out of the garrison stables and set out for the long ride back.

By the time five miles were covered, she realized how exhausted and emotionally drained she was. Every bone in her body ached and she found it hard to sit upright in the saddle. The new horse had an uneven gait and a hard mouth that made it difficult to ride and she had to settle for letting it go its own way.

Halfway through the terrible journey they blundered into a peat bog and her horse flailed around in mud up to its belly. While the men were hauling it out, it fell sideways and she tumbled off the saddle into black mire that threatened to suffocate her. Sobbng and hysterical, she was pulled free and mounted on another horse.

The mud on her clothes dried into thick crusts. She'd lost one of her silver spurs, her watch and riding stick, and feared that she would never see the town of Jedburgh again, but after a stop at a lonely farmhouse where she was given dry clothes by an astonished farmer's wife, she finished the last leg of her journey.

At last she looked down into the Jed valley and saw the lights of the town twinkling along the river bank, but she was so exhausted that she had to be carried into the house, where her concerned women washed and fed her and put her to bed.

That night she began to vomit and complained of an agonizing pain in her side.

The worried women rushed about ministering to her and whispering, 'It's the same pain as she always gets when she's tired.'

It often laid Mary low and was nearly always associated with her periods of deep depression. This time it could not be soothed but grew worse, and a trio of local doctors and apothecaries were called in but, to a man, they were so intimidated by having a queen for a patient that they could not agree among themselves what her trouble was or how to treat it.

On the second night she was worse, vomiting at least sixty times. Towards morning, her attendants saw with horror that she was vomiting blood. Moray sent a fast rider to Edinburgh to fetch one of the Queen's French doctors, as she lapsed into unconsciousness and her vomiting continued with such violence that people began to whisper she had been poisoned. The finger of suspicion pointed at Moray. who had the most to gain from her death.

Mary knew that her life was at risk and summoned a lawyer to whom she haltingly dictated a will giving her infant son into her half-brother's care. This was preferable to letting Darnley get his hands on the child.

For five days she hovered between life and death and panic seized her household when she lost her sight and the power of speech. A French doctor called Arnault, who had treated her for pains in her side before, arrived from Edinburgh and announced that her illness was coming from an ulcerated stomach and not from poison.

'You know what's wrong but not how to cure it,' said Mary Seton sharply.

Arnault shrugged. 'It is up to her. If she wants to live, she'll fight. If not, she will die.'

For a while it looked as if death were to be the victor. Only the arrival of Bothwell, in a stretcher slung between two horses, with an escort of 500 spearmen, made her rally. She was able to greet him and made him her chief Privy Councillor.

Because she wanted him near, he was installed in a room immediately below hers and above his head he heard the coming and going of her doctors and attendants. In the middle of one night he was wakened by the sound of running feet and opened his chamber door to see the doctor sprinting up the spiral staircase.

'What's wrong?' he asked.

'Her women say the Queen is dead,' was the terse reply.

Bothwell leaned back against the wall and closed his eyes. To be so close to absolute power and have it snatched from under his nose by death! He grieved for that loss but also for Mary. She was only twenty-four and her life had been tragic. If she lived, would he have been able to make it better?

The sound of women weeping came from her room and he slowly climbed the stone stairs to look in through the open door. Mary, with her glorious red hair spread out, was lying like a waxen image in the middle of a huge bed. Mary Seton, eyes swollen with weeping, ran about opening windows to let the Queen's spirit go free.

The Earl of Moray was rifling through a jewellery chest, letting a cascade of black pearls fall from the fingers of one hand into the palm of the other. He could barely hide his greedy satisfaction.

Bothwell walked over to the bed and gently lifted Mary's limp hand. To his surprise it felt warm.

'How long has she been like this?' he asked.

'An hour. I tried to wake her but she didn't move. We sent for her brother and her doctor but it took time because they were lodging up at the abbey,' sobbed Seton.

Bothwell said to Arnault, 'Feel her arm.' He had seen enough dead men to know that a body did not stay warm an hour after death, especially in the middle of a cold October night.

Arnault lifted Mary's arm and exclaimed, '*Mon dieu*! She was cold but now she's warm again. Help me, we must try to bring life back to her.'

Without thinking of her modesty, he and Bothwell threw off the bedclothes and Arnault began frantically massaging the Queen's body, giving orders to her women as he worked. 'Bring wine, bring herbs, bring hot water, bring bandages.'

Bothwell helped turn Mary on her side and they wrapped bandages tightly round her body while the women poured wine into her mouth. When she began to revive, Arnault administered a herbal enema and after three hours, he was jubilant when sweat broke out on her body. 'She lives, she lives!' he exulted.

When the joyful verdict was announced, Moray put down the jewellery box and walked out of the room.

Three days later, Mary was taking tottering steps around her chamber on Bothwell's arm, but there was no sign of her husband Lord Darnley and she did not enquire when he was coming.

Only on the fourteenth day of her illness did he come clattering into Jedburgh, brilliant in his gilded armour at the head of a retinue of gorgeously dressed young men.

His wife greeted him coldly. 'Where have you been?' she asked.

'Hunting near Glasgow.'

'Didn't you know I was ill?'

'They told me it was your old trouble – the pain in the side.'

'I nearly died.'

He said nothing and she went on, 'I might have been poisoned. Moray doesn't put it past you to organize that.'

'Moray hates me.'

'He's not the only one,' she replied and turned away from him.

Furious at her coldness, he stayed only one night. When he suggested that he share his wife's bed, he was told to seek lodgings elsewhere – not just in another room, but in another house.

'Where does Bothwell lodge?' he asked pointedly.

'In my house,' she said.

The next morning he rode out of Jedburgh, heading for Stirling.

Twenty-Eight

As the year drew to a close, rumours began to circulate in France that the Queen of Scots was dead.

People in Paris who remembered her as Francois' ill-fated wife shook their heads in pity and recalled how Nostradamus predicted tragedy for her.

A man who changed coinage for travellers and often dealt with Nathan's father heard the story when he was on his way to Amsterdam and it was fresh in his memory when he got there.

'You lived in Leith, didn't you?' he said to Nathan, who was helping Ezra with his business.

'Yes, my wife's family is still there.'

'It's sad about that poor young Queen.'

Nathan stared at the traveller. 'What's happened to her?' he asked.

'They say she's dead. There are rumours she was poisoned.'

Nathan's heart sank. 'Who did it?' he asked. He had his own possible candidates and top of the list was her foppish, feckless husband.

The traveller didn't know. 'In Paris they're only saying she's dead. Her Guise family are angry but can do nothing. Scotland is a wild place and it's best to stay out of it, if you ask me. She should never have left France.'

When Nathan passed the sad news on to Esther, she sympathized with him. 'I always felt that she was doomed to tragedy. I wonder what happened to her? There's been no word from my father, but he only writes about business,' she said.

The baby girl they had called Sarah was lying in her wicker basket on the table between them and they both looked at her with concern. They shared the suspicion about her real parentage but kept it a close secret, not even discussing it with each other. As far as Nathan's family was concerned, Sarah was a low-born foundling.

'What if...?' Esther whispered.

He held up a warning finger. 'No, we don't know.'

'I realize that, but remember what you heard before we left Leith about the Queen's baby girl being exchanged for a boy.'

'Stories like that always get about. My father was told that the Queen's grandfather was not killed on Flodden Field, but became a monk and lived in a monastery for years. That was nonsense. We don't want to know where our Sarah came from. We have her now.'

'If she were the Queen's daughter, she'd be a princess. What if we are cheating her of her birthright? She'll want to know if she's descended from a line of kings.'

Nathan smiled. 'Instead of from a line of pedlars and money lenders?'

He put his finger gently on the sleeping child's head and said, 'I wouldn't wish that terrible fate on her. Mary was an innocent child when I first saw her. All the fine clothes and jewellery don't make up for living a life like hers.'

'But I wish we knew the truth. Why don't you cross to Leith before the winter gales start and hear the news about the Queen at first hand,' suggested Esther.

It was good to be travelling again with a full pack. Hefting it over his shoulder, Nathan stepped briskly off the boat at Leith's quay and hurried to Leverson's, where he found work going on as usual and was greeted with much enthusiasm, patted on the back and taken home to be plied with food and drink by his wife's mother.

'Esther and I were sorry to hear about the Queen dying,' he said and Mr Leverson looked blank.

'She was ill but she's better now and certainly not dead, unless it happened today. Her son is to be christened in Stirling next week and everyone is being taxed to pay for the ceremony. She raised twelve thousand pounds to cover the expense. It's a waste of money,' said Leverson disapprovingly, 'And there's a rumour that she's planning to divorce the coxcomb king and marry again. No doubt there'll be more taxes to pay for that wedding. She has grandiose tastes.'

Nathan was glad Mary was not dead, but his main purpose in coming back was to try to get more information about Sarah. 'If there's to be a royal christening, every nobleman and woman in the country will be gathering at Stirling,' he said.

'Indeed they are. Edinburgh is empty. You'll be well advised to take your pack to Stirling to make yourself some money, for there's nothing to be made here at the moment.'

The worst of the winter weather had not started and he walked with pleasure, stopping at familiar inns and greeting old friends on the way. He made a detour by Falkland and dropped in on his friend Libby Mudie, who was delighted to see him and complimented him on his prosperous look and fine suiting. 'I knew the first time I set eyes on you that you'd do well in the world,' she said.

When he told her he had a daughter, she clapped her hands in delight. 'You'll be a good father,' she told him.

The words ran through his head when he was walking to Stirling next morning. 'A good father.' Would a good father deny his girl her birthright? But perhaps his suspicions were unfounded. Perhaps Sarah *was* a servant's child and he was giving her a better life than the one she was born into, but he must do his best to find out the truth.

Stirling was packed with people. The steep road leading up to the castle was crowded and servants ran to and fro buying provisions and exchanging gossip about who was in town for the christening of the little prince, which was due to take place in two days' time.

Flagpoles were erected on every corner and bunting drooped from them. Musicians tuned up while hopeful street performers and travelling players occupied any space where a stage could be cleared.

Gazing around in pleasure, Nathan walked along, noting the liveries of servants going to and fro. The Argylls would have a grand house, he knew, and it did not take long to find their flat-fronted three-storey building next door to a smaller one with a semicircular wing jutting out into the street that belonged to the Earl of Bothwell.

He asked a watchman if the Countess was in residence and the answer was 'yes'.

'Tell her that Nathan the smous has some fine goods to show her,' he said, knowing that his name would spark her attention. Soon he was invited in.

Lady Argyll was a hard-faced woman whose composure rarely cracked and she stared coldly at Nathan, obviously suspicious and expecting him to ask some favour of her.

He bent down and opened his pack to display his wares, but she was not interested. 'I have little time for stitching these days,' she said. Other women with her were interested, however, and they pored over his goods, passing things from hand to hand. When they had made their purchases, he started to lace up the pack again, aware that the lady of the house was still watching him intently.

'I've changed my mind. I want some small things,' she said as he was preparing to leave. Gesturing to her women to go away, she said, 'Just bring out your finest needles. That's all I need.'

When they were alone, she asked, 'Have you come about the child? If you pester me, I'll have you thrown in prison and you'll never be seen again.'

He straightened up and fearlessly stared into her eyes. 'I have no intention of pestering you about anything, Your Grace. I only came to tell you that the child you gave to my wife is healthy and well-loved.'

'You do not intend to bring her back?'

'Never.'

He saw her attitude soften and went on, 'We call her Sarah and she is a beautiful child with a highly bred look, but we are not high-born people and my wife is worried in case we are depriving our baby of her rightful place in life.'

'In my opinion the child will have a better life with you than she ever would have with her true parents,' said Lady Argyll carefully.

'You mean she will never have to be a scullery maid.'

'If that is what you think.'

'Please, my lady, I would like to know something about her origins to tell her when she is a grown woman.'

'She's not a kitchen maid's child. Try to make her a good marriage, for you're right, she is high-born,' said Lady Argyll.

Nathan bowed. He knew that was as much as he would ever be told.

'Thank you. Rest assured we'll take good care of her,' he said as he picked up his pack and made for the door.

As he walked down the steep hill again, he remembered the first time he saw the Queen as a terrified little child decked out in gold and gauze having a sceptre forced into her hand. What a destiny was given to her that day. He turned on his heel and stared back at the brooding citadel above him. The next King would be christened there tomorrow. How would fate treat him?

Though he was anxious to go home, he decided to stay another day and watch the ceremony, for it was as if his life and the life of the Queen were in some way interlinked.

On the morning of December seventeenth, he sat on his pack by the castle gateway watching a parade of horses draped in cloth of gold, marching bands in glorious liveries and richly dressed men and women trooping to the chapel.

He recognized the earls of Moray, Morton, Argyll and Rothesay. There were also Ruthvens, Arrans, Gordons, Huntlys and Douglases by the dozen.

Bothwell, glorious in purple and gold, was in charge of the parade, but the livid wound across his face and forehead made him look more dangerous than ever. Because he was a Protestant, he would not enter the chapel to hear Mass but stood among a group of other non-Catholics at the open door to watch the ceremony going on inside.

After the guests filed into the Chapel Royal, Nathan followed other bystanders into the courtyard and heard the gossip as they waited.

'The Queen of England has sent a golden font for the baby to be christened in. It's as big as a horse trough and there are jewels all around its rim.'

'Look, the Queen's coming now with her brother Moray and the baby. She looks ill, doesn't she, so white and thin.'

'That's Lady Mar carrying the child. She and her husband care for him here in Stirling Castle, because it's safer and easier to defend than Edinburgh and people say the Queen is not very motherly.' The crowd sent up a ragged cheer when Mary passed by, as gloriously dressed and jewelled as ever but pale and drawn, thinner and older looking than the last time Nathan saw her in Edinburgh.

'But where's the father? Where's Lord Darnley?' That question was asked over and over again by people in the crowd and a guard said loudly, 'He's sulking in his chamber. He won't come out because he says the child isn't his.'

Suggestions were put forward from the crowd about the baby prince's disputed parentage and most people favoured Rizzio, though one or two disagreed.

'It's that man Bothwell,' they said, pointing at the sturdy figure standing in the chapel doorway.

Nathan studied Bothwell. He'd seen him

before but never so close and now he was struck by the confident power of the man, by the hard set of his scarred face, by the way he stood four square on the earth, feet slightly apart in a characteristic fighting stance. Not a man to be gainsaid. If he was the Queen's lover, it was to be hoped he would take care of her, because she of all women was badly in need of protection, thought Nathan sadly.

And if, as he half suspected, his Sarah was the Queen's child, he was glad that she was not the one being carried up to the massive gold and jewelled christening font.

Twenty-Nine

'I hate him, I hate him! I wish he were dead,' Mary exclaimed to Bothwell as they sat together at the christening feast.

'Where is he?' he asked.

'He left after we came out of the chapel. He's been making threats that he'll run away to England. He rode off with a lot of noise and saying that the child isn't his, so why should he go to see it being baptized?'

Bothwell only shrugged and cut deeply into his slice of swan as if it were Darnley's neck.

The absentee father did not get far from Stirling before he leaned over in his saddle and vomited on to the ground.

267

'Too much Malmsey,' said one of his attendants unsympathetically, but half a mile farther on, Darnley vomited again.

'Do you want to stop?' the attendant asked but he shook his head. 'Let's go on to Glasgow. My father's waiting there.'

He vomited almost continuously after that and eventually had to be held propped in the saddle between the legs of a groom before he finally reached Lennox Castle.

As soon as Lord Lennox saw his son, he asked, 'Have you been poisoned?'

'If I have, my wife did it,' Darnley groaned as he was carried to bed. His father called in a local physician called James Abernethy who leaned over the patient and immediately recoiled, saying, 'He stinks!'

'What does that signify?' asked the anxious father.

'It could be poison – or...' said Abernethy doubtfully.

'Or what? I think it's poison and that woman the Queen has done it. She's evil incarnate!' exclaimed Lennox.

The news that her father-in-law had accused her of trying to murder her husband reached Mary as she was preparing to leave Stirling.

'That's nonsense. I haven't been close to him for weeks,' she exclaimed. Then she looked at Bothwell and added, 'You know how much I want rid of him. Did you do it?'

He raised his eyebrows. 'Not me! If I killed him it would be with cold steel.'

Mary wondered hopefully, 'Is he really near

death?'

'If he is, that'll solve your problem,' was Both-well's laconic reply.

It took an effort for her to pretend concern in front of Lennox's messengers who brought news of the patient in Glasgow, but she was a good actress and managed to persuade them that she was genuinely concerned for her husband.

'I must go to him!' she exclaimed when she heard his condition was grave.

Moray earnestly advised her against that. 'Wait and see if he does die, and anyway his illness might be caused by something other than poison. It could be catching,' he told her.

That proved to be good advice because more news came that Abernethy had revised his diagnosis. Darnley had not been poisoned. The stinking pustules breaking out on his body made the doctor suspect smallpox.

When Mary's doctors heard this diagnosis they looked at each other in speculation. 'Pustules?' queried Bourgoing.

'Stinking apparently,' agreed Arnault.

'If it isn't smallpox, it's the pox,' said Bourgoing.

'And he had that attack of what looked like measles before he married. Perhaps that was the first sign of syphilis. He told me about catching a dose of pox when he was young, and he ran wild here among some doubtful people...'

They advised the Queen that under no circumstances was she to go to Glasgow to see Darnley until the disease manifested itself properly.

'What do you think it is?' she asked.

'If it isn't smallpox, he might have syphilis,' Bourgoing told her.

She reeled. 'The dog! I pray he hasn't infected me or our child. This is all the more reason to be rid of him. I'll never get into a bed with him again.'

She was fuming when she rode with her retinue back to Edinburgh, and instead of going to Holyrood, which still brought back terrifying memories of Rizzio's killing, she took up residence in Craigmillar Castle, two miles south of the city. It was a pleasant place, set on a south-facing hillside, surrounded by woods, and most of the people she'd brought with her from France were housed there. It brought back memories of Fontainebleu.

While she waited for news from Glasgow, she spent time with Bothwell and summoned six other great Scots lords, including Moray, Mar and Morton, to Craigmillar to discuss her desire to be permanently rid of her husband.

'Why don't you ask your friend the Pope to grant you a divorce on the grounds of consanguity?' asked crafty Morton.

'That would take too long. I want the matter to be over with as soon as possible,' she told them. They finally agreed to drawing up a bond that committed them to helping the Queen rid herself of Darnley – exactly how was not specified.

'It must not arouse suspicion,' said Moray, who always watched his own back.

'Does that mean you think he should be mysteriously killed?' asked Bothwell, who called a spade a spade.

'If we sink our differences, we should be able to remove this problem from the Queen,' was Moray's cautious reply.

Darnley had no friends left among the great men of Scotland and one by one they signed the bond. He was to be eliminated, but by whom or by what method was not made clear. Morton became chief mover behind an assassination plot.

'If he survives this illness, the Queen must go to Glasgow and bring him back to Craigmillar, well away from his father and their friends in the west. It's quiet and secluded here and he could suffer an accident or become ill again without witnesses being involved,' he said.

To all their disappointments, Darnley survived and his fever subsided, leaving him with terrible scars, which could confirm both the smallpox or the syphilis fears.

'The infectious phase is over after three or four weeks and then you can go to see your husband,' Moray told the Queen, who was kept in apparent ignorance of the assassination plans, though she was well aware something was afoot, but adopted the attitude of looking the other way so that she could not be accused of complicity. The less she knew, the better the conspirators were pleased.

'Must I go to him?' she asked.

'Yes. It's necessary to get him away from the west. His father has too many supporters there. Bring him to Craigmillar,' she was told.

She set out for Glasgow with a large retinue

and even her ladies, who knew how much she loathed Darnley, were astonished by the skill with which she played her part as the concerned wife.

French endearments flew out of her mouth like little birds when she swept into his sickroom in Lennox Castle, where he lay in bed with a white cloth draped over his face. She bent over him, taking care, bystanders noted, not to touch him, and asked sweetly, 'Why are you veiled, my dearest?'

'Because I don't want you to see my face.'

'I'm sure you're as handsome as ever.'

'I'm not. I'm scarred.'

She looked down at the cloth over his face. It rose up and down with every breath he took and she found it hard not to laugh.

'Don't be vain. I'll still love you even if you have a few spots.'

'Of course you like scarred men, don't you? Why else could you sleep with Bothwell?'

She ignored this jibe and went on coaxing him till he consented to let her lift the cloth. What she saw chilled her. His face was covered with big, oozing scarlet pustules and when he turned to look in her direction, his breath smelt rank. Bourgoing had forewarned her that this was a sign of syphilis.

When Darnley said, 'Come into bed with me now and show you really love me,' an almost uncontrollable rage rose in her, but she fought it back and continued to smile.

'Not yet, dear one, you might still be infectious and I have our baby to think about. Until you're fully cured, I'll not sleep here but in Provand's Lordship, an old house in the middle of the town. It's nearby and I can nurse you every day. In fact, I'll start now.'

Coquettishly, she bent down, lifted her skirt and tore a wide strip off the hem of her white underskirt, then used it to wipe pus off his largest facial sore.

For three days she spent every waking hour with him, holding his hand, playing music to him on her lute, reading poetry and listening to his continual complaints. It was not too much of a chore for her, because in fact she loved nursing. If he hadn't fallen ill with measles and won her heart when he was sick and defenceless, she might never have married him.

On the fourth day of her visit, he was feeling better and she prevailed on him to agree to returning to the east. 'I'll take you to Craigmillar. It's so peaceful and beautiful there, you'll recover your health more quickly than you would in this crowded city,' she said.

'But how can I travel?'

'I've arranged for a stretcher to be slung between horses. You'll be very comfortable.'

'As long as I can lie in a covered litter and no one can see my face.'

'Cover it up with a piece of my underskirt,' she suggested.

Before he left Lennox Castle, he told his father, 'She's taking me to Craigmillar. The castle there is very large and comfortable. The baby is in Holyrood so I can't go there but she says she'll come to Craigmillar to visit me every day.'

Lennox frowned. 'But will she really? It's two miles from Holyrood. You'll be isolated among all the French people who live in that castle. People call it Little France because she houses her French court there and they have no love for you, do they?'

'I'll be perfectly safe. She loves me,' said his stupid son.

The tedious journey from Glasgow to Edinburgh had to be broken at Linlithgow and almost five days passed before they reached the outskirts. Far away on the horizon, the jagged silhouette of the dominating castle could be seen.

Darnley complained unendingly all the way and the Queen's patience was sorely tried, so it was with relief that she looked towards Edinburgh.

'I can see the castle! We're almost there. You'll be safe and comfortable at Craigmillar tomorrow,' she said.

He raised himself on one elbow and said sulkily, 'I've changed my mind, I don't want to go to Craigmillar.'

During his journey he'd had time to reflect on what his father said and had decided he would be safer in Holyrood or the castle. He'd also begun formulating plans to kill Mary, which would be easier to arrange if he were living beside her.

'But everything's been made ready for you at Craigmillar,' she protested. Her instructions from the lords had been definite. Craigmillar it was.

'I want to be with you,' he said petulantly.

'But you can't. The baby is in Holyrood.'

'Send it to the castle.'

'But then I'd go with him. He mustn't be exposed to infection of any kind.'

'You've become very maternal all of a sudden,' said Darnley sarcastically. She flushed, because for most of her son's life he had been in the charge of Lady Mar at Stirling, and she'd spent little time with him, making up for this by lavishing money on his christening.

With an effort, she assumed a sweetness she did not feel. 'Craigmillar is the best place for someone who has been ill and needs to recuperate.'

'It's full of French people and my father advises me against it,' he snapped back.

She turned her horse around, saying over her shoulder, 'In that case I must send a message to Edinburgh and another place will be found, because you can't be lodged in Holyrood or the castle.'

A fast rider was dispatched to tell Bothwell about this new development, and a few hours later, as the cavalcade was making its slow, swaying way along, another messenger arrived on a sweating horse to say that Earl Bothwell was on his way and would accompany them to a suitable lodging within the old town.

'Thank God,' Mary whispered fervently when Bothwell arrived with a group of pikemen.

'Where are you taking him?' she asked.

'Morton's found a house at Kirk o' Field. It's within walking distance of Holyrood. That should satisfy him.'

It didn't.

When his stretcher was lowered to the ground two hours later, Darnley sat up and looked around in disgust before he said, 'What's this? Am I expected to live in a hovel. I'm the King!'

Mary, sorely tried, snapped, 'This house belongs to the brother of Sir James Balfour. It's a nobleman's residence.'

He looked around. 'It was at one time perhaps, but now it's a hovel. The houses round about are much more suitable. The Hamiltons have a fine house here and I'd rather live there.'

'But their house isn't empty and this one is! Furniture has been sent up from Holyrood so you'll be living in great style,' Mary told him.

In fact, Balfour's house was very modest and dilapidated. Known as the Provost's House, it was stone-built and small, leaning up against the Flodden Wall, which the citizens of Edinburgh had hurriedly put up in 1513 when they feared the English would attack their town after the Battle of Flodden.

It had deep, capacious cellars and a kitchen on the bottom floor, a small bedroom and a few tiny rooms over the kitchen. Above that was a sixteen-foot long bed chamber for Darnley, with a wooden balcony between it and the top of the wall.

Surrounding the house was a paved courtyard and a sizeable, overgrown garden with an orchard of apple and pear trees.

'Look,' said Mary pointing at the Flodden Wall, 'A door opens off the garden and leads into

276

Blackfriars garden. I can use that as a secret way when I come to visit you from Holyrood, because it's very close.'

This suggestion mollified Darnley, who at last consented to being carried inside and installed in a great bed that had been rushed up from Holyrood for him. The bed, originally a present to him from the Queen, had previously belonged to her mother and was immense, hung with violet velvet curtains embroidered with golden flowers, and made comfortable with a purple damask coverlet and blue velvet pillows. Mary plumped her hand into the soft coverings and assured him, 'You'll be very comfortable here!'

'And where will you sleep?'

'Not with you yet, because there's still a risk of infection. Until it's safe I'll sleep in the room below. My bed is there already.'

When she left him, his manservant Taylor put him to bed, where he lay pondering his situation.

There was something about his wife's equanimity that disturbed him. No matter how awkward he made himself, she did not protest, but was still shutting him out of the business of government. He was King in name only. Mindful of his father's distrust of Mary, he knew what to do.

What if she died?

As her husband, he would be in a strong position to take over the throne. Their son was only an infant so he could rule as Regent – and infants were lucky if they lived to see adulthood.

If Mary dies? Then he'd be in a strong position to bend events to his will and a death would be

277

fairly easy to arrange, because she was agreeing to everything he wanted. If he set a good trap, she could well walk into it.

'Bring me a map of the layout of this house,' he ordered Taylor and as soon as he was able to walk, he explored the premises himself and stood in the bedroom that was to be his wife's, realizing that beneath his feet was the vast cavern of a kitchen.

If there were a fire or an explosion down there, Mary's little bed would be blown sky high or burned to a cinder. It was up to him to make sure she was in it at the time.

The trouble with Darnley was that he was massively indiscreet, talking to his servants about everything that came into his head. He was incapable of keeping a secret.

'I want you to send men out to buy gunpowder,' he told Taylor.

The valet looked confused. 'Gunpowder? What for?'

'I'm going to put it in the kitchen, set it alight and blow up my wife.' He laughed as he said it, but Taylor knew he was not joking. Because he liked Mary more than Darnley, he made sure that the news of this treasonable plan got out and inevitably it reached the ears of Moray, Morton and Bothwell, who seized on it. Darnley had provided them with the means of getting rid of him. They sent out to buy gunpowder too and also had it delivered to the Provost's House.

'There's no sense in not making the explosion as big as possible. We'll leave nothing to

278

chance,' said Morton.

Sacks were carried into the kitchens by men who were so careless that they wandered around the garden with sooty hands and faces, not even trying to hide what they were doing. Darnley watched their operations with satisfaction and suppliers of gunpowder in Edinburgh had not known such a good trade for years.

It was said later that the only person in the city who did not realize he was going to be a murder victim was Darnley himself.

Health began returning to the invalid, and he pestered his wife to prove her devotion to him by sharing his bed.

'I'll sleep with you,' she promised. 'But only after you've had a cleansing bath, and I'll soap you myself to make sure you're thoroughly clean. The infection must have disappeared.'

She was as good as her word, carefully lathering his back as he sat in a makeshift bath put up by the side of his bed. It was hard to hide her distaste for the job but she carried it off well.

'You'll come tomorrow?' he said as he was resettled in bed.

'Tonight I'll sleep in my little bed in the room below, and the night after that, when your scars are quite dry, I'll sleep with you,' she agreed, with a meaningful smile.

After she had returned to Holyrood, Darnley was busy in the kitchen organizing the laying of a long fuse to a sizeable pile of gunpowder sacks.

'We have plenty of fuel anyway. After my wife

279

goes to bed tonight in the room above, set the fuse alight,' he instructed his servants, adding anxiously, 'You understand what you have to do? Only set fire to the fuse when I send the order and when the Queen is in bed.'

They nodded, barely able to withhold their eagerness to get out of the house and carry the information to the Earl of Moray, who paid them well for it.

Mary arrived in the late afternoon to dine with her husband and went out of her way to be even more charming than usual. Deceived by her and sexually frustrated by weeks of abstinence, he tried again to persuade her to join him in bed but she shook her head, 'No, I promised it would be tomorrow! I can't sleep with you now because I promised to attend the wedding of one of my maids tonight.'

He was obviously disconcerted. 'So you're going to a wedding and leaving me here alone? But you said you'd sleep downstairs tonight.'

She soothed him. 'I will. I'll only stay at the wedding for a short while, but I must go because I promised the girl and she'll be disappointed if I'm not there. I'll be back in two hours and come in to say goodnight to you before I go to bed.'

Satisfied with that he sank back against the purple pillows. As he laid down his head, he noticed that his bed curtains had been changed. The beautiful gold embroidered ones had vanished and the bed was now hung with frayed and dusty brown velvet.

'Why have my bed curtains been changed?' he asked angrily.

'I ordered that. They're dirty and have gone to be cleaned. I don't want to sleep in a bed with dirty curtains tomorrow,' she told him.

When Bothwell heard about the curtain substitution, he laughed and said, 'That's typical of her. She values possessions more than people. Those curtains were too good to blow up.'

Before she left Darnley, Mary said sweetly, 'I want to give you something as a pledge of our love,' and she took off one of her rings, holding it out and slipping it on to his finger.

He turned his hand to and fro with obvious satisfaction. The ring was very distinctive because it was made of gold and enamel with a huge diamond set in it. The diamond was obviously valuable because it glittered beautifully in the candlelight. To him this was positive proof that the Queen, who was so fond of jewels, was completely won over to him again.

When she was halfway out of the door, she suddenly turned and looked back at him.

'My dear, have you remembered that this is the first anniversary of poor Davie's death?' she asked.

It was February ninth.

By midnight she had not returned and Darnley was furious.

'She's not coming. We'll have to put off our plan,' he stormed to Taylor. 'Go down and tell the servants to go to bed.'

At two o'clock in the morning, he suddenly sat up in bed and sniffed the air. 'I smell burning, Taylor! Get up. Those idiots have set off the fuse after all. We must get out of here,' he shouted, throwing his legs out of the bed and running for the door that led to the balcony. From there it was a short drop down into the garden.

Taylor, who had been sleeping on a mattress by his master's bed, sat up, blearily rubbing his eyes. 'It's all right, sire. The fuse is very long. It'll take at least ten minutes to burn through and we'll have plenty of time to get clear of the house.'

But Darnley, in his nightshirt, was panicking, running away and not listening. Grabbing a fur-lined mantle to keep his master warm and a pair of slippers for his bare feet, Taylor followed and found Darnley at the far end of the garden, staring back at the house, where nothing stirred.

'I'm not going back in there,' he said.

'I'll get you a chair to sit on then,' said his valet and ran back into the house. As he disappeared, Darnley was bending down to lift up the mantle and put it on when a dark figure stepped out from behind a crooked old pear tree. Other dark figures stood in the shadows behind him.

'I told you I'd take revenge,' said Ker of Fawdonside.

Dropping the mantle, Darnley jumped back and held out his hands, shouting, 'I'm unarmed. For the love of God and the sake of brotherhood, spare me! Spare me!'

Ker was as tall as Darnley. He laughed, reached out and grabbed him by the tail of his nightshirt, clamped his big strong hands round Darnley's neck and choked the life out of him.

Then he stuffed the torn nightshirt into the corpse's mouth and threw him aside, just as the hapless valet came staggering back under the weight of a wooden chair.

'You've been overly faithful,' Ker said, as he strangled him too.

Four minutes later the house at Kirk o' Field blew up with a massive explosion that shattered the windows of the houses round about, making crockery crash down from the shelves of neighbouring kitchens and rousing the citizens of Edinburgh from their sleep.

Mary, in bed at Holyrood, was wakened by the blast, but only turned on her side and did not get up.

She was one of the few people who did not want to investigate what had happened. The Town Guard turned out in force and Bothwell, with his brother-in-law Huntly, ran up from Holyrood where they had been playing cards, and found Darnley's house reduced to a heap of rubble. Even massive foundation stones were thrown up by the force of the blast and deposited on the other side of the Flodden Wall.

For two hours frantic men searched through the ruins looking for bodies. Whenever one was found – and there were three – either Bothwell or Huntly made a point of looking at the hands but seemed disappointed by what they found.

'She gave him her diamond ring. He'll be wearing it,' Bothwell said in a low voice and Huntly answered, 'Do you think he escaped?'

They were about to give up their search when a shout came from the garden, 'He's here, he's here,' and they ran to find the naked bodies of Darnley and his servant sprawled beneath the trees. On Darnley's finger glittered the Queen's ring.

Apart from the marks of strangulation on their necks, the bodies were unmarked and had not suffered in the explosion – but they were very dead.

When news was taken to Mary next morning that her husband had been killed, she was sitting up in bed eating a boiled egg and seemed neither very surprised nor upset. She dressed and for this bereavement decided on token mourning, a black overdress that swept aside showing bright yellow skirts underneath.

This was scandal enough, but neither did she withdraw from court life and was said to be enjoying her usual pastimes within Holyrood Palace – dancing, making music and laughing with her ladies.

When she heard the next day that John Knox had preached a sermon against her unseemly conduct, she announced she would start forty days of seclusion, but when the English ambassador arrived to pass on the condolences of his Queen, he reported that he was shown into a totally darkened room and suspected that the woman who received him with sobs and groans was not Mary but someone posing as her.

This scandalized Elizabeth, who was horrified at the thought of a king being assassinated, even though her opinion of Darnley was very low indeed. She was so outraged about what had happened that she freed Darnley's mother from the Tower of London where she had been incarcerated for disloyalty to the crown in plotting to marry her son to the Queen of Scotland.

More scandal was caused when Mary ordered that Darnley's body should be interred in Holyrood chapel in the same grave as Rizzio's.

Her half-brother Moray stepped in and told her, 'You can't do that. It's a deliberate insult. He must be buried with the appearance of propriety at least.'

In the end, she agreed that Darnley be laid to rest beside her father, James V, and at his funeral service, she burst out in dramatic, screaming hysterics which almost brought the proceedings to a halt.

Her hysterics however did not sway public opinion on to her side.

'I find it hard to believe that the common people are so upset about his death. No one liked or respected him in life,' she exclaimed when told that demonstrations were being held and protests raised against his murderers.

The ferment was worst in Edinburgh. Urged on by Knox, who called Mary a 'whore' and an 'adultress', mobs began to gather outside Holyrood, catcalling and jeering whenever she appeared.

Worse was to follow, because broadsheets were passed from hand to hand and stuck on doorways in the High Street. The Canongate and Cowgate were plastered with posters showing a crowned mermaid and a hare. 'Avenge me' was written on some of them.

Nathan's brother-in-law's printing press worked overtime because as soon as a poster was torn down, another took its place.

Moray showed one of the posters to the Queen and she asked, 'But what does it mean?'

He pointed at the printed figures, 'That mermaid signifies danger and promiscuity. She's wearing a crown, so she is you. The hare is the family crest of James Bothwell. The poster implies that you and he are adulterers who conspired together to murder your husband.'

She stared at him. 'But you know that isn't true. He was planning to kill me! Besides, you and the other lords signed a bond at Craigmillar agreeing to get rid of him for me. Which one of you did it?'

'I don't know. I didn't do the deed and nobody is sure who did. Nobody at all. But the towns-people are blaming Bothwell because they say he is your lover.'

Combative as usual, Bothwell reacted to the accusation with anger. 'Huntly will testify I was at Holyrood all that night. I couldn't have killed him,' he stormed and, true to form, issued an official challenge to fight in single combat any man who dared assert his guilt. 'I'll fight my accuser anywhere,' he raged.

Only one man took the challenge up, but Mary would not allow Bothwell to accept it. 'The man who says he'll fight you is base born. You're a nobleman and you can't stand up against him,' she ordered.

In Glasgow, Darnley's father Lord Lennox was

anguished and agitating for justice. He also accused Bothwell. All the accusations grew stronger and stronger till Bothwell said that, because no man of stature had accepted his challenge to fight, he was prepared to defend himself in a court of law.

The next day, he was officially accused of murdering Darnley and a trial was fixed for April twelfth at Edinburgh's Tolbooth. The cautious Earl of Moray went into self-imposed exile in England three days before the trial was due to begin.

The early days of April were terrible for Mary, whose depression and nervous incapacity became genuine. On the morning Bothwell rode out from Holyrood to stand trial, she was at her window to watch him go.

When he passed, he bent his head slightly and she collapsed in a storm of weeping. 'What if they hang him? I might never see him again,' she moaned to Seton, who was unable to soothe her.

Lord Lennox, intent on giving evidence at the trial, was advancing on Edinburgh with a large army but, fearing a serious affray, the Town Council stopped him outside the city and ordered his army to withdraw.

Discomfited and angry, he did as he was told and went back to Glasgow to await the verdict.

When the trial started, Bothwell stood in the dock looking so hangdog that one of his friends pulled at his sleeve and whispered, 'You must put on a better face or they'll be sure to judge you guilty.'

He straightened his shoulders, lowered his brows and assumed his normal combative stance, making several onlookers in the court draw back and hope his eye would not fall on them.

The trial dragged on for nearly seven hours, and in the end, because of the absence of witnesses, the accused man was acquitted. Then he gave a broad grin, ran from the Tolbooth and galloped in triumph back down the High Street with his entourage to a rapturous reception from the Queen.

When Lennox heard the verdict, he took ship and sailed for England.

Thirty

Although he had a difficult task ahead of him, the world looked beautiful to Bothwell as he and three old retainers whom he trusted completely rode to Crichton Castle.

He was dressed like them in a scuffed leather jerkin and homespun breeches instead of the grandiose clothes he wore at court and for his trial. He liked preening himself in finery but rough clothes turned him back into the fighting man he really was at heart.

Spring was his favourite season because the banks of streams were golden with primroses and, in glades beneath tall trees, harebells laid a carpet of such brilliant blue that they made him blink in delighted surprise.

The sun bathed everything in a kind of surreal peace and the silence was only broken by the lowing of a distant cow and the clucking of chickens that fled in front of his horse as he trotted past a cluster of cottages near the church. People came out to wave to him and called him Jamie, because they'd known him since he was born.

On his right, the squat steeple of Crichton church rose up, battlemented like a castle, and he smiled, as he always did, when he saw the grinning faces long dead masons had carved under the edge of the roof. They'd obviously enjoyed making those cheeky faces, some of which showed more mastery with the chisel than others, and it amused him to think of the stone carvers trying to outdo each other with their artistry. Some were obviously portraits of work-mates; one grinned showing ferocious teeth, one stuck out its tongue, and there were three elegant ladies with carefully folded, old-fashioned headdresses.

He turned to the man on his right and said, 'Pull the church bell. I want Jean to know I'm home.'

The man ran over the grass to the church door, where a long rope hung down from the belfry. He tugged hard and the bell pealed once. He tugged again and it pealed a second time. It had a true voice with no cracks in it.

Sitting with one hand on his knee, Bothwell stared around at the place he loved best in the world. His birthplace castle, not large or grand like other Scottish strongholds, squatted on the brow of a hill 200 yards away and stared down into a bottomless bog fringed by low-growing scrub. There was no need for a moat at Crichton Castle because that bog was impossible to cross.

Most of the fighting he'd done in his life had been around the Hermitage and he'd nearly lost his life there, but he'd never had to fight to keep Crichton, and God grant he never would.

Not Hermitage. This is the place I'll haunt when I die, he thought.

To drive away gloomy thoughts, he dug his spurs into the horse's sides and made it leap before going off at a gallop. The peals of the bell had warned the guards of his approach and the main gate was wide open when he clattered up to it.

Sweet-faced Jean was waiting for him in the inner courtyard. He jumped down and ran to her, sweeping her off her feet and hugging her close.

'Thank God you're better. You look well again,' he said when he let her loose.

She smiled through tears. 'I'm feeling very fit and it makes me even better to see you,' she said. She'd been ill for several months after a miscarriage and at one time, when he was taken away by the Queen's demands, there had been fears for her life. He looked lovingly into her face. She was a neat little person without guile or pretension, exactly the sort of woman he preferred, with skin as soft as silk, large trusting blue eyes and a sweetly curving mouth that made you want to plant a kiss on it. They had been married for only a year and in that time he'd grown to love her, much to his own surprise.

'I didn't expect you today. I only heard the verdict of the trial yesterday. I prayed for you to be found not guilty. My prayers were answered,' she told him.

She didn't ask if he had really killed Darnley, though she knew he'd killed many men in the past, but not by strangling them defenceless in their nightshirts in an orchard.

He took her hand and said, 'I've come to talk seriously with you. We must go where we can't be overheard.'

A shadow passed over her face as she looked up at him – what a joy it was to be with a woman who did not tower over him.

'Let's walk back to the church. It's empty and we can talk there,' she said.

They retraced his route slowly on foot, with her arm tucked into his, and she did not pester him with questions. She knew he would reveal what he'd come about soon enough and she was not sure she wanted to hear it.

'Are you happy here?' he asked, gesturing wide with one hand towards the east where the deep blue of the North Sea could be seen glinting beyond the hills.

'Very happy, it's a beautiful place. From my window I can see the lights of Edinburgh at night. I often sit and wonder where you are and what you're doing.'

He made no comment to that but walked in silence till they reached a little door that led into the church through a side chapel. When he turned the iron handle and swung it open, he caught sight of a bent figure scuttling away into a darkened corner.

'I thought you said the church was empty,' he said.

'It's only one of the old brothers. A few still live around about and come to pray here. Their whole lives were spent in this place and it's hard for them now that their order has been dispersed by the new religion,' she said.

He knew that her sympathies were more Catholic than Protestant, though she said otherwise, but he had adopted the new religion and stuck to it staunchly. If she wanted to support the brothers from the collegiate order who used to fill the air with their singing when he was a small boy, he would do nothing to stop her. In a way he was sorry that an old way of life was gone and could never return.

'You feed them I suppose,' he said.

'Yes.'

'That's all right. Just make sure John Knox doesn't get to hear about it,' he joked.

A vaulted stone roof arched over their heads and, by habit, they stared up at it, following the lines of the stone arches to their apex. In spite of the sun shining through the windows, it was icy cold inside and he shivered as if a shadow had fallen over him. Guttered candles lay on the stone benches by the walls. He lifted one, struck a flint and lit it. 'Not to worship. To warm my hands,' he said.

She watched in silence, waiting. He pulled her

down to sit with her back against the wall beside him. 'I want you to divorce me,' he said bluntly.

She stared at him in horror. 'But I love you,' she said.

He groaned. 'And I love you. I really do. I didn't when we first married, but I needed a wife and I needed your dowry. Before I knew what had happened to me I was in love with you. There has only been one other woman in my life that I truly loved – Janet of Buccleuch – but you know about her, don't you?'

'You said it was over.'

'It is. We haven't shared a bed for eight years.'

'Then why?'

'Because of the Queen.'

Jean flinched. She did not like Mary and had not been at court for the best part of a year. 'What has she got to do with it? Surely the lies and gossip people have been spreading about you and her aren't true, are they? I refused to believe them.'

'They are, in a way.'

She crossed both arms across her chest in a protective way and asked stonily, 'What do you mean?'

'She wants to marry me. She's fixed on it.'

'You mean she's besotted.'

'Yes. That's what she says. She says I'm the only man in Scotland she can trust. She needs me.'

'I need you. We've only been married for less than eighteen months and I didn't love you either when it started, but my brother persuaded me and I changed my mind when I got to know

293

you. I love you now.'

He groaned. 'Oh Jean. I've thought long and hard about this and there are so many advantages. I'm not a grand lord with vast estates like Moray and Argyll. I'm poor, I've always been poor, always battling to find the wages to pay my men, always trying to find the money for a good horse. If I marry the Queen my money troubles will be over – and I'll have power, more power than I ever dreamt of. I want it for you too. I'll set you up with a good estate – and my mother too. She's always short of money and has to re-stitch her clothes when they fray. Marrying the Queen will change everything for us all.'

'I don't care about clothes,' said Jean quietly.

He nodded. 'The Queen cares about them a lot. She has hundreds of gowns and she's kitted me out with Darnley's finery, cut down and remade for me – cloth of silver, cloth of gold, velvets and fancy furs. He's hardly dead and she's dressing me up in his wardrobe.'

His wife stared at his face and said, 'You enjoy looking fine, but how shaming for you.'

'She's fond of display and spends money like water. She gave me a hat of Darnley's that cost fifty pounds.'

'Have you worn it?'

'Once.'

If she had not been so miserable, she would have laughed at his expression.

'Will you divorce me?' he asked.

'On what grounds?'

'Janet would allow her name to be used, but most people know we are no longer lovers.
294

Name your sewing maid, Bessie.'

She stared at him aghast. 'My maid? Bessie?'

'Yes, the one with black hair who always wears a red kerchief tied around her head.'

'Why should I name her?'

'Because I've coupled with her.'

'When?'

'A year ago. Soon after we married – before you and I grew close.'

A red tide was flowing up her neck and into her cheeks. 'How often?'

He shuffled his boots on the floor and said, 'Maybe five or six times.'

Furious, she jumped to her feet and said, 'Or nine or ten! How shaming for me to divorce my husband because he slept with my maid. You can have your divorce and I wish you joy of your next wife.'

He tried to take her hand but she snatched it away.

'I still love you. I love you best of all. I don't want to lose you. Please let us stay close,' he pleaded.

'I think you've lost your senses,' she snapped and ran out of the church.

His mother was equally disapproving when he told her of his plans.

'The Queen is a manipulative woman. She's using you,' she said flatly.

'But people think I'm using her,' he replied.

'Why step into the lion's den? You're not duplicitous enough to survive among that company. You're forthright and outspoken, too blunt for your own good. Every enemy you've ever made will unite against you if you get into a position of power.'

'I'll fight them. I'll see them off,' he said, but she shook her head, 'Oh Jamie, you're a good fighting man but that's not enough. Don't let Mary Stewart use you. The Stewarts all have a treacherous streak – think about those half-brothers of hers. There's not a straightforward honest man among them.'

'She says she loves me.'

'She said she loved Darnley, and now she needs a strong protector because people suspect she arranged his murder,'

'She didn't.'

'How do you know?'

'Because I know who did.'

'And were you involved?'

'I knew what was planned but I didn't kill him.'

'Don't tell me who did, but I can guess the names. They made sure they didn't stand trial for the murder though. And would they have saved you if you'd been found guilty? No, of course they wouldn't.'

'I was not found guilty because I didn't kill him.'

'Do you know who did?'

'I'm not sure who actually throttled him but I have a note of the names of the conspirators.'

'You could be killed for that information alone. Don't marry the Queen, Jamie, if you want to live to have children and see them grow up.'

'I must. I've said I will. Think what it means. My father dissipated our property and left us with next to nothing. I'll be able to restore our fortunes.'

'I'd sooner stay poor than let you put your neck into a noose.'

He only shook his head.

Janet, Lady of Buccleuch, stared mournfully at him when he walked into her chamber.

'I knew you'd come,' she said.

'How did you know?'

'I saw it in the stars.'

'Did they tell you what I've come to say?'

'No, but I know it's of ill omen. You're setting out on a path to disaster but it's not too late to turn back. Go home to Crichton and stay there with your little wife.'

'I can't. She's divorcing me. I told her I've been sleeping with her sewing maid.'

'If every noblewoman divorced her husband for sleeping with a servant there wouldn't be a marriage left intact in Scotland,' said Janet.

'I'm going to marry the Queen.' It was said flatly and without jubilation.

'So that's it. I knew she would exert an evil influence on you. Do you love her?'

'No. I don't think I even like her very much.'

'She's trivial, hysterical and silly. I suspect she's more of a man than a woman, all that posturing around like a young gallant! I suppose you think you'll benefit from marrying her.'

'My debts will be paid. I'll have power and influence.'

297

'Do you want me to tell you you're doing the wrong thing for the right reasons? I can't. If you marry her it'll end in disaster.'

'Is your fortune telling always right?' he burst out angrily.

'I've read your future and grieve already because I love you,' she said.

He held up both hands. 'Don't tell me, don't tell me. But she's my Queen and she needs me. There really is no one else she can trust.'

'Be careful. This is the most dangerous thing you've ever done in your life and you've come through many hazards,' she warned.

Thirty-One

Usually Mary's charm eased away doubts and resentments but when she chose, she could switch from being an enchantress to a virago.

She was sweetness itself when she explained her latest plan to Bothwell. 'You must abduct me, take me prisoner and force me to marry you.'

He looked blank. 'But can't we marry like normal people when my divorce comes through?'

She shook her head. 'No. People must think I've been forced into it.'

'So I am to be the villain? What benefit is that to you?'

'People will think I'm innocent of plotting with you to get rid of Darnley. That's still being said in spite of your trial.'

'I didn't kill him.'

She snapped viciously, 'The ordinary people don't know that. They hear Moray's lies and believe them. People always believe the worst.'

'And I must be set up as the villain.'

She laughed. 'Aren't you that already? What difference will a little extra villainy make? I'll marry you to preserve my reputation.'

At the same time as Lady Bothwell's divorce case went to court, Mary and her retinue rode to Stirling so that she could see her son, who had been sent back there for security after Darnley died. He was now ten months old.

'He's growing well,' she exclaimed when the Countess of Mar proudly showed her the little boy asleep in his richly decorated cot.

'Do you want to hold him?' Lady Mar asked, but the Queen said, 'No, let him sleep. He looks so peaceful. I'll hold him later.'

Not for the first time, it struck the maids looking after the prince that his mother was not very maternal. Most women, returning to see her child after months of separation, would have been unable to restrain themselves from grabbing him, sleep or no sleep. Mary lavished riches and luxuries on the little boy, but spared him little love.

Later in the day, she returned to the nursery and found the baby awake, but when his nursemaid tried to give him to his mother, he stared at her and buried his face in the nurse's neck.

'Come to me,' coaxed Mary, holding out her arms, but he shrank back more and began to whimper.

'He doesn't know me,' she said in a broken voice.

'They have no memory at his age,' said the nurse defensively, thinking that the child could not be expected to leap into the arms of a woman he didn't recognize.

'I'll give him something to tempt him. What would he like?'

'He's fond of marchpane.'

'Bring me a bit and I'll give him that.'

But offering titbits also failed to work and when Mary tried to hold him, he struggled and grabbed frantically at her face, scratching her cheek. She wiped away a streak of blood and stared down at her baby's contorted face. *Even my son is against me*, she thought.

She stayed in Stirling for two days, by which time the baby had been cajoled by his carers into not screaming when she appeared. Before she left the castle, she ordered the Earl of Mar to guard the baby with his life, and to give him up to no one except herself.

When he reported these words to his wife, she said caustically, 'Of course she said that. Whoever holds the future king, holds Scotland. She knows how far out of favour she has fallen.'

After a night at Linlithgow Palace, Mary's party headed back to Edinburgh, and as they reached the village of Cramond, a few miles inland from the river Forth and six miles from the city, a large party of horsemen was seen waiting on the bridge across the river Almond.

Bothwell, in armour, rode out with his sword drawn and cried to Mary's guard, 'Stop! I'll take control of the Queen now.'

He rode up to her horse and grabbed its bridle, saying, 'There's an insurrection in Edinburgh. You must come with me to Dunbar.'

Mary appeared to be frightened and shrank back, shaking her head and protesting so loudly that some of her men drew their swords and rushed to protect her, but she turned in the saddle and told them to stay back.

'We'll have no bloodshed. I'll do as Lord Bothwell says,' she announced and rode off with her captor in the middle of his posse of warriors.

They did not stop till they reached the castle of Dunbar, where they stayed for a week. In the meantime, the divorce between Bothwell and his wife was finalized.

When news of the Queen's abduction reached Edinburgh, the Provost called out the Town Guard again but could do little except wait. Within a few days, information came back that Mary had been seen walking at Dunbar, practising archery and golfing with Bothwell. Both of them appeared to be in high spirits.

When they finally decided to return to Holyrood, Mary dressed as a man in armour and galloped at full tilt past the castle rock, while guns from the battlements above were fired down at them. They defied the resistance and rode straight into the castle, where Bothwell led her to her apartments and defied anyone to try to get at her without his permission.

Safely installed, Mary then issued a shocking statement. 'The Earl of Bothwell raped me during the first night I spent at Dunbar,' it said. 'So in order to preserve my character, there is nothing I can do but marry him.'

By doing this she showed terrible naivety in thinking anyone would be deceived by her rape story, for it was generally believed that she and Bothwell had begun sleeping together months before anyway.

All Scotland was astonished by this turn of events, and Bothwell's enemies, most of whom were Mary's relatives and supporters, were infuriated to be losing their hold over her. If anything could bind together the various factions in Scottish politics, she had given them the weapon.

Her enemies did not stay quiet. The placarding campaign against Bothwell and the Queen, which had lapsed for a while, started again and grew even more vicious. Street players, watched by enthralled crowds, enacted dramas about the pair's involvement in the murder of Darnley.

The country was in turmoil and something had to be done to calm the atmosphere, so Mary moved back to Holyrood and announced it was her intention to marry the Earl of Bothwell. To reassure people who feared that he was about to take over the throne, she said he would not take the title of King nor would he be allowed to make laws or grant any favours without her consent.

This was done at his insistence because he had

no ambition to rule her kingdom, for he knew that would have been like signing his own death warrant.

When he heard the rumours flying around Europe about the behaviour of his idolized Queen Mary, Nathan longed to make a return visit to Scotland and find out as much as possible.

Had she gone mad? Was she a murderess with her second husband's blood on her hands? Had she really been abducted by a wicked man who ravished her? Was her new protector a good man or an opportunistic villain? Was he another Darnley, only worse?

Esther was eager to accompany him home this time, because news came from Leith that her father was ill. They made the sea crossing with heavy hearts and when they landed in Leith, found to their dismay that her father's trading depot was closed and the house in the Kirkgate hushed in the peculiar cautious silence that surrounds dying people.

Esther's father, much depleted, lay in bed with his eyes closed with his women around him. When he heard Nathan's voice, he stirred and muttered, 'I was hoping you'd come. Lovely silks have arrived from China.'

Nathan lent over the bed and said, 'They can wait till you're better.'

'No, sell them for my wife and the girls. I spent a lot on them.'

'I'll do that before I return to Amsterdam.'

'Have you brought the miracle baby with

you?' asked Mr Leverson in a wavering voice.

'Yes, she's here,' said Esther, holding up the smiling little girl. Sarah had an equable nature and hardly ever cried.

'She's bonny. Very aristocratic looking,' quavered the old man. 'She must have her share of my fortune too. See to it, Nathan.'

Esther's mother, wiping back tears, said, 'Don't talk like that. You're not dying yet. You're better than you were.'

This seemed to rally the old fellow, who was propped up on pillows to sip a glass of wine, which infused some energy into him and made him eager to gossip with Nathan.

'Have you come back for the Queen's wedding?' he asked.

'Her wedding? No. We came to see you, but all sorts of stories are going around about her in Amsterdam,' Nathan replied.

'I'm not surprised,' said Esther's mother, 'She's been carrying on like a loose woman since that popinjay husband of hers was murdered.'

'What's the next husband like?' asked Nathan curiously.

'From what I hear, he speaks his mind and curses like a trooper, but he's not the villain his enemies paint him,' said the old man, who gestured that Nathan lean close so he could whisper, 'And he's a MAN.'

Nathan nodded. It struck him that pleasure in sex might be something the Queen had never experienced.

'They're getting married tomorrow at the

church in the Canongate. You should go up there and watch,' said Esther's mother.

On the night before their marriage, Bothwell and Mary held a banquet, at which he got very drunk and used rough language peppered with a generous amount of obscenities towards her. For her part, the Queen behaved in such a strange distracted way that observers thought she'd finally lost her senses.

Their marriage was celebrated at ten o'clock in the morning of May fifteenth in Greyfriars Church, where Bothwell had married Jean Gordon eighteen months before.

Mary would have preferred to marry in a Catholic church but the groom adamantly refused to agree to that.

'If you are so anxious to wed me, it must be in a church of my religion,' he said and added with a sarcastic smile, 'After all, if you decide to get rid of me, you can always have the marriage annulled, and you won't have to blow me up.'

For this ceremony, he did not dress up like 'an ape in purple', nor would he wear any of Darnley's refurbished garments Mary pressed on him. Instead, he wore a plain yellow doublet buttoned up tight and to his neck, and rimmed by a narrow frill.

As when she had married Darnley, Mary wore a black mourning gown, but again it was trimmed with yellow. Her new husband was not lavished with expensive gifts and the only thing he accepted was enough fur to trim a night robe. The fur was taken off an old cloak of her

305

mother's.

Most of the nobility deliberately stayed away from the ceremony and the newly wed pair walked the short distance from the half empty church in the Canongate to Holyrood where they dined in public.

People off the street were permitted to watch the half-hearted celebration, and among the crowd stood the Queen's smous.

Mary sat at one end of a long table with Bothwell at the other, both looking exceedingly glum. A feeling of disquiet filled Nathan as he watched his adored Queen.

What had happened to her? She was different, sharper-edged. The softness had gone out of her and she seemed to be on the verge of tears. The bridegroom was little better, for he started off half-drunk and as the feast progressed, grew drunker.

Nathan walked away while the banquet was still going on. 'No good can come of this wedding,' he thought sadly. In a strange way, he felt as much disquiet for the groom as for the bride.

As he walked down Leith Walk, he noticed that his eyes were blurring, and not with tears. Everything seemed to shiver slightly and dark blotches swam around in his field of vision.

'My God, I'm going blind,' he thought, with terrible conviction.

Both his father and grandfather had lost their sight when quite young and he'd hoped he might escape, but now he knew that he too was suffering from their disability. He said nothing to Esther, but when he saw her, he stared hard into her face, trying to imprint it on his memory.

How pretty she was, and their baby was lovely too, with her curling dark hair and cherubic face. They were more valuable to him than anyone or anything else in the world. *Until I stop seeing, I'll look closely at them every day and when my eyes are clouded with white like my father's, I'll still see them in memory*, he promised himself.

Thirty-Two

'Wantons wed in May!'

Placards and handbills bearing that message were passed from hand to hand or stuck on walls in Edinburgh. The Queen had married because of carnal passion and now was regretting it, said her detractors.

Mary's behaviour backed up this opinion. She stayed out of sight in Holyrood, weeping and wailing, furious because she suspected Bothwell still visited his ex-wife, and was even sleeping with her.

'Get me a knife so I can cut my throat,' she screamed to her ladies, but she had threatened suicide too often in the past for anyone to take her threat very seriously so, as usual, she retreated into one of her depressions, demanding the services of doctors, who were also growing sceptical.

As soon as Bothwell returned and cajoled her

to walk out with him however, she recovered.

When he was with her in company he politely doffed his bonnet, and sometimes, if they were both in a good humour, she playfully put his hat back on again, saying, 'There's no need to go uncovered before me.'

Tactfully he spiked the malice of his enemies by taking little part in the deliberations of the royal Council. Unlike Darnley, he demanded no riches nor to be crowned King. The Queen made him Earl of Orkney, and Lord High Admiral, but he asked for nothing more.

When he sent one of his fluent and well-expressed letters to the rulers of France and England, he never used the royal 'we', but always inferred that Mary alone was the head of state in Scotland.

Moray stayed abroad, but the other lords Morton, Mar and Maitland were determined to destroy Bothwell and to keep hold of the infant prince. Armies began gathering on both sides.

'We'll have to leave Edinburgh,' he told Mary in June.

'Where will we go?' she asked.

As always, his mind turned to his power base in the Borders. 'To Borthwick Castle. It's secure and the owner is loyal to you. I'll collect more men there and we can then march on to Melrose.'

Borthwick Castle was ten miles from Edinburgh and two from Crichton. They reached it just in time, for close on their heels rode Morton and Kerr of Cessford at the head of a thousand troopers who surrounded the castle and fired their muskets at its massive walls, with little effect.

Thwarted, the besiegers rode up and down outside the walls shouting insults at the Queen and her new husband. There was no courtly politeness now, for they called her a whore and made lewd jokes, which made her rush into an inner room with her hands over her ears.

Knowing the best way to provoke Bothwell, Kerr shouted challenges to him. 'Come out and meet one of us in single combat,' he jeered and the Queen had to hold on to him to stop him rising to the taunt.

'They'll have to go away eventually,' she told him, but he shook his head.

'While they're holding us here, others on their side are gathering more men. I have to get out to rouse the men of the Borders. They'll follow me,' he said.

When darkness fell that night, a bent old washerwoman scuttled out of the back of the castle and made her way by foot to a cluster of cottages farther down the narrow valley. The besiegers, sitting around fires in front of the great gate, paid no attention to her, but the old woman was Jamie Hepburn. He'd escaped from a tight situation once before in the dress of a maid and was doing it again.

Safely out, he recruited aid from local land-owners who knew him, before setting out for Haddington. When the besieging party learned that the man they wanted most of all was on the run again, they left Borthwick in pursuit of him and Mary took the opportunity to send a message to her husband's friend Lord Huntly in Edinburgh, telling him to rouse the city on her behalf.

Unfortunately, the canny folk of the capital wanted to be sure they were on the winning side and told Huntly they were not prepared to turn out on behalf of a wanton Queen. He had to retreat into the castle and sit tight to await events. Mary's magic worked no longer and she knew she must escape from Borthwick too.

At ten o'clock at night, she dressed herself in man's clothing, and, as she buckled on her spurs, a serving man said, 'You make a good soldier, Your Majesty.'

She laughed. 'I've dressed as a man often in the past, but this time it's serious.'

It was hard having to run a mile in armour across rough country. Bothwell was waiting with a cob wearing a man's saddle but that did not deter Mary, who had ridden astride many times.

Though she realized the danger, she enjoyed the headlong chase across country to Dunbar castle, where they would be safe. At three o'clock in the morning they finally reached sanctuary, and fell into each other's arms, laughing and more loving and trusting than they had been for months.

'We'll stay here and gather a bigger force. We can't ride into Edinburgh with only a couple of hundred men,' Bothwell told her the next morning.

She was more reckless. 'Nonsense. We should go now. As soon as I show my face in the city, the people will rally to me. They always do,' she said.

She disliked waiting and the dash from Borth-wick had made her feel invincible. 'I want to march on Edinburgh. The townspeople love me,' she insisted.

Her conviction seemed correct when a messenger arrived from the capital and asked for an audience with her. Bothwell stood at her side with a hand on his sword hilt, saying nothing while they conversed in French.

'He says I can safely go back to Holyrood,' she said, turning to him with her face looking younger than it had for months.

'I know what he said. I speak good French,' was his surly reply.

She ignored his ill humour. 'He's our friend and a Jesuit. He says my enemies are disbanding and the city will welcome me back.'

He shook his head in disbelief. 'He's a decoy. He looks like a Protestant spy to me. He has a shifty eye and I don't trust him. I'd rather wait.'

'I'm sure he's genuine. He blessed me with the Jesuit blessing. Have you lost your courage and prefer skulking here? We'll go and gather men on the way.' She was in a state of high excitement.

With bad grace, he stalked out of the room and gave the marching orders to his supporters, who numbered only 250 fighting men. Not enough to take a city!

Thirty-Three

15th June 1567

In spite of the tension, the sight of the Queen when she emerged to start their ride to Edinburgh made Bothwell smile.

Because she'd escaped Borthwick dressed as a man, with her fine gowns left behind, she'd been forced to borrow a change of clothes from a serving woman in Dunbar castle and was wearing a blouse and a red skirt that was much too short and showed her bare calves. Over the blouse was a shawl, knotted in fisherwoman style, and on her head a floppy bonnet.

'You look very fine,' he said and she curtsied in a mocking way, which he found endearing.

Before they set out, he took the precaution of adding three cannons to their army but that meant they progressed slowly through Prestonpans, stopping for the night at their familiar haunt, Seton House where they slept together, holding each other close and making love, not knowing it would be for the last time.

In the morning, Bothwell's army was increased by the arrival of some minor landowners from the Borders, who brought a couple of hundred men to his support. He noticed with alarm, however, that others from his ranks had already disappeared, drifting away overnight without taking leave.

Why? he wondered. What had they heard to make them defect? He wished he had not left Dunbar without a bigger force.

The sun was blazing down as they approached the ancient humpbacked bridge that crossed the river Esk at Musselburgh, and his heart sank even more when he saw a massive force lined up on the flat plain that ran along the seashore. There were at least two thousand men there, with a large contingent of cavalry, all armed to the teeth and blocking his approach to Edinburgh.

'So much for your lying Jesuit,' he said bitterly to Mary.

Ignoring that, she was pointing ahead with a stricken look on her face. 'Look, look!' she gasped. Held in front of the opposing army was a huge banner, a white sheet stretched out between two long poles. It was at least eight feet across and five wide, crudely painted and showing a naked body lying beneath a tree. Beside the body sat a small child wearing a crown – the baby prince of course – out of whose mouth came the words, 'Judge and revenge my cause, oh Lord.'

As they stared at it, a small party carrying a flag of truce detached itself from the hostile force and rode towards them. The rebel lords obviously wanted to parley and the intermediary they had chosen to carry their terms was Du Croc, the French ambassador, whom Mary knew and trusted.

His face was unsmiling when he drew his horse up at her side and kissed her hand. 'Your Majesty, I've been instructed to tell you that if you wish to avoid bloodshed, come with me now and cross over to the other side,' he said in a sorrowful voice.

She shook her head violently, but he persisted. 'If you come, the men opposing you will serve you on bended knee and remain your obedient servants forever.'

'They're traitors,' she said.

'You have forgiven traitors before,' said the Frenchman flatly.

'What will happen to my husband if I agree?' she asked.

This was the point on which Du Croc knew her enemies would not shift.

'They are his mortal enemies. They are challenging him to come out between the armies and meet their champion in single combat. If one antagonist is not enough to quell him, another will follow.'

She was horrified. 'In other words, they intend to kill him, come what may.'

'They are his mortal enemies,' Du Croc repeated sadly. Like most Frenchmen, he had a strong respect for Bothwell, both as a man and a warrior, but now he was an emissary for others.

Bothwell himself intervened and said forcefully, 'Let them send their champion. I'll meet him. Go back and tell them that.'

It was a sweltering hot day and the sun was beating down so hard that his men had to lay down their arms and strip off their armour as they waited for Du Croc's return. He came back with an offer from a man called John Murray to fight Bothwell. He would have accepted there and then, but again Mary protested on the same basis as before. 'You can't fight a man who is not of your own rank. Tell them you'll only take the field against the Earl of Morton.'

The challenge was accepted and Morton made a show of buckling on the great sword that belonged to his ancestor Archibald Bell the Cat, but did not leave his tent even though Bothwell waited in the cleared space between the armies for almost an hour.

The longer he waited, more and more of Mary's army drained away, while the rebel army slowly advanced, with their insulting propaganda banner held up in front of them.

In despair, seeing there would be no personal combat, Bothwell eventually withdrew his force to Carberry Hill, preferring to fight a pitched battle from rising ground. The cannons, hauled so painfully from Dunbar, were pulled up the hill too, and turned on his enemies.

He looked at the woman in red by his side and accepted failure. When hand-to-hand fighting began she would be a liability, because she would certainly be the first object of murderous attack.

'Make terms with them now,' he ordered.

She protested hysterically, 'No, no. Never!'

'Make terms or they'll kill you. If you don't make terms, I'll ride away and leave you to your fate.'

She saw he was deadly serious and asked, 'And if I do make terms, what about you?'

'It doesn't matter about me.'

She was thinking desperately, trying to find some way out. 'It does to me. I know what to do. I'll send a message saying that I forgive them for their treachery. They accepted when I forgave them for the killing of Rizzio and if I forgive them again, they'll do as I say like they did before,' she said.

He shook his head, astonished at her naivety. 'Marie, you've never learned to understand people, have you? Not all men are trustworthy.'

She stared at him. The scar on his forehead blazed scarlet, and exhaustion and disillusion marked his face, but his gaze was steadfast.

'Is yielding all I can do?' she asked.

'Either that, or ride with me back to Dunbar and we'll hold out there till we gather a bigger army.'

She quailed at the effort required for retreating to Dunbar and shook her head. 'It's best to parley. I'm their Queen. They'll do as I say. You go to Dunbar and I'll join you there later.'

He groaned. 'That's fool's thinking.'

'Then I'm a fool,' she snapped and jumped off her horse. He dismounted too and for a brief moment they held each other, kissing for the last time as he said, 'Stay loyal to me Marie. I'll come back for you. Promise you'll stay loyal.'

She watched him riding away with tears pouring down her cheeks. 'I promise, I promise,' were her last words.

Now there was nothing for it. She turned and

faced her enemies, who were lined along the foot of the hill staring up at her.

She picked out hard-eyed Morton, Maitland, Ker and the weasley faced Hume, whose ancestor had betrayed her grandfather James IV at Flodden, then she remounted her horse and cantered down to them.

The animosity they felt towards her was visible but they performed the usual courtly pretensions, bowing and addressing her as 'Your Majesty'.

'You've come back to your rightful place, among your loyal subjects,' said Morton sarcastically.

She glared at him. 'I'll have you hanged,' she snapped.

As she spoke, some soldiers raised a jeer, yelling, 'Hang the whore!' and the cry was taken up by the rest of the throng, till it became deafening.

'Hang the whore. Burn the murderess!' Men carrying the banner raised it higher and waved it in front of her. In that instant she knew she had made a terrible mistake by throwing herself into the hands of those who hated her.

Defenceless in ridiculous clothes, without the trappings of power or riches, she was only a vulnerable woman, prey to whatever men chose to inflict on her. Her soul shrank.

Her ride into Edinburgh was a nightmare. Only the fact that she was riding in the middle of an escort prevented her being injured by stones and rubbish thrown at her by bystanders along the way. There were no sympathetic faces among the throng.

Do they hate me because of Darnley? He wasn't worth their loyalty, she thought over and over again.

Eyes fixed, she held her head high and tried to close her ears to the taunts and jeers as she passed familiar places without a sideways glance. At last her guards stopped at a small house in the Grassmarket and gestured to her to dismount.

'Not here. I want to go to my own chambers at Holyrood,' she protested.

'Get down here,' said Morton and roughly pulled her foot out of the stirrup. They put her into a barely furnished room with one window overlooking the street. The banner carriers stationed themselves opposite that window so, when she looked out, all she saw was the image of Darnley's naked body beneath the green tree.

'Where are my women?' she asked, looking around, but no one replied and she was left alone. When the key turned in the lock with a clunking noise a chill struck her heart. Food was brought, but she refused to eat.

'Bothwell will rescue me,' she said and her guard smiled sarcastically.

'Don't be so sure. He's probably with his other wife in Crichton now. He always spent three nights a week with her even after he married you,' he told her.

'You're a liar,' she stormed, but he only shook his head at her stupidity and took away the tray of untouched food, leaving her with doubts and fears.

Dawn broke in glory. Early sun burnished the

tall buildings that huddled in the middle of Edinburgh and woke her from a fitful sleep. Galvanized with febrile energy, she rushed to the window and started screaming down at the street below, 'Save me, save the Queen, get me out of here!'

The terrible banner had disappeared, but a few early risers were on the roadway below and a woman stopped to stare up at the window. Several others joined her and when they recognized the frantic Mary, they began to laugh and point fingers at her. One old hag drew her forefinger across her throat in a mime of slashing and yelled, 'Whore!'

Mary fell across the bed in a storm of weeping, and was still sobbing an hour later when the door was unlocked and Mary Seton was shown in.

'Oh my Queen!' she exclaimed and held out her arms. Mary ran into them and they clung together. Seton, the most devoted of Mary's women, washed the Queen, combed her disordered hair and dressed her in the fine clothes she'd brought with her, hanging the precious black pearls and a diamond crucifix around Mary's neck.

'We must make you look regal,' she said.

Surreptitiously, for she knew they were being spied on through the door, she gave Mary writing materials and paper hidden in a half finished piece of embroidery brought to beguile the time. 'Write Bothwell a letter and I'll send it off for you. Where is he?' she whispered.

'Dunbar I think.'

'Write then.'

Mary scrawled, 'Dear heart, I will never forget or abandon you ... Come and save me.' Seton folded the paper small and slipped it in her bodice seconds before the guard ordered her to leave.

At midnight, Morton arrived with an escort and ordered Mary to dress and go with him. 'Where to?' she asked but the only answer she received was, 'Wait and see.'

When dawn broke again, she saw sunlight glittering on the smooth waters of Lochleven near Kinross. She recognized the place because, as a small child, she'd been taken there by her mother for safety, to a castle built on a small island in the middle of the loch and surrounded by a high curtain wall that was impossible to breach. As well as being a safe sanctuary, it was the perfect prison.

'Pray for my soul, for my body is now worth very little,' Mary said to the boatman who ferried her across to the castle.

Bothwell did not hide out in Dunbar or wait for the arrival of his enemies. The day after the encounter at Carberry, he was officially put to the horn by Moray and declared an outlaw, so he headed for the Borderland with twelve loyal companions, only stopping on the way to bid farewell to his mother and first wife.

At Crichton, he yanked the church bell himself to alert Jean of his arrival and they hugged each other as he said, 'I can't stay. You must leave here at once and go north to your mother. You'll

320

be safe there, for Moray and Morton will certainly seize my home as soon as they can.'

She laid her face on his chest and said, 'This is a tragedy. We could have been happy and raised our children here.'

'I know, but destiny intervened. Go home. Marry again and forget me. Be happy.'

He stared around, before laying a hand flat on the great gate of the castle and closing his eyes. After a few moments, without a backward wave, he clattered off to the south.

He had friends in Liddesdale, but their power was nothing compared to the forces of Moray and Morton. He stopped at Hermitage and told his garrison there to keep the castle safe for his return, before he rode off to see his first mistress Janet for the last time.

She was in the Buccleuch stronghold at Hawick and her face went white when she saw him. 'What will you do now?' she asked.

'I'm going to raise a force and rescue the Queen.'

'Don't waste your time.'

'You don't like her. You've never liked her.'

'True. Nostradamus saw her soaked in blood and she taints everyone she draws into her orbit with disaster.'

'Nevertheless, I have to try to save her.'

Janet closed her eyes and shook her head. 'I know. I'm sorry, Jamie.'

'What have you seen?'

She lied. 'Nothing. Go with my love and always remember me.'

'I hope we meet again,' he said.

'I hope so too, but I don't think we will,' was her reply.

His travels in search of support for Mary took him to the west of Scotland and the Highlands, but there was little enthusiasm anywhere for raising a rebellion on her behalf, especially after news started to circulate that a silver casket containing letters from her had been discovered and they proved that she was involved in the plot to kill Darnley. The letters implicated Bothwell too, though he swore they were forgeries.

Details of what was in the letters and who they were to and from were vague and contradictory, but because his name was involved, no great landowner wanted to antagonize his enemy, the all powerful Moray, who was a vengeful man.

Even Huntly, Bothwell's long-time friend and brother-in-law, who bore him no ill will in spite of the divorce from Jean, would not leave his Aberdeenshire lands and advised, 'Get out of this country, Jamie. Moray and his gang will stop at nothing. They've stripped you of your titles and lands. Don't let them take your life as well.'

But Bothwell was thirty-two years old, strong and vigorous in spite of his battle wounds, and he felt invincible. Provided by Huntly with money and fresh horses, he decided to head for his mother's birthplace, Orkney. He was hereditary High Admiral of Scotland, after all, and hoped the independently minded fishing people would pay little heed to sentences of outlawry passed by a Stewart bastard son in Edinburgh.

In the Cromarty Firth, he managed to get control of five ships and recruit three hundred men. In Shetland, he rented another large, two-masted vessel called *The Pelican* and took to the high seas in it, but his enemies were hot on his heels. After a short naval battle, his fleet was destroyed and he was left with only the badly damaged *Pelican*, now little more than a hulk, which a storm fortuitously blew across the North Sea to Norway.

Standing on the deck of the ravaged *Pelican*, he stared ashore at a group of huddled wooden houses fringing Karm Sound and the snow-capped Norwegian mountains rising precipitously behind them.

'I've been lucky to escape with my life, but what do I do now?' he said aloud. The decision was made for him by the captain of a Danish warship lying in Karm, who spotted the wallowing *Pelican* and rowed over to investigate and offer help.

The ragged ruffian who met him looked like a fugitive pirate and had no official papers. When asked for his identity, he said, 'I'm the King of Scotland!' and the Danish captain laughed as he said, 'I think you'd better come with me to Bergen till we sort this out.'

Bergen was a pretty town of traders' brightly painted wooden houses and warehouses grouped beneath a castle and around a semicircular harbour. Bothwell's heart sank when he discovered that the governor of the castle was Erik Rosencrantz, uncle of his rejected mistress Anna.

When they met, he tried to bluff it out and

asked cordially, 'Where is Anna now?'

'She and her mother, my sister, are living on a farm just outside the town. I've sent word to tell her you're here,' said Uncle Erik.

She was still beautiful when she walked into the room. He went towards her with his hands outstretched and a smile on his face but she drew back and her hard-faced mother asked, 'Have you come to repay my daughter's dowry?'

'I have nothing except the clothes I stand up in, unfortunately,' he told her and she sniffed, 'And you're meant to be the King of Scotland! In that case, we'll bring a court case against you for the dowry's return.'

To put off the prospect of a court case, he promised to pay Anna a yearly stipend and give her the damaged *Pelican*. She accepted this inadequate payment because she was not vengeful and still had a soft spot for her lover, like most of Bothwell's women.

Her uncle, too, liked him and put him up in comfort in the castle till it was decided what to do with him. One morning Anna arrived with a dark-haired little girl hanging on to her skirts.

He smiled at the child and asked, 'Who is this?'

'Don't you know? She's your daughter.'

Bothwell knelt on the floor and stared into the child's eyes. *My daughter, my only child,* he thought. He remembered Anna saying she was pregnant before she left Scotland for the last time but she'd said that before and it never came to anything.

'What's your name?' he asked the little girl.

'Marget.'

'Marget, always remember the name James Hepburn, Earl of Bothwell, for I have nothing else to give you. My crew sailed off with the little I had on board,' he told the child.

Anna said, 'At least give me a letter acknowledging her paternity.' He strode across to his writing table and, in his beautiful, clear hand, wrote out a statement saying that Marget, daughter of Anna was his true daughter and entitled to his estate.

'I hope it means something in the end, because my lands have been sequestrated but perhaps one day she can claim her share,' he said as he passed the paper over.

'Even if it doesn't, I'll make sure that she grows up proud of her father,' said Anna and the couple kissed in farewell.

The next day, the authorities sent him to Copenhagen, passing on the responsibility for him to King Frederick of Denmark. The King was a manly fellow who listened sympathetically to Bothwell's story, for he was the sort of man that Frederick appreciated – bold, foul-mouthed and plain-spoken.

Nor was Frederick convinced by Moray's argument that Mary's husband was guilty of Darnley's murder and asked his prisoner to write an account of his side of the story, which he read with interest. It put him more on the Scottish earl's side than before.

'Moray, the Regent of Scotland, wants me to extradite you,' he said at one of their friendly conferences.

'He hates me because he knows I'll tell that he was as involved in Darnley's death as I was, if not more. He'll kill me the moment I set foot on Scottish soil.'

'I thought as much but I'm in a difficult position. The best thing for me to do is hold you safely here and ask you for a guarantee that you won't try to escape.'

King Frederick was really hoping either England or Scotland would offer him ransom money for Bothwell but neither showed any inclination to do so. It was in all their interests to keep him well away from home.

The prisoner looked levelly at him. 'I won't give any guarantees. If I can escape, I'll go. It's my duty to try to rescue Queen Mary.'

'I thought so. If she is restored to the throne, I'd want to be in her good graces, so the best I can do is hold you at Malmoe Castle till events work out. It won't be rigorous imprisonment but even an accomplished escaper like you, Lord Bothwell, won't get away from there.'

Frederick thought it shaming that a man who was used to the best of everything only had ragged clothes and no money, so he granted his prisoner an allowance to pay for good cloth and a skilled tailor, before he exiled him to Malmoe where his chambers were secure, but spacious and comfortable.

Thirty-Four

Before Mary was taken away from Edinburgh, she was told by the cruel and gloating Morton that a Highland seer had predicted she would be burned at the stake as a husband killer. This obsessed her, and within days of moving into Lochleven, she succumbed to another of her hysterical collapses, and once again doctors feared for her life.

But again she revived and when she was able to sip some wine, her jailer, Sir William Douglas, Moray's half-brother and owner of the castle, sent his mother to sit by her bed and say, 'The doctor thinks you're having another child. Did you know that?'

'I suspected as much,' said Mary.

Lady Douglas eyed the Queen's outline beneath the blanket. Her belly was bulging, yet she had been married to Bothwell for less than three months.

'Have you any idea when it is due?' she enquired.

Mary shook her head. In fact she was five months gone, and the child had been conceived before she and Bothwell married, even before Darnley died, but she was not prepared to admit that and provide her enemies with another weapon against her.

At the end of July, she went into premature labour and was delivered of dead twins. The midwife who showed the foetuses to Lady Douglas said, 'They are at half term, perhaps even five months.'

'So she and Bothwell were lovers before they married,' said Lady Douglas and told her son, who sent the news to Edinburgh, where it provided ammunition for John Knox to preach against Mary from the pulpit of St Giles, calling her 'a scarlet adventuress and a whore of Babylon'. Fortunately she knew nothing of what he said.

While she was ill in bed, and whey-faced from loss of blood, a group of rebel lords, including her old enemies Ruthven and Morton, arrived at Lochleven with lawyers and legal papers for her to sign.

'What am I signing?' she asked.

'Your abdication,' Ruthven told her.

'But I've no intention of abdicating.'

He leaned over the bed and told her, 'Sign it. If you don't I'll pull you out of this bed and either drown you in the loch or cut your throat.'

She knew he meant what he said so she put her name at the bottom of the page, but not before asking, 'What will happen to my son?'

'He becomes King immediately and Moray is to be his Regent. You'll sign to agree to that too.'

Again she did as she was told but retaliated by saying to the watching lawyers, 'I'm only signing under duress. Take note of that.'

Alone that night with the faithful Seton, who

had been allowed to share her imprisonment, she broke down in tears and sobbed, 'I'm cursed. Everything goes wrong for me and I lose everyone I love. You're the only person in the world who stands by me. What have I done to attract such ill luck?'

Seton stroked the Queen's glorious hair. She loved Mary but felt powerless to help except by joining her in prayer and hoping that God was listening to them.

Five days later, with little ceremony and watched by only a few people, Mary's son was crowned King James VI at the parish church in Stirling and John Knox preached the sermon. It was the second anniversary of her wedding to Darnley and she was not present to see her son crowned King.

In August, Moray, the new Regent, arrived in Lochleven to speak with his half-sister. She dressed with care and Seton spent a great deal of time arranging her hair in the most becoming style. When she saw Moray's stern face however, she burst into a storm of tears, but her emotion did not soften him.

There was now no sympathy between them, though she found it bitter to remember how much she had once trusted the man. Before they parted, he ordered her to hand over her most precious jewels to him so that he could take charge of them for her son.

Once again, he was particularly covetous of her string of twenty-four grape-sized black pearls. With great reluctance she handed them over, remembering how her Guise uncles had also wanted the necklace.

'Who will wear them next?' she asked, tenderly rubbing her fingertips over the smooth beads for the last time.

'The woman who marries your son, I hope,' he said, though he secretly intended to give them to his wife.

The Countess of Moray had more scruples than her husband, however. and refused to accept the pearls. 'In that case,' said her husband, 'I'll sell them to Elizabeth of England.'

And he did.

Thirty-Five

1568

Mary was an exploiter.

Growing into womanhood in France, she had watched how women like Diane de Poitiers won men to her side. She studied and perfected the art of cajolery, which was not the same as seduction because, in fact, sex was not a major motivation for her. She enjoyed having people, mostly men, in thrall to her, but until she was swept away by momentary desire for Bothwell, she was largely untouched by physical longing for any particular person.

Because she had little understanding of the powerful forces that brought men and women together, she managed to persuade herself that she loved Francois, and later Darnley. Love to her was something written about by poets, not something she herself experienced.

Even in Lochleven, it was essential for her to seduce people, and to make them her slaves. All the other Marys except Seton were married by now, but she had a small court of three ladies to share her captivity who gave her total devotion. Tall, lanky Seton never had a suitor, and did not seem to want one. Her love was all for Mary and it was unwavering.

Like most exploiters, Mary had a sharp eye for potential victims. As the weeks of her imprisonment passed, she regained her spirits and enchanted her companions by gaiety in dancing, singing and making music. Even some of the guards fell in love with her and a shy little girl who brought the laundry was enchanted, as was an awkward sixteen-year-old called Willie – 'Little Douglas' to everyone.

He was an unwanted by-blow produced by a female member of the castle owner's family who'd been taken in and drifted around looking aimless and unloved. By January he was madly in love with the glamorous Queen, whose bloom and good looks had returned during her time of enforced leisure, and who was prepared to pass hours talking to him about poetry and pet dogs.

Though she seemed resigned, that was only a facade. Using Little Douglas to carry notes to the mainland, she made contact with the Hamilton and Seton families who were her supporters, and they contacted a cousin of Bothwell who agreed to help her if she could get on to the mainland. She watched and looked around, wondering how to escape.

'Where do you wash the clothes?' she asked the little laundress on a breezy March morning.

'In my mother's house on the shore. She and I wash them and I bring them back when they're dry and pressed.'

'Do you row the boat yourself?'

'Oh no, there's a ferry. My father rows sometimes and he shares the work with other men.'

'How often do you come across?'

'Every day.'

It did not take long before the girl was persuaded to change places with Mary on a dark evening when she was going home with a basket full of dirty sheets. They chose a night when a new boatman was on duty because they hoped he would not notice that he was ferrying a different laundry maid to the one who'd been taken across in the morning.

The plan worked perfectly. Dressed in working women's clothes, Mary lugged the clothes basket on to the jetty and settled down with it in the shallow hull. When the boatman jumped in, she sat with a scarf over her bowed head and acknowledged his greeting with a grunt.

'Bad temper?' he said lightly, and pulled on the oars, but there was something about the laundry maid that made him suspicious and he leaned over to pull the scarf away from her face. She reacted quickly, pulling it back, but he saw that her hand was long and very white. Not a hand that scrubbed dirty linen every day.

'Show me your face. You're no laundry maid,' he said, resting on the oars.

She stared at him with sheer terror in her eyes.

'Please don't betray me,' she sobbed.

Though he'd never seen the captive Queen, he knew immediately who she was. People working in the castle all spoke well of her and pity filled him when she said, 'If you take me back, they'll kill me.'

'I'm sorry. I have to take you back,' he said.

'Please, no. Douglas will have me drowned and Moray will cut his throat if he finds out I almost got away.'

The boatman groaned. He did not want her death on his conscience, but knew that he'd be a dead man himself if he ferried her to safety.

'I'll take you back and put you off at the castle jetty. No one'll see you. I promise I won't tell what's happened,' he told her.

When Mary climbed out of the boat, the laundry maid was watching to see if the fugitive reached land safely. Without speaking they changed places and Mary slipped disconsolately back to her prison chambers.

Six weeks later, she tried again. This time she and Seton slipped out of her chamber on a night when the family were enjoying a banquet in honour of the Lady Douglas's birthday. Little Douglas had a boat tied up waiting for her and he'd also stolen the castle's massive keys, locking every gate and door before he rowed her away.

Halfway across the stretch of moonlit water, raising his arm high in a jubilant gesture, he threw the bunch of keys up in the air and they all watched in delight as they splashed into the water, sending out ring after concentric ring of silver. Mary clasped her hands in delight and told him, 'When I regain the throne, I'll give you an earldom for this.'

The plan went without a hitch. The Hamiltons, along with Mary Seton's father and brother, were waiting with horses to whisk them away to freedom at Broxburn on the other side of the River Forth. They had a head start too, for when the garrison tried to go in pursuit, they found they were prisoners themselves, because all the gates were locked and the keys gone forever.

Her main jailer, Sir William Douglas, was so ashamed of failing in his duty that he tried to cut his own throat and was only saved by his mother snatching the knife out of his hand.

The first thing the freed Queen did was issue an edict declaring that she had been made to abdicate by force and intended to take back her throne. In a few days the Hamiltons had raised an army of 10,000 men, and, led by a refreshed and jubilant Mary mounted on a spirited steed called Rosabelle, they set out for Dumbarton, where the castle guardian was loyal to her.

In Glasgow, Moray reacted with disbelief when he heard that his half-sister had escaped from Lochleven, but he moved fast and also raised a larger force. His men travelled with an extra musketeer riding pillion behind each horseman. On the thirteenth of May, 1568, the two armies met at Langside, a little village on the south side of Glasgow.

Like Carberry almost a year before, this battle was a fiasco. It lasted forty-five minutes and soon became a rout when Mary's main force allowed themselves to be trapped in a narrow sunken road and were mown down before her eyes as she watched from a nearby hill.

The men of Argyll who'd joined in her support, took little part in the fighting because Argyll himself suffered an epileptic fit just as the battle began and was powerless to exert any authority over his men.

Bleak-faced Mary watched her supporters drifting away. 'We lack a commander,' she said and wished with all her heart that Bothwell was at her side. Only he would know how to turn this defeat into a victory.

She turned to the faithful Little Douglas who had stayed in her company since he rowed her across the loch and said to him, 'Save yourself. Run now.'

He shook his head. 'Wherever you go, I'll go with you,' he told her.

Along with him, a dozen loyal men, including Seton's brother, stayed too and escorted her and Rosabelle off the field, heading south as fast as they could ride.

When night fell, they drew rein in the middle of a wooden valley and stared at each other in confusion.

'Where can we go?' Mary asked.

One of the Hamiltons suggested, 'To the coast. There you can get a boat and sail back to France.'

335

That prospect did not appeal to her, for she knew that she'd receive a lukewarm welcome there even from her own Guise family. 'Must I leave my kingdom to Moray?' she asked.

'You have property in France, Your Majesty. You'll be able to live there in comfort and safety for the rest of your life,' said Little Douglas.

'But I'm the Queen! I don't want to run away. I'm the Queen of Scotland.'

'If you don't get out when you can you'll be hunted down like a dog – and your enemies won't spare you even though you're a woman,' Lord Seton told her.

Then he pointed at her red hair and said, 'You won't get far if you try to stay in Scotland. You're too easily recognized.'

What he said was true. A beautiful, six-foot tall woman with startling red hair turned heads wherever she went.

She grabbed at a thick strand of her own hair and said desperately, 'I'll cut it off. Help me cut it now!'

They all drew back in alarm and she turned to Little Douglas, ordering, 'You cut it for me. Take your knife and cut it all off.'

She sat on a tree stump while he hacked away at the beautiful hair and it fell around her feet like autumn leaves. Every man in the party took a strand and tucked it into his purse as a memento of the lovely Queen. Little Douglas wanted to stop when her hair was as short as a boy's but she urged him on.

'Make my head as bare as a bald man's. I want it all to go,' she ordered and that was done. Only a dusting of red covered her skull and the strange thing was that, without the mass of thick hair, her face looked even more beautiful and striking than before.

'To the coast,' she said, rising to her feet, and they rode on till exhaustion forced them to lie on the ground beneath scrubby trees and sleep till dawn broke.

After sixty miles, when they were within sight of the sea, and she was exhausted to dropping point, one of the outriders saw spires and turrets rising above the trees in front of them.

'It's Dundrennan Abbey,' he called.

'Thank God. They'll take me in,' sobbed Mary.

The abbey was an old Cistercian house and a few monks were still living there, for the tolerant locals hadn't driven them out. She rode to the gatehouse and hammered on its door with the end of her riding stick. An old man who opened it to her fell on the ground and kissed her feet. In spite of the shaven head, he recognized her.

Life in the abbey was a poor version of what it had been thirty years before, but the monks provided chambers and food for the Queen and her supporters. Her presence was kept secret while she came to a decision about where to go next.

Everyone but Mary herself thought she ought to take ship and go to France. She would have none of that, however.

'I'm going to cross to England and ask for sanctuary from my cousin Elizabeth. As a woman and a queen she'll not turn me away, and from England I have a better chance of returning to my own kingdom again,' she said firmly.

No argument was entertained. She was going to England.

On sixteenth of May, she sent off most of her followers, telling them, 'Save yourselves. Go to France.'

With Mary Seton and Little Douglas, she boarded a small boat at Port Mary and crossed the Solway Firth, landing at Whitehaven and causing consternation when the news of her arrival reached her cousin Elizabeth.

Thirty-Six

Malmoe was on the southern tip of Sweden, a short distance across the strait from Denmark, to which it belonged. The climate was good and the outlook to the sea eternally changing and beautiful. Being of an optimistic nature, and sure that he would either escape or be set free eventually, Bothwell did not fret too much in his captivity until news came of Mary's escape from Lochleven and her disastrous military engagement at Langside.

For days he sat in his room with his head in his hands. 'If I'd been there, she wouldn't have run off into England. I'd have made sure she defeated Moray first,' he told the friends who tried to cheer him out of his depression.

It was hard for him to accept, but in his heart he knew the great enterprise was over.

Mr Leverson died that summer, so Nathan and Esther returned to Leith with their small daughter to take part in the family mourning rituals. Nathan, more bothered than ever by his failing sight, took on the task of settling his father-in-law's estate and clearing the warehouse. It was a nostalgic pleasure to pass hanks of soft silks through his hands again and part of him longed for the road. Before he went completely blind, he wished he could make a few trips over his old routes. Perhaps Sarah would lead him around when she was big enough. He'd like that.

Esther's father turned out to have been rich and his wife and daughters were left goodly sums, so there was no problem about money.

'Do you want to come back to Amsterdam with us?' he asked his mother-in-law when the thirty-day period of intense mourning was over.

She shook her head. 'I've lived here all my life. I'll stay in Edinburgh with Ruth. Help me move there before you go back to Amsterdam.'

Ruth's husband Stern owned a thriving printing press and their house in the Lawnmarket was always full of chattering people who brought in the latest news. Nathan enjoyed sitting there listening to the gossip but the city had gone very quiet and subdued. 'Nothing seems to be happening these days,' Nathan said to his brother-in-law who agreed.

'Yes, everything's calm because Queen Mary and her court have run away to England. Her son is on the throne and Knox's church rules Edinburgh now so we must behave ourselves!'

'Where is Queen Mary?'

'In Carlisle Castle, waiting to see what the English Queen will do with her.'

'Do you think the English Queen will send her back to us?'

'I doubt it. The Scottish lords don't want her here and neither does the Protestant church. She should have gone to France. People say the English will keep her locked up in case she raises Catholic support and causes trouble for Elizabeth. She isn't helping her own cause, because she keeps on saying she's the rightful ruler of England as well as Scotland. That woman is impossible to gag.' Stern did not share his brother-in-law's devotion to Mary.

Nathan shook his head in despair, remembering the brilliant and hopeful young woman he'd watched landing in Scotland only eight years ago. So much had happened since. It seemed as if her life had gone from disaster to disaster ever since she stepped on to Leith jetty. Poor girl – he still thought of her as a girl – how she loved pretty things! He remembered her bejewelled fingers sorting out his silks and always picking the prettiest and best.

'Her son is only a baby, so who rules Scotland?' he asked.

'The Earl of Moray,' was the reply.

'Perhaps when her son is old enough he'll bring his mother back,' suggested Nathan.

'I doubt it. Anyway no one is sure he really is her son,' said Stern mysteriously, relishing the

340

surprised expressions on Esther and Nathan's faces.

'What do you mean?' asked Esther.

'There's talk that she gave birth to a daughter and it was exchanged for a boy born to a kitchen woman.'

'What happened to it?' Esther asked in a breathless voice.

'People say it went to the nuns and has been sent away to France to be brought up.'

A pain gripped Nathan's heart and he wanted to put an end to the conversation. 'That's only speculation,' he said shortly, but Stern loved gossip.

'People talk. There was a woman called Lady Reres at the delivery and she drinks too much. The sister of a woman I know is her sewing maid and she's heard the lady talking about the Queen's daughter. Apparently Lady Argyll took it away to give to the nuns, but Lady Argyll's dead now and no one knows the truth.'

Nathan caught his wife's eye and saw how she clutched Sarah defensively to her. 'If the nuns have the child it'll be better off than it would be in the royal court,' he said shortly.

The next day, he and his family hurriedly boarded a boat sailing out of Leith for the Low Countries. As they were passing the Bass Rock, a small rowing boat came alongside with a sailor standing in the hull yelling up to their skipper, and asking him to take on another passenger.

In a wildly tossing sea, a tall, thin man clambered up a rope ladder on to the bigger boat's deck and shook himself like a dog, for he was soaking wet. Nathan, who was watching, threw a blanket over his shoulders and said, 'Rub yourself dry if you don't want to catch your death of cold.'

Teeth chattering, the man gave a wry smile and said, 'It wouldn't matter much if I did die, I'm afraid.'

'Where there's life there's hope,' said Nathan facetiously but saw from the stranger's face that he was in dire trouble. He carried a rapier and his clothes had once been good but were now torn and dirty. Nathan thought he'd seen him before but could not be sure.

It soon turned out that the new arrival was travelling without proper papers, but the master of the freighter was well-disposed towards him and silently clapped him on the shoulder in sympathy when he admitted his lack of official accreditation.

'Where do you want to go?' he asked.

'Anywhere in France.'

'Anywhere?'

'Anywhere,' said the stranger, staring fixedly at the disappearing coast of Scotland as if he'd never see it again.

They made slow passage in the rough seas and three mornings later, when a coastline hove into view, the captain called out, 'This is Le Havre. I'm putting in because the weather is so bad.'

Nathan and the stranger stood together watching the shore and waiting for the pilot. 'Forgive my curiosity, but have you any money?' asked Nathan.

The stranger's sharp grey eyes had a hopeless

look in them. 'Not much,' he said sadly.

'Are you on the run? Are you a Marian?'

'What does it matter if I tell you now? Yes, I was with the Queen at Langside.'

'That was before she escaped into England?'

'If you can call going into imprisonment an escape. She should have taken our advice and run for France.'

'I'm a supporter of the Queen, too. How was she when you last saw her?'

'Wild and optimistic. I don't know how she is now but my sister is with her and she'll take good care of Queen Mary.'

'Your sister?'

'Lady Mary Seton.'

'Is she the tallest of the royal ladies?'

'Yes, that's her. She stayed with the Queen but I made it back to Seton Castle. Then Morton and Moray sent men to seize our property and I escaped. My wife and children have gone to her father's stronghold in the Borders because he played safe and stayed out of the trouble.'

'What will you do in France?' Nathan wondered.

'Work. I'm good with horses. It's all I know really, for I've never been much of a scholar.'

Nathan reached into his purse and brought out some golden coins. 'Take these on behalf of the Queen. My name is Nathan, son of Ezra, and we have a counting house in Jodenbreestraat, Amsterdam. If you want to send messages to your family or your sister, bring them to me. Money passes to and fro all the time and it doesn't need passports or papers.'

After landing at Le Havre, Esther and Nathan found another boat to take them north, and Lord Seton shook their hands before they left.

Nathan doubted he'd ever see the tall man again, but he was wrong. Two years later, Seton turned up in the counting house to repay the money Nathan had given him – which was refused – and passed on news from home.

He looked leaner than ever, but tanned and healthy, and the hopeless look had gone from his eyes. 'The Queen and my sister are at Tutbury in Staffordshire now. They seem to be quite comfortable there,' he told Nathan.

'But not free?'

'Not free alas. Even my sister thinks Queen Mary is too outspoken about her claims to the English throne, and of course her piety worries Elizabeth Tudor. There are too many Catholics in England who'd be happy to see one of their own faith back on the throne.'

'Are you in touch with your family?'

'I travel around a lot because I drive a coach and four for a living now, and sometimes I receive letters if a friend is in France.'

'Will you send a gift to the Queen from me? Before I went blind, I used to sell her sewing silks and still have some. Send them to Tutbury and say they come from the smous the Queen met at Falkland.'

Seton laughed. 'I'll do that. They're always sewing. It passes the time, I expect.'

He took the silks and from time to time turned up at the counting house to pass on news of Scotland. It was he who told Nathan that Mary had finally antagonized her English jailers too much by involving herself in a plot to marry an English duke and raise a rebellion against Elizabeth.

'Whatever possessed her?' Nathan asked.

Lord Seton shrugged. 'I'm afraid that though she's my Queen, she's not a cautious or a clever woman. The Stewarts have all been the same – so rash and headstrong that they destroy themselves.'

'Let's hope it doesn't come to that,' said Nathan fervently.

Thirty-Seven

1572

'What day is it? What month? What year?' Mary was on the verge of hysteria when she asked the questions over and over again. Her women knew how to soothe her: brushing her hair, playing music, rolling balls for her collection of little dogs, decking her with what was left of her jewellery collection, putting drops of perfume on the palms of her hands and holding them to her face so she could smell them.

She was always at her most fretful if there were no men around, and when a man appeared, she reverted to her charming persona, holding his hands and listening to every word he said as if he were as wise as Solomon.

'It's a Friday, in August 1572, and you are in Chatsworth,' said Mary Seton patiently.

'Where is Shrewsbury? Where's my jailer?'

'I'll send for him.'

'He'll only come if his wife Bess lets him. That woman is a dragon and ugly, fat and bulging-eyed. Yet she's snared four husbands, each one richer than the one before. I've had three husbands. I think it's about time I took a fourth.'

Seton looked over her shoulder in alarm in case they were overheard. 'You're still married,' she reminded the distraught woman.

'The Pope will give me a dispensation. Bothwell forced me to marry him by raping me, so it'll be easy to get a divorce.' Mary often talked now of divorcing Bothwell, and seemed to find it impossible to remember the truth of their relationship or that she once felt passion for him. The tenderness of their last embrace on Carberry Hill was gone from her memory.

Seton tried to soothe her, fearing that she was about to lapse into one of her terrible bouts of hysterical rage, or even worse, a debilitating depression and catatonic physical collapse like the terrifying episode at Jedburgh.

Fortunately, as her attendants often commented, the attacks of painful sickness and bloody vomiting that used to plague her were less frequent. A reclusive life suited her body, if not her mind.

'I'll ask Shrewsbury if she can be taken to Buxton for the waters. She's fortunate that conditions here are not too harsh. She isn't closely confined,' Mary's doctor Bourgoing said to Seton when she told him the Queen was in a distraught state again.

'I worry in case her constant troublemaking will make Elizabeth more strict,' Seton agreed.

He nodded. 'She can't help herself. She has Shrewsbury eating out of her hand and his wife is so furious she's threatening to divorce him because she says he's fallen in love with our Queen.'

Bess, Countess of Shrewsbury, had begun by befriending the royal captive. The two women rode out together and spent hours doing their embroidery in the pleasant surroundings of the various rural strongholds round which Mary travelled, spending time in the castles of Sheffield, Wingfield and Chatsworth – but as Bess's husband fell more and more under the Scottish Queen's enchantment, the friendship withered.

'And there's the Duke of Norfolk to worry about now. The Queen's put Bothwell out of her mind and is making plans to marry Norfolk if she can get a divorce. She's led Norfolk so much by the nose that Elizabeth has sent him to the Tower.'

'Won't she listen to reason?' Bourgoing asked and Seton shook her head.

'She's set on the Norfolk marriage. She thinks he'll raise a rebellion on her behalf and put her back on the Scottish throne, if not the English one.'

'Queen Elizabeth's advisers won't put up with much more of it,' the doctor said and Seton groaned, because she knew that even if Norfolk stopped responding to Mary, she'd find another victim. There was no point advising her to accept detention with resignation. She did not care whom she sacrificed in pursuit of her own ends.

Mary shouted in delight when news came that her hated half-brother Moray had been stabbed to death by Hamilton of Bothwellhaugh, one of the Queen's supporters who'd been in their company at Dundrennan. Seeing the Queen's exaltation about the murder, Seton's heart sank. *When will the bloodletting cease?* she wondered.

'You look tired,' the doctor said solicitously, seeing the strained look on Seton's face. He felt pity for this most devoted of Mary's women. Others came and went but Seton stayed.

'I am tired but I must serve the Queen,' was the weary reply.

'Let me feel your pulse,' he said, lifting her wrist and counting the heartbeats with a concerned look on his face.

'How is your cough?' he asked.

'It plagues me at night.'

'And you're very thin. I think you must leave this place.'

'I can't. Who will care for the Queen if I go away?'

'She always finds someone to do her bidding,' he said sadly, for he was as much in thrall to Mary as Seton was.

The Duke of Norfolk died at the block two months later. Typically, Mary grieved for a while, but was soon involved in yet another plot. It was as if she were driven by senseless demons.

Thirty-Eight

All the time that she was under the care of the tolerant Earl of Shrewsbury, Mary was able to send and receive letters from Bothwell, many of them carried by his Danish page.

He waited eagerly for communications from her, even when all she wrote about were proposals for a legal separation from him because that would be in her best interests.

As the months and years passed, she returned more and more to the subject, writing about diplomatic alliances with powerful men like Don Juan of Austria or the Duc of Anjou, who would be able to secure her freedom. Bothwell was powerless to help in that matter now that he was in prison himself, of course, and she made no pleas to anyone on his behalf.

More politically astute than she, and used to her flights of fancy, he doubted if any of those important suitors would take on such a problematic bride, though he replied that if divorce was what she wanted he would go along with it.

'Take care that you don't antagonize Elizabeth Tudor by your plans,' he warned. 'I'm only a pawn in a royal chess game,' he told his page and laughed uproariously as if he'd made a tremendous joke.

He'd taken to walking for hours round the castle battlements every day, staring out to sea with a yearning look on his face.

'The sea is beautiful but though I was High Admiral, I'm a landsman, and I prefer empty moors to open water,' he said, when darkness forced him back to his chambers.

After three years of imprisonment, he took to laughing out loud when no one was about and conducting strange, animated conversations with himself. No wonder, thought people who sympathized with him. Frequent raising of his hopes for freedom were always followed by disappointment.

King Frederick seemed to have lost interest in him and the gifts of clothes and money no longer arrived. As the months became years, he became more and more shabby, which grieved a man who'd enjoyed presenting a good front to the world.

Sometimes visitors from the outside world came to see him, and he sparkled, enjoying their conversation and avid for news, but when they left he sank into even more disabling glooms.

When he was alone, his mind always wandered back to Scotland, to Crichton and the Hermitage. He'd close his eyes and think himself there. *What season is it now?* he always asked himself.

If it was spring, he remembered Crichton, with primroses sparkling like scattered gold on the green grass round the ancient church; if autumn, he went back to Hermitage where the bracken would be rust red on the hills around the fortress and the sky a pale, pale blue.

He yearned, how he yearned. Sometimes he sat with his eyes shut for hours, watching scenes of his homeland passing behind his eyelids. When he finally accepted that he would probably never see Scotland again, it became important to him that his body at least should be returned home. He wanted to lie by Crichton Church, with the grinning stone heads looking down at him and the one-tongued bell ringing above his head.

'When I die, please ask the King to send my body back to my own place,' he said to his jailer.

'Where is that?'

'Crichton.' He pronounced it Scottish style with a thick burr on the R, so the jailer had no idea what he said but promised to send him back there, wherever it was.

Some people, a few of them informers, came to see him from time to time and asked questions, but he never admitted to the murder of Darnley. 'Moray's men did it,' he said.

If asked about Queen Mary, he seemed confused, but often said, 'She's never known desire for anyone or anything except jewellery.'

'His mind is going,' his servants reported back to the King, but Frederick would not turn him loose. Too many outside forces were involved, and no one really wanted him enough to pay a ransom.

Bothwell, the archetypal man of action, was left to rot away with nothing to occupy his mind but memories. Sometimes he could be heard yelling out in frustrated fury when he was alone, especially in the middle of the night, 'You were right, Janet. I shouldn't have married her. She never cared a fig for anyone but herself.'

Then, suddenly, like a storm breaking, he went berserk. In the middle of the night, he rose from his bed and started to wreck the chamber, tearing panelling from the walls, ripping down bed curtains and smashing furniture. When two pages tried to stop him, he stabbed one of them to death, though he'd liked the man.

The dagger was eventually wrenched from his grasp and he was put in chains.

The next day he was taken to an ancient castle called Dragsholm, also on the edge of the sea. He fought every inch of the way, flailing out with his still powerful arms, even when they chained him to a stone pillar in the middle of a small room on the ground floor. The chain was only long enough to allow him to walk three short steps in any direction.

He was a difficult prisoner, shouting and screaming terrible profane curses day and night. When anyone tried to approach him, he lashed out and almost succeeded in gouging out the eyes of a soldier who was taking food to him.

The retainers in the castle kitchens regarded their new charge with extreme caution but knew little about him. 'He told me that he was once married to a queen. As if I'd believe that!' the sergeant of arms said scornfully.

'Nonsense, he's only an old pirate. Look at the rags he's wearing. He hasn't even got proper boots,' said another.

A pretty little kitchen maid with curly dark

hair and dimpled cheeks said, 'I'm sorry for him. I think he was once a gentleman.' As usual, Bothwell won a woman's heart, even in his most dire extremity.

'A gentleman!' scoffed the sergeant. 'He's an animal. We can't even give him food. The man who carries it to him has to put it down on the floor and run for his life.'

'Let me take it,' said the maid. The men refused to allow her to try for many weeks but eventually she wore them down and, to everyone's amazement, Bothwell allowed her into his cell without cursing. He stood silent and stared as she approached him with a platter of bread and cheese, smiled and laid it down at his feet.

'Ah Bessie,' he said in a soft voice. 'You're a bonny lassie, Bessie.'

She did not know what he said but was delighted because he sat down quietly on the ground and ate the food. After that she took him his food every day and he was always quiet when she was in the cell.

Physically he deteriorated horribly. His long reddish hair was streaked with grey and his beard grew so thick that his features were hidden. He stank because, like an animal, he slept in his own ordure, and unlike an animal, no man could get close enough to him to clean out the cell.

It took eight years before he died, on April fourteenth, 1578, skeletal thin and mindless. People in the castle felt pity for their captive, even though he'd tried to kill several of them. He was forty-four years old when they laid him to rest in the crypt of Faarevejie church, in a plain pine coffin with his body wrapped in a white sheet. On to the sheet the pretty kitchen maid pinned dozens of little bows of black ribbon.

The promise to send him back to Scotland was forgotten. The salty sea air turned his body into a husk-like mummy, and the only sign he had ever been in Dragsholm castle was a groove in his dungeon's stone floor, worn away by his feet during year after year of pacing to and fro.

Thirty-Nine

1584

Mary's constant refusal to accept imprisonment with good grace antagonized Elizabeth's advisers.

No matter how hard they tried to restrict her contact with the outside world, she still managed to send and receive illicit messages. One was even smuggled to her in a cask of ale. Warnings were ignored, and Shrewsbury, whose marriage was ruined by Mary, worried about his own head if his captive continued running rings round him, and he at last succeeded in relinquishing the responsibility by pleading that his health would fail completely if he was not relieved.

His replacement was Sir Amyas Paulet, a hard-hearted man who was impervious to female charm. He moved the royal prisoner to a more secure prison at Tutbury, a damp and draughty house where a Spartan regime was imposed.

'I'm not allowed out, not even to walk in the gardens. I cannot ride. I cannot see visitors. You've taken away my money so I can't even give alms to the beggars at the gate,' she mourned.

'It's your own fault,' Paulet snapped.

Mary Seton, and Little Douglas who was still with her, tried to offer comfort. 'Perhaps if you stay quiet and give no trouble, the rules will be relaxed again,' they said.

The trouble was that Mary had no intention of staying quiet, but the discomfort of Tutbury affected her health and she fell into one of her perplexing illnesses. Her state became so pitiable that she was again moved, this time to a more comfortable prison at Chartley, and Paulet relaxed his rules enough to allow her to be carried outside by Little Douglas to sit by the side of a pleasant pond and watch the water fowl.

A young page called Anthony Babington joined the household, and like so many young men before him, became entranced by Mary, who retained her power to enchant even though she was swelling up with dropsy as her mother had done.

Like Little Douglas, Babington was filled with the desire to rescue her from the miserable circumstances in which she found herself, and with ten friends he formed a rescue plot. He was young and reckless and his zeal was so intense that he decided the first thing to do was assassinate the woman who was Mary's chief persecutor – Queen Elizabeth herself.

Mary enjoyed the intrigue, and encouraged him. Listening to his plans and receiving illicit letters from him brought interest into her life. Past experience had taught her nothing and the naivety that marked her early life was as strong as ever. It did not occur to her that Elizabeth's spies read every letter that came in or went out.

Loyal and loving Mary Seton, whose health was failing visibly, watched what was going on with deepening despair. For the first time, she acknowledged to herself that the Queen's faults were ineradicable, and had deepened over the years.

She remembered the terrible day when they had watched Hamilton's hanging and hardness and cruelty showed for the first time on Mary's face. It hurt Seton now to watch the deliberate enchantment and exploitation of young Babington.

'Your Majesty, have a care for the young man. If you involve him in a dangerous enterprise, he'll pay a terrible price,' she warned.

'I know nothing of what he's doing,' said Mary blandly, but Seton was not deceived and knew the Queen was deeply involved. She looked around at the small circle of people who remained loyal – Dr Bourgoing, Little Douglas and his uncle, the two secretaries, three women and herself, the last of the original Marys. They were giving up their lives for the Queen.

When the news of Bothwell's dreadful death came through, Seton was more affected than his wife, who had consigned him to the past like so many others.

'I liked him. He was a romantic and loyal to the Queen. They often stayed at Seton with my father and brother, who respected him too,' she said to Dr Bourgoing who shook his head in sympathy.

'You're looking worse,' he said. 'Let me give you a remedy for your terrible cough. The damp has affected your lungs and breathing. You should leave us soon or you will die.'

'I've stayed with my Queen for thirty-eight years and I can't leave her now.'

'Someone else can dress her hair,' he said shortly, but Seton continued to protest so he went to Mary and said forcibly, 'Seton is very ill. If she doesn't leave this prison, she'll die. You must send her away, because she'll not leave without you ordering her to go.'

Mary realized what he said was true and told Seton, 'I've arranged for you to go into a nunnery at Douai. You'll recover your health there.'

They stared at each other for a few moments till Seton asked, 'Are you sending me away?'

'Yes. My cousin is a Jesuit at Douai, and your aunt is abbess of a convent in the town, isn't she? You'll be among friends.'

Seton nodded with tears in her eyes but said nothing and Mary persisted, 'Go as soon as possible. Dr Bourgoing says you need looking after. My cousin has contacted your brother and he'll meet you when you land in France and take you to Douai.'

'I haven't seen my brother since we left Scotland.'

'It's all arranged. Please go without a fuss.'

'I'll miss you,' sobbed Seton and Mary, also weeping, replied, 'No more than I'll miss you. You're my most faithful friend but it'll be a comfort to know you're safe in a nunnery, praying for me.'

Nathan was in the counting house when a noise alerted him to someone coming through the door and a Scottish voice said, 'Do you remember me?'

'I'm afraid my sight has gone but I know your voice. Is it Lord Seton?'

'It is indeed. You have a good memory.'

Seton had looked in at the counting house a few times over the past years and Nathan never forgot a voice.

Hearing them, Sarah, who was in a back room, came through to help her father and saw a tall, lean man, dressed like a French coach driver with a cocked hat and a long caped overcoat, leaning on the counter. When he looked up at her, a strange expression came over his face and it was obvious he was taken aback.

Nathan, being blind, did not see how much his daughter had surprised Seton, who asked in a changed voice, 'Who is this young lady?'

'My daughter Sarah,' said Nathan proudly.

'Your daughter?' He sounded surprised. *Why?* Sarah wondered. *I've never seen him before.*

'My daughter,' repeated Nathan firmly. When

his eyes last gave him a sight of Sarah, she'd been a gangly girl. He had never seen her as an adult.

Seton stared hard at her again and bowed his head as if in obeisance. 'Is your wife a very tall woman?' he asked Nathan.

Nathan laughed. 'She's five foot tall and I'm five foot six.'

'Yet your daughter is so tall...' He seemed to be on the verge of saying something more but changed his mind.

Nathan recoiled. What did his daughter look like now, he wondered? He and Esther had always told her they were not her real parents and that she was given to them as a baby. Was it possible she looked like someone Seton knew?

'It's not what they feed me on that makes me tall. I'm a foundling,' she laughed.

'An Amsterdam foundling?' queried Seton.

'A Scottish foundling,' she said proudly.

Seton turned to Nathan and asked, 'How old is your daughter? Where did you get her?'

Nathan's friendly attitude changed and he stiffened as he turned to Sarah to say sharply, 'Leave us to carry out our business please, my dear.'

She backed out of the room and closed the door. It was too stout to allow anything said in the front office to come through.

'Why do you ask about Sarah?' he said to Seton.

'Because she looks like a woman I knew once.'

'A lady in Edinburgh gave her to me,' Nathan said.

'A *lady*?'

'She did not want the child. My wife had just lost a baby and was grieving. Sarah filled the gap in our lives.'

'She looks like Queen Mary,' Seton said flatly.

'My wife tells me her hair is not red,' Nathan replied.

'Perhaps not, but she's about six feet tall and has the same pale skin and long hands. People say the Queen had twins by Bothwell at Loch-leven. Is she one of them?'

Nathan put both hands palm down on the wooden counter and said slowly, 'She was born the year before Lochleven. I swear to you she is not Bothwell's child.'

Seton shook his head. 'The likeness is un-canny. I'm on my way to meet my sister at Rotterdam. She was one of the Queen's Marys since they were five years old, but she's sick now and has to retire to a nunnery. Can I bring her to see your daughter?'

Nathan's white-sheened eyes were hard as he stared back and shook his head. 'I beseech you to leave my daughter alone, Lord Seton. Don't probe into matters that don't concern you.'

Seton knew what he was being told and said, 'I respect your wishes. You're a good man and your daughter is fortunate that she fell into your care.'

Forty

The Babington plot was a farce. A spy called Gilbert Gifford was planted in Mary's household and, again, she was completely deceived, using him as a go-between and passer on of letters, which went, of course, to Elizabeth's advisers.

Mary's pen proved to be as indiscreet as her tongue, and when Babington proposed killing Elizabeth, she replied enthusiastically to the idea. She wrote her own death warrant.

What to do with her? Her cousin Elizabeth, who was against any suggestion that kings or queens could be executed, would have preferred the troublesome Mary to suffer a fatal accident. Poisoning was the usual way and easy enough to arrange. Darnley's mother Lady Lennox had recently died in mysterious circumstances after dining with a 'friend'.

Amyas Paulet, however, refused to agree to this way of disposing of his inconvenient charge. He wanted Mary's importunate conduct made public to prevent pro-Marians taking revenge on him.

Unaware that her hated jailer was protecting her life, a protesting Mary was again moved, going this time to Fotheringhay Castle, a semi ruin that was even more inhospitable than Tutbury.

'I hate this place!' she announced when she looked around her new chambers.

'Perhaps you'll not be here long,' was Paulet's reply.

In October it was announced that she was to be put on trial, and during the presentation of evidence all manner of charges were laid against her, including involvement in the murder of Darnley.

The Casket Letters, the box of forged and altered letters, were produced and they purported to prove that she and Bothwell plotted the killing at Kirk o' Field, and that they had been lovers before Darnley died.

The letters were only a decoy, however. Mary Stewart was really on trial for plotting to kill Elizabeth Tudor and trying to incite the King of Spain to invade England on her behalf. Murder and treason combined were unforgivable.

She was pronounced guilty, as were Babington and his seven co-conspirators, who were dealt with quickly and suffered the terrible deaths of being hung, drawn and quartered. Another seven plotters escaped with only being hung. Once again Nostradamus's prediction was proved accurate. Those who associated with Mary Stewart were drenched in blood.

'What will be done with me?' Mary asked Paulet when she was escorted back to her chamber after the verdict was announced.

'It's out of my hands,' he said, with relief in

his voice.

'The only person who can pronounce a sentence on me is another Queen,' said Mary grandly.

Elizabeth Tudor did not want to be the one who signed the order to kill her cousin and though her courtiers persisted in pressing her for action, she refused to do it.

'Let us wait and see what she does next. Perhaps she'll die soon,' was all she would say when the death warrant was pushed beneath her nose.

Lord Seton sent a message to Amsterdam to tell Nathan that Mary was on trial. 'Her son James does nothing to save her. He is anxious to stay in the good graces of the English Queen, because she might name him as her heir. The French and the Spaniards are making bellicose noises but they're only bluffing. No one cares any more what happens to our Scottish Queen,' he wrote.

Through information coming from Elizabeth's court, all Europe knew that she was reluctant to kill her cousin, but when a new year dawned, the pressure on her increased and the decision could not be postponed much longer.

Nathan sat in his counting house, listening to travellers' tales, and said, 'I've followed Queen Mary's life from the day she was christened. It is a tragedy what has happened to her.'

Esther shook her head in sympathy. 'Don't upset yourself. It was inevitable that she would end like this.'

'I wish I could see it through to the end,' he

363

said mournfully.

Sarah, who was listening, said, 'Then why don't you go back to Scotland once more? I'll go with you.'

'I suppose I could. I'll dress in my old travelling clothes and fill a pack. I'll be a smous again...' The idea appealed to him. Then he remembered Seton's reaction to the sight of Sarah.

'But I can't take you,' he told his daughter.

'Don't be silly. Of course you can. You need someone to lead you around and I take you all over Amsterdam, don't I? You haven't fallen into a canal yet,' she said with a laugh.

'You're too beautiful,' he said.

'Nonsense, I'm not beautiful. I'm too tall for one thing. You want to go, don't you, and I'm the only one who can take you.'

'You'd attract attention,' said Nathan mournfully.

'Not if I dress like a poor woman.'

'You're too tall.'

'Are all the Scots dwarfs? I'll walk with a stoop. I'll pretend to be a halfwit! I want to take you back. I know how much you admire the Queen. Let me do this for you. We'll walk the roads as pedlars and no one will spare us a glance.'

Forty-One

Fotheringhay
1587

They landed in Hull on a bitter January day and Nathan insisted on putting up in comfortable inns until they drew near to Fotheringhay on February first, the day a frustrated Sir Francis Walsingham forged the Queen's signature on Mary Stewart's death warrant and sent it north to Paulet.

When Elizabeth heard what he had done she burst into furious tears, but did not rescind the order.

The weather was cold but bright with a winter sun making frost-covered twigs on the trees sparkle as if they were coated in diamond dust. Nathan made no effort to sell anything from his pack but enjoyed the road beneath his feet again and asked Sarah to describe the countryside to him as they walked along. She did so in such vivid words that he exclaimed, 'You speak like a painter. You're making the world come back to me, my dear.'

'I want to be a painter, father,' she said, 'In fact I've met a painter who says I have talent.'

'Who is this person?' asked Nathan suspiciously.

'It's a woman called Mayken Verhulst. She's old now but well known and highly respected as a good teacher.'

'In Amsterdam?'

'Not far away. In Mechlen near Antwerp.'

'What do you want to paint? A blind man knows nothing about painting,' he said.

'I like painting flowers, especially tulips.'

'Tulips? Those costly flowers! I've heard enough about them but have never seen them.'

'They're lovely. They come in all colours, some are striped or frilled, some are pointed. They're all very elegant.'

'Elegant,' repeated Nathan in approval, thinking that elegant flowers would appeal to the daughter of a queen.

Then he asked, 'Does this woman charge money to teach people to paint?'

'She does, but she only takes students with real talent.'

'Your mother and I don't want you to leave home, not even to go to Mechlen. We've been talking about arranging a good marriage for you.'

She stopped in mid-stride. 'I thought so. I'm not ready to marry yet. I'd rather paint and be a student of Mayken.'

'I'll think about it,' said Nathan. He had a lot to think about. One of his reasons for wanting to go to Fotheringhay was because he was unsure about how much he should tell Sarah about her true background.

He also wanted her to see the woman who was possibly her mother – not just possibly, he corrected himself, almost certainly.

It was not his intention to expose her or himself to the actual execution, but when he found himself in the courtyard of Fotheringhay, he was impelled to follow the tragedy through to the end.

Unfortunately, it was even more harrowing and terrible than he could have imagined and when he walked away, leaning on his daughter's arm, he was weeping.

'Oh father, don't grieve so. She said she was glad to die,' Sarah tried to soothe him.

'What did she look like? Tell me what she looked like,' he pleaded.

'She was old and bent, and rather fat. She was wearing a wig...'

He stopped in the middle of the road. 'Old, bent, fat? A wig? Are you sure?'

'Yes, I'm sure.'

'But she's almost twenty years younger than I am.'

'She seemed much older and she looked ill, as if she had not many years of life left.'

He groaned. 'My beautiful Queen with the red, red hair and beautiful pale skin!' Sarah hugged him and said softly, 'I shouldn't have told you. Keep on remembering her like that.'

At that moment, he made up his mind. He'd take his secret to the grave. Sarah need never be told about her ancestry. He had to save her from the curse of the Stewarts.

They were back at Hull, about to board the

ship that would carry them home, when he put his hand on her arm and asked, 'That woman in Mechlen, how much does she charge to teach painting?'

'I don't know.'

'It doesn't matter. Whatever it is, I'll pay.'